ADRENALINE

JAMES DILLINGER

A PLUME BOOK

NEW AMERICAN LIBRARY

NEW YORK AND SCARBOROUGH, ONTARIO

NAL BOOKS ARE AVAILABLE AT QUANTITY DISCOUNTS WHEN USED TO PROMOTE PRODUCTS OR SERVICES. FOR INFORMATION PLEASE WRITE TO PREMIUM MARKETING DIVISION, NEW AMERICAN LIBRARY, 1633 BROADWAY, NEW YORK, NEW YORK 10019.

 PLUME TRADEMARK REG. U.S. PAT. OFF. AND FOREIGN COUNTRIES REG.D TRADEMARK—MARCA REGISTRADA HECHO EN BRATTLEBORO, VA., U.S.A.

SIGNET, SIGNET CLASSIC, MENTOR, ONYX, PLUME, MERIDIAN and NAL BOOKS are published *in the United States* by NAL PENGUIN INC., 1633 Broadway, New York, New York 10019, *in Canada* by The New American Library of Canada Limited, 81 Mack Avenue, Scarborough, Ontario M1L 1M8

Library of Congress Cataloging-in-Publication Data

Dillinger, James.
     Adrenaline / James Dillinger.
         p.   cm.
     ISBN: 0-452-26075-2
     I. Title.
PS3554.I418A66   1988   87-30162
813'.54—dc19   CIP

First Plume Printing, August, 1988

1 2 3 4 5 6 7 8 9

PRINTED IN THE UNITED STATES OF AMERICA

It was hot. The sun pounded down through the smog and the ash from the brush fires, saturating Los Angeles with an eerie metallic orange light. It made everything look fake, as if all the streets and cars and buildings were part of a massive set for a movie about a nuclear apocalypse.

Sweat matted Nick's short black hair and dripped from his sunburnt nose and thick black mustache. It glistened on his hairy chest and trickled down his hard stomach, soaking into his filthy button-fly Levi's. He couldn't finish his soggy catering-truck ham-and-cheese. He tossed it in the trashbin, leaned back in the shade by the loading dock, and polished off his warm Coke. Then he lit a Marlboro, even though it felt like a slug in the chest, and watched the cream-colored 1969 Eldorado lumber up 104th Street near LAX.

It was a real piece of shit: scraped, primered, right rear fender mangled, air-conditioning shot—he could tell as it got closer, because the woman at the wheel had all the windows rolled down.

At first he figured she was one of the other guys' girlfriends, but he could tell by the way they started acting when she pulled up and got out that she wasn't. They started snorting and swallowing laughs—in general acting like a bunch of assholes.

All she had on was a red nylon bikini. A lot of people would have said she should have been wear-

ing more than that bikini—she was about twenty
pounds overweight—but her attitude said she didn't
give a shit, and Nick liked her right away. She reminded him of the tough girls he'd known in high
school in Detroit, girls who could laugh without trying
to act like refined little ladies.

"Hey, look," she said, trying to ignore the fact that
the other guys were acting like assholes, "could you
guys tell me how to get to Marina Del Rey?"

She smiled in the harsh sunlight. Sweat trickled
down the cleft of her breasts. A few pubic hairs stuck
out around the edge of her red nylon crotch.

The other guys couldn't control themselves. Ernie
and that other black guy, the new guy, were cracking
up and making for-blacks-only-type comments. Louie
and Immanuel were doing the same thing in Spanish.
Botts and Dwayne were doing it in Okie, but Botts
finally made a stab at civility. "Well, now, doll, what's
a sweet little tomato like you want to do in Marina
Del Rey? You going to one of them swingin' singles
bars, sweet thing?" He grinned, showing bad teeth.

"If you wanna party, baby," Ernie said, "I got a
little somethin' in my glove compartment—"

"If she ain't prejudiced 'gainst dark meat," the new
black guy joked.

Louie was the wittiest. "Hey, baby. You wanna
suck on my cock for a while?"

Her smile began to look forced. Then she gave
them a look that was more puzzled than offended,
and turned to go back to her car.

"Listen," Nick called to her, "go back to Sepulveda
and take a left—"

The other guys squinted at Nick. What was wrong
with *him*?

She turned and looked at him, too. She liked what
she saw, but she was cautious. "Yeah—"

"Then take Sepulveda till it veers off into Lincoln,
you'll see the sign. Then just stay on Lincoln. It's
about six miles."

She kept looking at Nick, longer than she had to. "Okay. Thanks."

"Nick'll go along and show you, honey." Botts cackled and leered at Nick. "Go on, man. We'll punch you out."

The other guys broke up.

"You guys are full of shit," Nick said.

The woman gave Nick a brief, poignant smile. Then she walked back to her Cadillac.

Ernie and Dwayne whistled as they watched the red nylon bikini ride up over the cheeks of her butt.

They watched her pull out before they let loose.

"Hot fuckin' *bitch*, man!"

"She was beggin' for it, jack. Somebody oughta done that skunk a favor."

"That pussy was *smokin'*!" Louie hooted. "You see all the hairs stickin' out, man?"

Nick got up and threw his Coke in the trash. It was time to go back to work. "You guys are a bunch of animals," he said.

"What's wrong with *you*, Krieger?" Botts said. "Man, she was practically *oozing* all over you—"

Nick grinned at Botts. "She wasn't my type." He stubbed out his cigarette and started to go back into the warehouse.

"The way I hear it," Botts said, "*no* type is *your* type, if you get my meaning."

Nick stopped, glaring at Botts.

"Un-oh," Ernie said. The other guys snickered, as if they knew what Botts meant—as if they'd known, or at least suspected, for a while.

That made Nick doubly pissed off. "I don't give a fuck *what* you mean, Botts."

Botts snorted and turned away. Nick watched him for a second, then turned to go back inside. The tension seemed to have passed.

Then Botts snuck up behind Nick and said offhandedly, "I just heard you like to *suck cock*, that's all."

Nick swung around and slugged him in the face.

When Botts tried to defend himself, Nick slugged him again. "You fucking piece of shit—"

Botts' nose started bleeding. He tried to slug Nick. Nick grabbed him around the neck. Then the foreman saw what was happening and came running from his air-conditioned office. The other guys pulled Nick and Botts apart.

Twenty minutes later, Nick was sitting in his metallic-blue 1968 Camaro SS, suffocating in the boiling car, trying to start the engine. He had the radio on, blasting ZZ Top, to drown out whatever comments Botts and the foreman and the other guys were making about him over at the warehouse. A check for a hundred and forty-two dollars was folded and jabbed in the crack of the scalding black vinyl seat.

The engine finally started and Nick lurched out to the street. He could see Botts and the other guys laughing in his rearview mirror as he floored it. Breathing hard, slippery with sweat, he burned rubber up 104th Street, hauling ass out of there, absently, reassuringly, squeezing his cock through his Levi's.

Nick's guts were still grinding a half-hour later when he stopped at the Security Pacific Bank in Westchester to cash his check. Since he hadn't bothered to put on his shirt before he went in, he drew a few glances from the people, mostly businessmen, in the long line. There were going to be long lines everywhere tonight. Not only was it Friday, it was the start of the three-day Labor Day weekend.

One of the tellers was a dead ringer for Randy—at least from the neck up. From the neck down, the teller was a fat polyester slob.

Randy. *Fuck*. It was—what?—almost five years now, and Nick still felt sick with longing every time he thought about Randy. It was stupid. You ought to live in the present and all that. But it was hard, because the time he'd spent with Randy was the best time of his life. And the present sucked.

The time he'd spent with Randy had begun shortly after his arrival in San Francisco in 1976. He'd pulled into town in a smoking GTO, an amphetamine-ravaged fugitive from justice with fifty bucks, a dishonorable discharge (for butt-fucking another marine), and a hypersensitivity to shrill and sudden noises.

He got a job at an ARCO and rented a room in a Castro district flat he shared with two leather guys and a Chinese concert pianist. He quit taking speed and started to drink.

He was in a Western bar one night, drunk, when Randy stepped through the swinging doors. He was dressed like a cowboy, as were many of the other patrons, but Randy's clothes looked real. They were worn and dirty in a way you couldn't fake. He had a walrus mustache, like a gunslinger in a tintype. And a body that made Nick spill his drink. He was *hot*.

Randy evidently thought the same thing about Nick. They checked each other out for a while before Randy finally came over and ordered a Jack Daniel's. Glancing at Nick's ARCO uniform, he said casually, "So, is this real? You really work there?"

"What about *this*?" Nick said, playfully tugging Randy's mustache. "Is this real?"

They both laughed. Then, impulsively—a plaintive Tammy Wynette song playing in the background—Nick leaned over and gently kissed Randy on the mouth.

Randy, it turned out, was a law student at Berkeley. He'd grown up on a ranch in Oregon, and he went back a lot, still on good terms with his parents. They knew he was gay but loved him anyway.

"What about you?" he asked Nick as they smoked a joint in bed after sex.

"Detroit," Nick said. "My dad worked at GM. So did my mom. My dad killed my mom on the Fourth of July when I was eight. He hit her with a frying pan. It was more or less an accident, they used to fight a lot. He's still in prison. I went to live with my uncle after that. He was kind of a prick."

The first year, at Randy's insistence, they kept it light. No romantic melodrama, no stifling commitments. "I can't afford a draining relationship right now," Randy said. "I need all my energies for school." That was fine with Nick. The friendship was what he really needed more than anything, and the casual sex, which they had a lot of, just kept getting better, which astonished Nick. Before Randy, most of Nick's sex had been impersonal: in movie theaters as a kid in Detroit, in cars, tea rooms, parks. Being with the same person a number of times and getting to know them was a revelation.

They did other things, too. They both liked movies a lot: Clint Eastwood films, which Randy considered politically despicable but amusing as macho trash, and which Nick just plain liked. They went dancing. They spent a couple of weekends up at Russian River. They smoked dope and joked around, affecting a mock-tough manner with each other, enjoying the illusion that they were like a couple of straight buddies. Although they never got mushy or exchanged I-love-you's, it became increasingly apparent to their friends that they were totally wrapped up in each other.

Randy had been a leader in the Gay Students Union at Berkeley, but the gay movement was changing, the "Brady Bunch generation," as Randy called them, denouncing the old guard as radicals whose time had passed. Randy became disgruntled. "I've quit law school," he announced one night; actually he'd just taken a year's leave of absence. "I'm getting out of here, my sanity's at stake. I've got some inheritance money I've been saving, and I'm going to buy some land in Mendocino. You want to come?"

Together, they looked at property and picked out a ten-acre spread with a two-story wood-frame house that needed fixing up. They fixed it up. They stripped the floors and refinished the woodwork and put on a new roof. They poured a new driveway and planted a vegetable garden. They worked together during the day (Nick liked to say they were *partners*; he didn't like the term *lovers*), and at night they slept together under a patch quilt in a brass bed. When they finished their house, Nick got a job fixing up another house in the area. It looked like the start of an ongoing business.

One day Nick was watching Randy chop wood behind the house. It had just stopped raining, there was a rainbow making everything look fresh and idyllic. It suddenly hit Nick that after a grim childhood being raised by his uncle, after the bullshit with the marine corps, and the life-of-crime crap in L.A., he'd finally lucked out totally. He'd fallen in love, settled down, and he fucking had it made. Watching Randy through the window, Nick wept for the first time since he was eight years old.

Randy had been getting increasingly edgy as his leave-of-absence expiration date approached. One day he came back from a trip to the city and said, as gently as he could, "Nick, the last thing in the world I want to do is hurt you—" He'd decided to go back and get his degree. Although it wasn't completely unexpected, it still hit Nick like a punch in the gut.

If it was only the degree, they could just move back to Berkeley. But it wasn't quite that simple.

"I've met this guy, Nick. A younger guy. He's a law student. We have a lot in common. I think you'll like him. He's a lot like you in many respects. Relationships evolve, Nick. I know we're both mature, non-possessive—"

Instead of slugging Randy in the face, Nick went for a long walk. It was raining lightly; the Mendocino countryside looked like an illustration on a crate of peaches. It was as close to any of that paradise crap as Nick ever figured he'd come. The next day, while Randy was off in the city again, Nick packed what little stuff was his, threw everything in the Camaro, and hauled ass out of paradise. He mowed down the

vegetable garden as he went—not that it mattered.
The corn, they'd already discovered, was diseased.

"Next." It was Nick's turn at the window; of course,
he got the fat slob teller with the walrus mustache.
"Give me all twenties," Nick said, and for a second
he was tempted to close his account. And do what?
Split L.A.? No, fuck it, he'd wait till Tuesday. There
was no point in doing anything now; trying to get out
of L.A. this weekend would be totally insane. Besides,
something might happen.
Like what? Nick wondered, sticking the bills in his
wallet, stepping back into the blast furnace Santa
Ana heat. Shit wasn't going to happen, it never did.
Still, for some reason, Nick had a feeling of nervous
anticipation in the pit of his stomach. Was it just this
weather? It shredded your nerves, it made your skin
feel like cracked vinyl, but it was also strangely
exciting. And sexual. Everywhere you drove, there'd
be hot-looking guys wearing next to nothing. That
was one thing you had to admit about L.A.; it was a
cheap plastic turd of a town, but it sure had a lot of
hot-looking guys.
Nick got back in his car, squirting water on the
windshield, briefly running the wipers to get rid of
the brush-fire ash.

Nick had had vague high hopes when he'd come
back to L.A. this time. Everything had seemed new:
new condos and chain stores and fast-food places
everywhere. New people. It was easy to forget the
shit from the past: the speed-ravaged summer of '76
when, unable to get work because of his dishonorable discharge from the marines, he'd stuck up the
7–11s. It was the stupidest fucking thing he'd ever
done. He must have been insane. Thinking back on it
as he shot under the San Diego Freeway into Culver
City, it seemed like ancient history. Remembering
the last time he'd done it was like looking at closed-
circuit TV pictures of somebody else: running out of

the store on Olympic just as the squad car pulled up, dashing up the alley, the cops opening fire, shitting in his pants. Back home, counting the take: $12.52. Selling the gun, taking off for San Francisco. No, that wasn't him. That was some crazed asshole who almost got his brains blown out for twelve bucks.

Nick felt a surge of elation as he roared up an empty side street in Culver City. He still thought Botts was a piece of dried wino shit, and the other guys were a bunch of stupid pukes—and losing the job for the reason he'd lost it completely fucked him in terms of getting another job, but at least he'd stood up to them. At least now he was free.

It was scary. His rent was past due, so were the utilities, the Camaro needed serious work, but fuck all that. He'd figure something out, he always did. *Something* would happen. Nobody starved in America, did they?

Nick saw the 7–11 ahead, one of the stores he'd robbed in '76. I need some dinner and some booze, he thought, impulsively turning into the lot.

He walked into the 7–11 and went back to the frozen-foods case and dug out a Rosarita Mexican dinner. The place was crowded—a bunch of screaming Mexican kids, blacks, an elderly black security guard on a stool by the door. Bright and vibrant with color, the store made Nick very much aware that he was in the present, safely removed from what had happened six years before.

Until he stepped up to the counter. He nearly shit. It was the same lady clerk he'd robbed in '76. He could never forget that splotchy face, lower lip quivering with fear as she'd opened the register.

And she was definitely checking him out very closely. Below the neck. Nick still had his shirt off and her eyes were practically burning the sweat off his chest and stomach. Other people stole looks at him, too; he had that kind of body. Gay or straight, male or female, everybody admired his looks: his hairy defined chest, his smooth back, his tight hairy stomach, his muscular arms. Women and gay guys fantasized fucking him, straight guys wished they were like him. When Nick realized that was the case with the clerk, he managed to say, with some semblance of casualness, "And a fifth of Jack Daniel's."

When she turned to get it, Nick realized why he hadn't recognized her before; she'd lost at least a hundred pounds. In '76, she'd been a tub in a floral muumuu. She'd also had a face-lift, he realized, and not a very good one.

He gave her a twenty, and when she gave him his change, he smiled at her. Nick had a winning, somewhat wistful smile. Few people could resist, and she was no exception.

With a tinge of embarrassment, her eyes flitting over his body, she compulsively tugged a metallic-red curl down behind her ear and smiled back.

2

Jeff sat at his desk on the sixth floor of the 9000
building on Sunset, talking on the phone to his
best friend, Victor. "So, anyway, we'd stopped
for ice cream when we noticed that this Zody's
store was still open. So we went in and we did
this tour number, like we were a couple from the
Valley or something, looking at all the tacky crap.
There'd be these little hand towels with 'I love L.A.'
and a heart, and we'd say, 'These will be perfect for
the half-bath off the rumpus room.' Or there'd be
these little Day-Glo figurines from Hong Kong that
looked like Phyllis Diller having DTs and we were
practically rolling around, holding our stomachs, like
we were loaded or something. *We couldn't quit laughing.* People were staring, and finally the assistant
manager came over and said, if we're not going to
buy anything, would we please leave. And we *still*
couldn't quit laughing. It was too much. And we
weren't even high or anything."

Jeff paused, then laughed at Victor's response. He
had an effusive adolescent laugh.

Thin from working off several pounds a week on
the dance floor, Jeff wore a faded pair of ten-year-old
Levi's and a blue T-shirt with a Polygram logo. He
was clean-shaven, suntanned, boyishly handsome; his
curly blond hair was cut expensively in Beverly Hills
in, "you know, kind of a short, no-bullshit surfer/intellectual style." It was lunchtime; he was alone in

15

the frigidly air-conditioned office, an empty carton of cottage cheese on the desk in front of him.

"I don't know, Victor. I'm sick of Studio. There's too many tourists. I think Grayline stops there now. You glance over and there's Ma and Pa Kettle gawking at you from the sidelines." Jeff absently bent his white plastic spoon till it snapped. "Anyway, I almost forgot. I'm invited to a dinner party tonight. At my boss's. It's kind of important *politically*, if you know what I mean. There's a lot of competition around here."

Another clerk typist came back from lunch, a fat sweaty man with styled hair. He didn't look very competitive. He burped loudly and sat down at his desk.

Jeff turned to the window, trying to make his phone conversation more confidential. He stared at the billboard across the street, an ad for the hit movie *Summer and Sweat*: a shirtless young stud in a '58 Cadillac convertible, his arm wrapped around a pouty blond babydoll.

"So . . . you're going to the Apache? Yeah, I wish I could. People are so much more real once you get west of Sepulveda. I've had it with this ghetto mentality, I mean it. If I see one more bulging basket, I think I'm going to fall asleep." Jeff saw his boss come in. "Victor, gotta go. Talk to you later. Okay, 'bye."

Jeff's boss was a skinny forty-year-old guy, also with styled hair, a tan leisure suit, and a tropical Qiana shirt open to reveal a Mexican gold-coin medallion dangling against a bony, hairless chest. He drove a shrill canary-yellow Porsche 914 and lived in Marina Del Rey. "So, you all set for tonight?" he said to Jeff.

"Sure. Seven."

"Tell your lady friend to dress cool and sexy. I thought we might go dancing later."

Jeff was stunned for a second. "Yeah, sure," was all he said.

But he didn't have a lady friend, not the kind his boss meant. He hadn't even thought about bringing a date for the dinner party; now he realized it had been taken for granted. Not that he was obvious, but for some reason Jeff had always assumed that his boss realized he was gay. Now he saw how wrong he'd been; perhaps he wasn't obvious enough.

Periodically, throughout the rest of the afternoon, Jeff called a dozen women friends who might be able to bail him out. But they were either not home or not free. It was, after all, Labor Day weekend.

At five-fifteen, Jeff took the elevator down to the underground garage. His boss was with him, making insinuating conversation with a pretty new secretary for the entire ride. Only as Jeff headed across the garage did his boss call out, "See you tonight, Jeff."

Jeff waved without looking back and unlocked his dirty green Honda civic. He started the engine, other cars roaring to life around him, filling the garage with exhaust fumes. He waited for a chance to pull out; it didn't come. "Come on," he said under his breath, not loud enough for any of the other drivers to actually hear. "Hurry up, asshole. Come on, you fuck. Come on, come on."

He finally made it out to Sunset, which was clogged. Even after rolling the windows down, the Honda was still a sweatbox. He crept along, a few feet for every light change, forced to look at that fucking La Cienega billboard. It had to be *the* choice billboard on the Strip, dead ahead for at least seven blocks, but it wasn't the current ad copy—an arrogant Winston blond—that bothered Jeff. It was the memory of how it had looked, briefly, in '77, when the leasee had been a major record company and the illustrated image in the sky had been a likeness of the woman he adored. A *version* of her anyway.

Not the version he'd seen a few months earlier at the Whisky. That night Jennifer had been an ethereal debauched beauty, dressed like a forties torch singer—Ida Lupino in *Road House*—wilted pink carnation stuck in her long blond hair, looking like she'd just come off a five-day drunk, yet unnaturally, narcissistically gorgeous, delivering a howling, near-insane rhythm-and-blues plea, fervently begging somebody to "Roll me, baby! Oh, good God Almighty! Roll me *all* night long!"

He had rolled her. So, in different ways, had everyone else.

He could still remember vividly the afternoon when, contracts signed, studio dates set, her discovery official, they'd come back from their honeymoon in Acapulco and driven down to look at the La Cienega billboard. It should have been an ecstatic moment, a milestone, the ultimate evidence of blind faith and serious hype on the part of the record company. But right there in broad daylight, right there in front of everybody on the Source patio, she had become hysterical. "What has he done to me? That's not me! That's garbage!"

She'd had a point. The young record mogul who'd signed her had, in his word, transmogrified her from a raunchy bohemian blues singer into a depraved imitation of Cher: glittery bikini and jewelry, baroque hairdo, Vampira makeup. Her eyes rolling, her tongue licking wet blow-job lips, she was down on all fours, chained, shackled, and bound, bruised butt to the breeze, beckoning all masters and dogs and dog-style devotees. JENNIFER SWAY, it said (her real name was Stumpfel), SWEET SURRENDER.

"I *know* that I'm doing," insisted the young record-mogul, who at twenty-five was already responsible for the meteoric rise of several major disco stars. "People are sick of all that hardcore blues shit. It's the seventies! People want class and kinky glamour. Trust me."

Jeff, with nothing but good intentions and a fanatical desire to see Jennifer make it big, persuaded her to go along. He loved her—he worshiped her—and more than anyone he understood what she was trying to do. Their backgrounds were very similar: Jeff growing up in Santa Barbara, Jennifer in Pacific Palisades. Both their dads were work-obsessed corporate executives. Jeff's mom drank, Jennifer's took pills. Home had been a color TV. He knew the feeling of wanting to do something special and dangerous, even *mythic*, of wanting to prove you weren't just another middle-class mediocrity, of wanting to grow up and become something more than a vaguely hip version of Ozzie and Harriet. He knew she was going to do it, she was so much more than an entertainer—she was an artist, for Christ's sake, a female Rimbaud! She was destined for the very top and he was convinced the depraved Cher persona was just a temporary commercial expediency necessary to launch her career. He assured her of that constantly through the long recording sessions for her first album. It was a grueling, tedious period, but the amenities helped smooth the way: a house in Brentwood, a vintage Porsche Speedster, silly, extravagant clothes, coke and Courvoisier—and, of course, the people, *big people*, in music and films, Jeff met through the young record-mogul who'd put him on salary as an executive trainee. It was all very heady. Until then, Jeff had worked a series of dull clerical jobs and had always disparaged material excess; if he made enough to be able to kick back and get high on the weekends, he was happy. But he got a taste of *real* success—of being able to *stay high* all the time—during the summer and fall of '77. It changed him, and continued to haunt him, long after it had all disappeared

It disappeared shortly after Jennifer's album was released.

The night of the big party celebrating the release, the young record-mogul got Jeff coked, drunk, and naked, in a Bel Air pool house. Jeff had known he was gay for a long time, at least since junior high; he just hadn't done anything about it. Or rather, he'd done everything he could to deny it, almost convincing himself his gay feelings were just a slight psychic aberrance that would go away with persistent hetero-sexual conditioning. He had been very persistent, but making it with the young record mogul—who besides being a "genius" was also very cute and ingenious in bed—was like knocking out a dam in a disaster movie. Jeff went berserk: doing the bars and baths every night, cruising Robertson Boulevard in the Porsche Speedster, shirtless at three A.M.; sucking and fucking his brains out, doping heavily.

Ultimately, he got a case of herpes and, one drunken night, broke down and told Jennifer everything. She became hysterical.

Then Jennifer's album was released. A horrendously overproduced collection of disco-fied oldies, and turgid, grotesquely ornate originals. *Rolling Stone* called it "a piece of low kitsch garbage," comparing the production to "Phil Spector on angel dust." The single, a bizarre, unintentionally funny cover of Brenda Lee's "Sweet Nothings," died a quick but expensive death.

Jeff got into a physical altercation with the young mogul, lost his job, and went on a colossal binge. Several months later, he was convalescing in the alcoholism-detox unit of a hospital in Santa Monica and Jennifer was singing at a restaurant in Florida. He told people she had a lot of fans down there.

Although he recovered from his bout with alcoholic excess, he still had show-business fever. He decided to become an agent—agents, after all, ran this town—and he still knew a lot of big people. But they didn't return his calls. He went around to the agencies, inquiring about their intern programs. Finally, he got a job at ICM, in the mailroom. After several agents complained that he was badgering them with questions, being too aggressive, and trying to work his way up too fast, he was fired. There followed another series of clerical jobs as he persistently, frustratingly pushed for something better, cultivating the moderately successful gay show-business people he met on the disco/nightlife circuit. He hung out at Studio One, the Motherlode, sometimes hitting the baths.

Jeff had affairs—affairs and crushes. Recently, he'd had an affair with one of the bartenders at the Motherlode and a crush on a twenty-three-year-old beauty who was already a partner in a contracting firm and drove a baby-blue Maserati. On occasion he would also go home with guys he wasn't really attracted to—producers, agents, young hotshots with obvious futures—if he thought it might lead to something later. Sex was no big deal. "I see a lot of people," he was fond of saying.

Jeff took a left on La Brea, skirting the edge of scum city: downtown Hollywood. It was a part of town that always made him cringe: the land of the losers and no-talents, the mediocrities who never really had a chance.

He had a chance, he had to believe that. A good chance. Perseverance did pay off. He was just experiencing a temporary fall from grace. He still knew everybody. He still had the contacts. He was still charming, intelligent, quick-witted and, at twenty-nine, people were always telling him, "Boyishly good-looking," *hot*. He couldn't afford to think of himself as a has-been. The best had to be yet to come. Besides, most guys didn't really get successful till they were around thirty. He still had three, maybe four years before anybody could really consider him a bona-fide failure.

Jeff took a right on Catalina Street, pulling up to a seedy Spanish-court apartment building. "Very *In a Lonely Place*" was how Victor described it. But Gloria Grahame didn't live across the court. The tenants were a mix of old people, Hollywood punks, and El Salvador death-squad refugees.

Jeff waved to Michelle, the landlady's teenage daughter, as he crossed the court to his garage apartment. She waved back from the steps of the other garage apartment, where she was talking with her boyfriend.

As soon as he entered, Jeff punched on the stereo and picked up the phone. "Victor? Yeah, listen. I've changed my mind. Fuck the dinner. Fuck my boss. Fuck it all. Let's have some *fun!*"

3

Nick pulled into the alley behind the run-down, white-stucco-with-glitter apartment building in Culver City. His parking space was full of trash barrels, so he parked in the next one over. As he got out, a guy shouted down from his shower window, "Hey, you can't park there. That's where my wife parks."

Nick glared up at the guy. "Get fucked." He walked past the cracked empty swimming-pool basin in the court and climbed the reverberating wrought-iron stairs. A baby was screaming in one of the apartments he passed. He unlocked the deadbolt, went in, and closed the door.

The living room was dark, hot, and empty. There was no furniture, just a bunch of unpacked cardboard boxes, a pile of dirty clothes, and a pile of clean clothes. The beige walls were bare.

Nick walked across the pistachio-green carpet to the kitchenette, where he opened the louvered window to let in some fresh air. He looked at the dirty-orange sunset for a second. Then he turned on the oven and stuck in the Rosarita Mexican dinner.

There was a hammer on the counter. Nick opened the refrigerator and used the hammer to knock ice off the freezer. The refrigerator was empty, except for a bloated can of Springfield orange juice and an empty box of Vaporole poppers. He threw some of the freezer ice in a glass, pouring Jack Daniel's over it. Then he went into the bedroom.

There was just a mattress on the bedroom floor, some disheveled blue sheets and a pillow, and a Colt Publications magazine beside the mattress.

Nick unlaced his boots and took them off, going to open the window. A eucalyptus tree rustled in the hot breeze outside the window, and in the driveway below, a couple of Mexicans laughed and drank beer, working on a '63 Impala.

Nick dropped onto the mattress and took a sip of whiskey, staring at the blank cream-colored wall. He leafed through the Colt magazine, looking at the pictures of the naked butch men: truckers, cowboys, linemen, studs.

Nick rubbed his cock through his Levi's. It started getting bigger. Finally he unfastened his belt and unbuttoned his Levi's, pulling out his hard cock, slowly jacking off.

The phone rang. He was tempted not to answer it, but he stumbled into the living room. "Yeah, hello—"

Some dip wanted to know if Nick was familiar with the Big Brother program. Nick hung up on him.

He could smell his dinner heating. He stuffed his cock back in his Levi's and went and got the Rosarita Mexican-dinner carton out of the trash and reread the instructions.

Then he leaned against the counter, drank his whiskey, and looked at the greasy Mickey Mouse clock over the stove, thinking about the night ahead.

⌇⌇⌇⌇⌇⌇⌇⌇⌇⌇⌇⌇⌇⌇⌇⌇⌇⌇⌇⌇⌇⌇⌇⌇⌇⌇⌇⌇ **4**

Jeff and Victor got to the Apache at eleven. The place was packed with good-looking young men, the air thick with smoke and the smell of sweat and amyl. The B-52s sang with nerdish elation about a party gone out of bounds.

Jeff liked the Apache. There was an area away from the dance floor where you could actually carry on a conversation. Though Jeff liked to dance, he also liked to talk, especially when he came with Victor. Victor was a small, cute Chicano, twenty-four, who worked as a driver at Paramount. At first Jeff had found him shallow, and for a while Victor had had a crush on Jeff. Now they were like brothers. As Victor said, "You can find a lover anywhere, but good friends are hard to come by." And a friend was all Jeff wanted tonight.

Until he saw Nick.

Nick had his shirt off. In the bar's amber light he was a sight to behold. He looked, Jeff thought, like one of those hunky, hyper-macho Colt models. Fantasies did come true. He was dancing with a bearded guy he'd probably just met. The bearded guy was a good dancer, but he was conserving his energy. Nick wasn't. He was dancing his brains out. But he did it with so much style—losing control on purpose, instead of because he was too loaded—that everyone was getting off on him.

Jeff stared at Nick for a long time. Would a guy as

hot as Nick give him the time of day—or night? Why not? He was hot too, he knew he was. But when Victor made a comment about the way Jeff was looking at Nick, Jeff felt a rush of self-consciousness. Did everybody in the place see him stare at Nick, practically drooling? Thank God Nick hadn't looked over at him.

Then the B-52s segued into the Go-Gos, and Nick looked directly at Jeff. Separating from the bearded guy, he started toward Jeff.

Jeff panicked. What was he going to say? What would Nick say? Yet all Nick did was brush past him, pushing against him deliberately, saying, "Excuse me."

For a second Nick was right in Jeff's face, and Jeff could feel the heat from his body, he could see Nick's mouth glistening in the amber light. His cock jerked and he wanted to kiss Nick. But he didn't. And Nick kept moving.

Jeff felt his Hawaiian shirt, damp with Nick's sweat. He watched Nick polish off his Coors, trying not to look at Nick's body. Nick's face gave no clue as to what he was like; he was just too fucking good-looking. Something about the black mustache and beard growth framing Nick's sensuous pink mouth drove Jeff crazy, filling his mind with ideas both raunchy and tender. Jeff realized he was staring again, but Nick seemed oblivious. Was it part of the game or did he really not give a shit?

"Dance?" Victor asked.

Why not? It was his turn to show off while Nick watched. But when Jeff glanced over to see what Nick thought of his dancing, he realized—with more of a sinking, desolate feeling than usual—that Nick had taken off.

Nick leaned against his car and wiped the sweat off his chest with his T-shirt. The hot wind rustled the palm trees and blew dust and leaves across the asphalt of the Apache parking lot. A cop car warbled in the distance. This was race-riot weather, he thought. The kind of night when best friends punched each other out over imagined insults, when wives shot burglars who turned out to be their husbands, when guys jacked up on speed sucked cock in public places till their lips went numb.

Nick sat in his car and smoked a cigarette and thought about where to go next. He looked at the men lined up to get into the Apache. He thought about going into Hollywood. He thought about the guy in the Hawaiian shirt.

He'd been attracted to Jeff at first, but after he'd brushed past him, he'd checked him out again. Jeff's friend had turned him off. Although Victor was technically macho, he still struck Nick as a typical West Hollywood queen, shallow and bitchy. Although Jeff didn't project that sensibility, the association was enough to discourage Nick from the protracted cruising game the situation seemed to call for. Nick just didn't have the patience for that crap.

Since Randy, he'd gone back to impersonal sex. He wasn't bitter or scared of intimacy; he just didn't have time to play a lot of bullshit games. It was lonely in a way, but it was better than being desperate, always hoping the next guy who walked in the bar would be the love of your life. Fuck all that.

At least with the impersonal scenes you knew why you were there.

He had several options. Griffith Park was closed for the night, but there was that smaller park in West Hollywood. Still, the last time he'd been there, the pickings had been slim. Unemployed hustlers, a Latino drag queen stuck in a Charo fantasy who'd asked him for a light, and some old guy in lederhosen constantly scolding a terrified chow.

There was the alley behind the Pit on Santa Monica Boulevard. Definitely a lot of action, and most of the guys were reasonably attractive. But it was also one of the harshest scenes Nick had ever encountered. Hollywood veterans, exhausted and bitter. You didn't get fondled, you got yanked.

Nick thought about the Ocean Park lot. His luck had been pretty good there. It was more of a beach crowd, more like the San Francisco–style atmosphere of Ocean Park itself. Semihip UCLA students from Venice, who liked to step out once in a while between cramming sessions for a quick blow-job. Or else they were "between relationships" and came to the beach only when they were so fucking horny they couldn't stand it.

That's when it's fun, Nick thought. That was when you felt renewed afterward. He started the engine.

Jeff sipped a glass of white wine and watched the Eurythmics on the big Revolver screen. But it was hard to keep his attention on the video. Revolver, a hot new bar on Santa Monica Boulevard, was a gallery of incredibly hot-looking men.

Practically everybody seemed to have come with friends, somebody to stand with while being watched by everybody else. Watching was what Revolver was all about. Watching the videos and covertly checking out the other guys as they watched.

"So what about Suzanne? Why didn't you ask her?" Victor said.

It was late. They'd been all over town.

"I did. She was going to a party in Bel-Air."

"What about Paula? She's a good sport."

"She's in New York."

Jeff checked out the guys by the bar. The situation was hopeless. Everybody looked good in the soft light, but no one was going to make the first move.

When Victor got into a conversation with a silly designer, Jeff tossed back his drink and left. Victor was puzzled, but knew it was best to let him go. They could talk about it later.

Jeff walked up Larrabee to his car. It was almost two. His body was slick with sweat. Was it from the heat or his nerves?

He was depressed and angry. The events of the day

and the possible repercussions clogged his mind. What would he tell his boss? Why did he have to care what that moron thought?

He had thought things were on the upswing. Acting informally as an agent for a writer friend with a TV series idea, he'd given the outline to a producer he'd tricked with. That was almost a month ago, but something still might come of it.

Then there was the daughter of a famous and bankable English movie director whom he'd recently met. She was pretty, fun, and a fag hag with ulterior designs. Another possibility.

It was a strange town. Things happened out of the blue.

Yet suddenly Jeff felt overcome with failure. He thought of different successful show-business people his own age or younger, and felt a rush of rage and frustration.

He thought of the pretty narcissistic young men back at Revolver. He decided to go home, jerk off in the mirror, take two valium, and go to bed.

But somewhere between Revolver and home, he changed his mind.

Things were slow for a Friday night. A few cars cruised through the Ocean Park lot; a few others were parked and empty. The temperature was still in the eighties.

Nick sat in his Camaro and smoked his next-to-last cigarette. In just under two hours he'd seen an old guy pull up in a pickup, walk out to the beach, and come back with another older guy. Back in the pickup, the second guy's head had disappeared from view. They were still going at it.

He'd seen a man with styled hair and polyester slacks get out of an Olds Cutlass. He was still out on the beach.

A young student type on a bicycle had swooped around the lot a few times and left.

A Japanese kid in a Toyota had driven past Nick seven or eight times, slowing down each time and checking him out, long after Nick made it clear the interest was not mutual. Finally the kid had parked and gone out to the beach.

Now Nick watched a tricked-up VW bug with a surfboard rack move slowly up the lot. He figured it was a straight surfer at first, because the straight surfers used the lot farther up. But when the VW pulled up and parked in the gay cruising area—at two in the morning—the driver's intentions were clear.

Nick watched the surfer get out and stretch and lean against the VW, giving Nick a better look.

Nick liked what he saw.

Although the beach lights could be deceptive, the surfer looked good. The unbuttoned print shirt and powder-blue cords, the blond hair worn over the ears, suggested a guy who passed for straight with his buddies during the day. He exuded self-confidence, pumping his leg impatiently as he leaned against the car.

Suddenly, as if tired of the game that had barely started, the surfer looked right at Nick and then got back into the VW. But he didn't drive off. Instead, he sat tapping his hand on the roof in time to a song playing on his radio.

Nick got out and walked over. He had at least two options, and one was just to talk. As he got closer, his cock chose the other option.

The surfer was very good-looking, about twenty. He was tanned and his nose and cheeks and mouth were rosy. Looking up at Nick, he smiled faintly, pleased with what Nick was doing.

Nick had pulled out his hard cock and shoved it in the surfer's face. The surfer sucked like he'd been dying to suck a cock for a long time.

Suddenly the headlights of an approaching car washed over them. Nick pulled away and stuffed his cock back in his pants, watching apprehensively as the headlights approached. The Santa Monica police patrolled the lot periodically. But it was just a regular car. Nick turned back to the surfer.

Now the surfer was holding his incredibly hard thick cock in his fist. The big head shone like chrome under the beach light. Nick wanted to suck the surfer's cock—badly.

"Wanna go out on the beach?" Nick said.

The surfer looked down at his cock and then at Nick, grinning. "Yeah, okay."

Nick headed out first. Glancing over at the car that had interrupted him, he saw the driver getting out a few hundred yards up the lot. It was too dark to make out the man's features. He would never have guessed it was Jeff had it not been for the Hawaiian shirt.

Nick kept walking toward the beach. After all, there were a lot of guys wearing Hawaiian shirts that summer. It wasn't necessarily that guy he'd seen at the Apache. But he kept looking over, and when Jeff passed directly under the light, Nick made out his features and knew for sure.

Jeff didn't recognize Nick. He saw some guy heading out to the beach, but was too self-conscious to look over. He crossed the bike trail and plodded out across the sand.

Nick heard a car door close and looked back. It was the surfer, following him.

Nick was torn. Reaching the sand, he started out toward the jetty. The moon was full, the sand luminous. The dark figures standing around the lifeguard station were more numerous than Nick had expected. Maybe they'd come in from the Venice side. They were definitely avoiding the campfire. The partying Chicanos out by the jetty were potential queer-bashers.

A straight couple walked a dog by the water, heading toward the lifeguard station. There, as Nick looked more closely, he could see a guy fucking another guy in silhouette. He wondered if the guys would stop fucking when the straight couple passed. He also wondered what had happened to Jeff. He seemed to have disappeared.

Nick scanned the beach for Jeff's Hawaiian shirt, a smear of tropical color in the moonlight. He saw a dark form among the palm trees behind the men's room, but had to look hard to make sure it wasn't just a shadow. He took a few steps. The shadow sat down. Then Nick saw the shirt and knew it was Jeff.

Nick trudged over, aware that the surfer was still following him.

Although he heard someone trudging over, Jeff couldn't bring himself to look up.

Christ, what am I doing here? he thought. He didn't

feel like going home, that was for sure. He didn't want to be alone tonight. But the last thing he really felt like was getting a frantic blow-job from some desperate old troll down on the goddamn beach. He was beginning to feel he just came down here by rote. What else does a gay guy do when he's depressed and wants to escape his feelings? He fucks his brains out, of course. He picks up a trick. *Trick*. Jeff hated that word. "I'll be right with you," Victor had said more than once when Jeff called, "as soon as I kick out my trick." Of course, when Victor said it, it was funny, almost facetious. This is absurd, Jeff thought, the trudging footsteps getting closer. He wished Victor were here right now, or that it was later, so they could joke about it.

I probably won't even be able to get a hard-on, Jeff thought. It was probably some horrible creep. For a second before he finally looked up, Jeff actually thought about Nick, the hot number at the Apache. If I'd just asked him to dance—instead of trying to play it cool and show off first—I could have avoided all this shit. Why didn't I?

Nick sensed Jeff's nervousness and liked him for it. Nick was a little nervous himself. "Hello," he said.

Jeff looked up. He was stunned. Then he laughed. So did Nick.

"I guess there wasn't much going on at the Apache tonight," Nick said. His tone of voice indicated he was ready to break the code of minimal speech that went with impersonal sex.

"Yeah, I guess not," Jeff said. He hesitated, reluctant to dissipate whatever tension might still be there with talk. But he quickly decided: if he wants to talk, he's probably not interested in me sexually, so we might as well at least talk. "Not much going on anywhere else either."

"Yeah? Where'd you go?"

The surfer watched Nick sit down next to Jeff and introduce himself with a handshake. What the fuck was going on? The surfer kept his distance and waited, rubbing his cock through his pocket, hoping Nick would change his mind. When he realized that Nick and Jeff were having an extended conversation, punctuated with soft laughter, he snorted in disgust and plodded on out toward the lifeguard station.

"So, you come down here very often?" Jeff said. Then he laughed. "What a cliché. Sorry about that."

Nick grinned. "Oh, I come here every once in a while. What about you?"

"No. It's not really my scene. I mainly just go to the bars. Or out dancing."

"I don't know. It's kind of exciting down here sometimes. Not the almost-being caught part. Just never knowing who you're gonna run into next. It's kind of an adventure in a way—"

Jeff pointed to the lifeguard station. "I guess that's where most of the action is."

"Yeah. Pretty much."

Jeff dug out a cigarette and lit it. "Shit. I don't even know why I came down here tonight. I'm really not into it. I guess I was just depressed. I didn't want to go home."

Nick hesitated. Up to now it had been small talk, nothing personal. Would it be worth it to get to know this guy? "What are you depressed about?"

"Just bullshit. Work. My career."

"*Career*. Wasn't that a movie once?"

"Yeah. Dean Martin and Shirley MacLaine. About fifty-nine."

"Yeah, I think I saw part of it on TV. Gee, you must really be into movies to remember something like that."

"Well, yeah, I guess I am. It's part of my work."

"Oh, yeah? What do you do?"

"I'm kind of an agent."

"You mean like a Hollywood agent?"

"Yeah."

"No kidding. That must be real exciting."

"For the most part, it is. But it's also incredibly vicious. People are your friend one day and shit on you the next. A lot of people go crazy—literally. There's an incredible amount of pressure."

"Yeah, it's got to be real hectic. Always on the phone, making deals, jacking each other off."

"Yeah, there's a lot of that. The whole town is built on phoniness."

"It must be a turn-on, though. You probably meet a lot of big stars."

"Oh, yeah. But they're just people."

"Lots of coke, too."

"Yeah."

"Are you with one of those big agencies?"

"Well, I was with ICM for a while. But it was too big, too impersonal. I'm kind of working on my own now."

"Well, I don't see what you're depressed about. It sounds like you know what you want and you're going for it."

But Jeff was suddenly tired of his own hype. "The truth is, I'm not on top of shit. In fact, I'm not even a real agent. It's a shit-ass oral agreement with some moron who thinks he's a writer. Trying to peddle a sitcom idea about a sitcom writer who's a moron. This drip in Encino probably used it for toilet paper a month ago. The grim truth is, I've got a crummy little job as a clerk typist. That's reality. At least for now. Success takes time."

Jeff paused. What the hell was he ranting at Nick for? But Nick didn't seem put off. And it was nice to be able to just talk to somebody for a while.

"At least you have a job," Nick said. "And something going for your future. What's fucked is when you take a shit job that's going nowhere and the only thing in your future is another shit job. I feel real sorry for people like that."

"What do you do?" Jeff asked.

"I've got a salon. In La Habra. Mr. Nick's for Hair. We do men, too."

"Really? That's great," Jeff said. But he was

thinking: Oh, crud. Another hairdresser, another macho poseur.

"I'm just kidding. Did you really think I was serious? I wouldn't do any pansy shit like that. No, actually I have a hard-driving muscle job in a warehouse out by the airport. At least I did till this afternoon."

"What happened?"

"I got canned. Fight."

"A fight?"

"Yeah, I caught this Okie staring at my dick while we were taking a leak at the urinal. Had to beat the shit out of him."

Jeff laughed. This time he figured Nick was at least partially joking. "Well, there's always another job, that's what I've found out. And there's always unemployment."

"Yeah, but I think I'm gonna split L.A. All this good-natured greed, I don't know. Nobody gives a shit anymore. People just want to check out your car, your cock, that's all. They don't give a fuck about anything else."

"So where would you go?"

"I don't know. Not Frisco. Not New York. Maybe out of the country. Work on a sailboat or something. Something romantic. Like your shirt." Nick smiled. "Maybe go to Jamaica. Smoke some good dope and get over being jaded. You think that's possible?"

It seemed like a strange question to Jeff. Sometimes he wondered if he was jaded, but he usually decided it was a B-movie concept:

Jaded (1946) Ida Lupino, Richard Widmark, Gloria Grahame. An alcoholic torch singer helps her demented boyfriend accidentally kill a poor sweet kid who got knocked up.

Besides, Jeff thought, nowadays if jaded meant anything, it meant being into S&M.

"It's possible," Jeff said. "If you don't go too far."

"How far is too far?"

"I don't know. Are you into S&M?"

"No. Not since basic training. What about you?"

Jeff laughed. "I don't think so. At least not consciously."

"Shit." Nick laughed and leaned back on his elbows. "Who cares about all that crap anyway? That's the least of my worries now."

For a long time, they looked at the ocean and watched the dark figures move across the sand. The heat enveloped the beach and made the slapping of the waves sound flat and artificial. It reminded Jeff of a huge soundstage and the ocean itself looked strangely fake.

"I don't believe this weather, do you?" Jeff finally said.

"Yeah," Nick said. "Great for the beach."

"Especially at night."

"Yeah."

"Yeah."

Nick leaned over and kissed Jeff. Jeff hugged Nick and kissed him back. It felt good. They kissed gently at first and then they really went at it. They wanted each other and it wasn't just looks. There was something else going on, too—something special—though they didn't really know what it was or what it meant.

"You wanna go someplace?" Jeff said.

"Yeah," Nick said, "I guess we ought to. This beach isn't very private tonight."

They were crossing the bike trail when three Chicano guys came around from behind the men's room where they'd been taking a leak by the locked door.

The Chicano guys glared at Nick and Jeff, figuring two guys like that were probably homos, but nothing happened.

Although Nick's place in Culver City was much closer, he accepted Jeff's invitation to follow him back to Hollywood. Nick seldom took guys home. He usually didn't want them to know that much about him.

By the time they reached Jeff's place, it was three-thirty, and the wind had died down completely. The sound of the car doors slamming and their footsteps climbing the stairs reverberated through the hot still air with almost irritating clarity.

Jeff switched on a light and turned on the radio. "You want to smoke some dope?" he said.

"Sure, why not?"

Nick looked around the apartment while Jeff went to get the grass. It was cluttered but comfortable. Lots of books. Old movie posters: *Detour*, *The Big Heat*, *Kiss Me Deadly*.

Nick sang along with the Police song on the radio, which was poignant and forlorn in a way that matched the dead hour. Nick was glad he wasn't alone.

Jeff lit a couple of candles in the bedroom and opened the window to get rid of the hot stale air. Then he picked up a shoebox full of grass and went back into the living room.

He never got a chance to roll the grass. Nick went over to him and started to unbutton his Hawaiian shirt.

Jeff set the grass down. He pulled Nick to him,

running his hands down over the Levi's that cupped Nick's butt.

Nick kissed Jeff all around his mouth, all down his neck. He took Jeff's shirt off and ate his way down Jeff's hairy chest and stomach.

Jeff pulled Nick's T-shirt up and ran his hands over Nick's smooth shoulders.

Nick opened Jeff's pants. Jeff's cock flopped out, jerking to a full erection. Nick seemed to study Jeff's cock for a long time, drawing out the suspense. Jeff could hardly stand it.

Then Nick licked the sun-bleached hair on Jeff's thighs, working his way around to Jeff's butt.

Jeff groaned as Nick's hot tongue moved over him. He felt like he was going to shoot off any second and his cock hadn't even been touched yet. He stepped away from Nick and said, "Let's go into the bedroom."

Nick got up and kissed Jeff. They went into the bedroom and took off the rest of their clothes. Jeff was folding back the spread when Nick came up behind him.

Jeff felt Nick's hard cock push between his legs. He turned around and sat down on the bed, worshiping Nick's cock. He sucked and licked for a long time. When Nick reached down to squeeze Jeff's cock, Jeff brushed his hand away. Jeff still felt on the verge of coming.

Finally, Nick lifted Jeff's legs and lowered him back on the bed. Nick bent down and kissed Jeff. Then, very slowly, Nick eased his wet cock into Jeff's tight ass.

Jeff moaned. "Oh, wow. Easy."

Nick moaned too. He leaned down and kissed Jeff again. *Jesus*, Jeff looked so good. Talk about your fucking dolls, man. *Shit*. If this wasn't heaven, it'd sure do.

Nick pushed his cock in further and further. Then, with long deep strokes, he started fucking Jeff very slowly. Jeff started going crazy, moaning and groaning.

Nick leaned down and sucked the head of Jeff's

cock, still fucking him. Jeff moaned louder. Then Nick started going hard and fast. He groaned, out of control.

"Fuck me, man," Jeff shouted. "Fuck me."

Suddenly Nick stopped, high on the brink of orgasm. He wanted to hold the moment as long as possible.

Jeff filled the excruciating lull with a loud delirious groan.

Nick went crazy. The wet slapping sounds reverberated through Jeff's apartment—through the hot still air . . .

"I'm gonna come. Oh, man, fuck me! Jesus!"

"Jesus, Lord Jesus, oh, please, Lord Jesus," Doris, the building manager, whispered fervently, kneeling in prayer at her bed. Her hands were clasped together as she cringed by her open window. She could hear the sex sounds, the two male voices moaning and groaning, and she unclasped her hands and used them to cover her ears. She pressed her forehead against a black Bible and ground her teeth.

"Jesus Jesus Jesus Jesus Jesus," she said when she heard Jeff shout, "Oh, Christ, I'm gonna shoot!"

Doris' Pekingese, watching her from its doggie basket across the room, emitted a high-pitched growl and yapped twice.

Jeff exploded across his own chest.

Nick came in hard jolts that seemed to shake the whole room. "Shit!" He couldn't believe how good it felt. It was better than anything.

Nick collapsed on top of Jeff. Jeff lowered his legs and hugged Nick. They were both out of breath, covered with sweat, exhausted, and happy. Nick let out a deliberately melodramatic joyful yowl of satisfaction.

Nick's yowl struck Doris like a physical blow. He might as well have been towering over her like a demon, shaking a huge bludgeoning prick in her face, chortling.

Nick slowly pulled out of Jeff and lay back beside him on the bed. "Whew! That was too much. I'm not just saying that either."

Jeff leaned over and kissed Nick. "Yeah, I kind of enjoyed it myself. For the most part."

"For the most part?" Nick laughed. Then he kissed Jeff very tenderly.

Doris' bedroom was empty. There was a lamp on in the living room.

Doris sat beside the lamp, dialing a number on the sticker on the pink telephone. Her cheeks were smeared with tears and she held her Bible tightly. Whispering rapidly to Jesus, she stroked her Pekingese, and waited for the call to click through.

Doris blew her nose. When a voice came on the line, she said, "Yes, this is an emergency. I want to report a crime-in-progress."

───∿∿∿∿∿∿∿∿∿∿∿∿∿∿∿∿∿── 9

"**D**id you say you had some dope?"
"Yeah," Jeff said. "It's in the other room. I'll get it."
Watching Jeff pad into the living room, Nick felt good. He liked Jeff, and Jeff seemed to like him. They'd sure hit if off sexually. Plus Jeff was easy to talk to. He'd be fun to see again, if they could keep it light. If Jeff wanted to. It was hard to tell; everything could seem perfect, then they'd give you a fake phone number.

Only a few feet away in the next apartment, Doris was talking to a cop over the phone.
"Well, that's not technically against the law, ma'am," said the cop. "Of course, if they're disturbing the peace—"
Doris wasn't getting results. "Well, they're killing each other, if you call that disturbing the peace."
"They're fighting?"
"They're shouting, they're carrying on, it woke me out of a sound sleep. I thought maybe you'd like to know if someone was being killed. Or would you rather wait until it's all over?"
"We'll send someone out."

10

Officers Burke and Rodríguez loved each other and hated queers.

Once Burke had let a queer suck him off in the May Company men's room when he was working Vice. Then he'd kicked the guy's teeth in and busted him on assault. Back in high school, Burke used to go out with his buddies in Long Beach and beat up queers coming out of downtown bars. One time they caught a guy in the alley; they tried to make the queer blow 'em first, but they were all too drunk to get it up. So they wasted him. The guy had looked familiar. Turned out he was the high-school music teacher. Nothing happened. What was he going to do, tell the principal? Report it to the cops?

Rodríguez hated queers because of his pretty looks. "Hey, señorita," the cruel kids in high school used to joke. He'd been too shy and nervous to ever be considered for a club or gang. He'd showed them, the guys who used to call him a *pussy*. He'd joined the ultimate gang.

Burke was crazy about his baby-faced Chicano partner. Cops often loved their partners. When you spent that much time in a car with another person, going through all the things cops went through together, it was hard not to.

But the way Burke felt about Rodríguez was different; it went a little farther. Like one time at a

party when everybody was drunk and Burke pulled
out his cock and dangled it over a passed-out Rodríguez' open mouth. Some joke. Everybody had laughed
about it later, except Rodríguez. It had pissed him
off. For several days after that he had been sullen,
sulking like a lover, giving his partner the silent
treatment. The incident had triggered his old anxiety
about being effeminate. He hated his pretty looks
and couldn't stand it that Burke had treated him like
a girlie queer, even in jest. Nobody treated him that
way *now*. Not when they saw his gun and his badge
and his uniform, you bet your ass they didn't. For a
guy he worshiped and was willing to die for to treat
him that way was intolerable.

He'd shown Burke, though, the night the black guy
pulled the gun at the Pup 'n' Taco. He'd greased that
dusted fuck just in time. He'd never forget the look
on Burke's face that night: sitting in the car afterward,
pale and trembling, his eyes full of resentment and
gratitude. All right, asshole, treat me like a faggot
now, Rodríguez had thought, grinning cockily at Burke
in the flashing red light.

They were cruising a deserted Western Avenue when
they picked up the Cataline Street call. "A pair of
fruits fighting. Fuckin' *shit*." Burke laughed loudly,
as if the idea of two pansies trying to act like a
regular couple having a lover's quarrel was intrinsi-
cally hilarious.

They took a left on Franklin. Burke's lips were
moving slightly, as if he was talking to himself, and
he breathed heavily. He was speeding, Rodríguez
knew. He'd seen Burke wash down a couple of Dexedrines when they'd stopped at Winchell's.

"Did I tell you about the queer we caught once?"
Burke said with a bark that made Rodríguez flinch.

"Which one?"

Burke's sharp laugh echoed. "When I was on Vice.
In one of those uniform bars. That place out on
Melrose—"

"Uniform bars?" Rodríguez pretended not to understand, playing rookie to Burke's veteran.

"You know. Where the fags dress up. We caught a guy in there in a CHP uniform. He had the whole deal. Boots, leather jacket, gold helmet, all the insignia, everything but the piece."

"You're shittin' me."

"And guess what? He's got a real badge. And we trace the badge, and guess what? Turns out it belonged to an officer shot in the line of duty several months prior. The queer stole it off the slain officer's widow."

"You gotta be shittin' me."

"No. I'm telling you, there's *nothing* lower than a queer in heat. They're fucking *animals!*"

Rodríguez shook his head.

"I could tell you some stories about queers you wouldn't even fuckin' believe." Burke snorted.

Rodríguez stared out the window at the dead street. The night was almost over. He wanted to go home and get drunk, fuck his ulcer.

Burke reached in his pocket. When he was sure Rodríguez wasn't looking, he stuck two more Dexedrines tablets in his mouth and swallowed them dry.

11

"**M**om, what's going on?" Michelle shielded her eyes from the living-room lamp.

"Nothing." Doris steered her daughter back to the bedroom. "There's just some trouble next door. The police will handle it."

"What do you mean? At Jeff's? What happened?"

"It's nothing that concerns you, young lady. You just march straight back to bed."

Michelle marched straight to her bedroom window. In a few minutes, she saw her mother meet two uniformed police officers in the court below.

One look at Doris' ravaged face and Burke figured her for a lush. She had been, until her born-again experience the previous spring. She was hysterical, rattling on in a whiny, grating voice Burke found nearly unbearable. Even so, the speed and his exhaustion combined to make him believe her.

"It sounded like one was raping the other one. And there was screaming, horrible screaming. And more hitting. He screamed, 'No, no, don't!' Then it stopped. I think he's dead. It just made me sick, sick to my stomach—"

Burke felt queasy, starting to sweat. He imagined: a mutilated teenage boy, his cock hacked off with a machete. A color glossy of another boy's hacked-up torso. The severed arm of a Chicano youth they'd found wrapped in a green plastic bag in a field in

Duarte. The head of the blond-haired surfer kid, skin turned gray, tongue lopping out, they'd found off Mulholland Drive. The trashbag murders! The dismemberments performed by two prissy S&M fruits in an innocuous Gold Medallion all-electric apartment.

Burke looked up at Jeff's apartment, at the bland stucco facade, the chipped tile steps, the Spanish door—and his heart started pounding. "Has anybody come out?" he said to Doris.

"No."

"Do you have a passkey?"

Nick and Jeff sat up in bed, finishing a joint. They talked and laughed as David Bowie crooned softly on the radio in the other room.

Jeff stroked Nick's hairy stomach. "You know, at the risk of being trite, I'm really glad I ran into you."

Nick smiled. "I'm glad you did, too."

Jeff laughed softly. Then he kissed Nick. They both got hard again. Jeff rolled over as Nick reached for the Vaseline.

Soon Nick was on top of Jeff, his hairy chest sliding against Jeff's sweat-slick back, as he moved with slow, steady thrusts, feeling as if he could go on forever.

Burke and Rodríguez climbed the stairs to Jeff's apartment. Burke had Doris' passkey in his hand. At the top of the stairs they heard Jeff groan. To them, it sounded like a groan of agony. They drew their .38s.

Nick was going fast and hard. Lost in Jeff, he'd quit thinking, he was just fucking. It made everything all right; no matter what else happened, they couldn't take this away from him. No matter what else happened, he could still fuck, he could still fuck, it was so much more than all right.

Nick was bucking toward a blinding orgasm when he heard somebody in the hall. Before he could even wonder who it was, the overhead light snapped on. Two cops lunged into the room.

Jeff saw them first. "What the fuck—"

Nick was turning when he felt a gun against the back of his neck. A hand grabbed his shoulder and pulled him up. He saw the wall ...

Burke smashed Nick's head against the wall, pulling Nick's arms behind his back. The cuffs dug into his wrists. His mind imploded with pain and shock.

Jeff sat up. "What the fuck are you doing?"

Rodríguez straight-armed his gun in Jeff's face. "Shut up, you fucking faggot!"

Burke turned Nick around. Nick saw Burke's squinched-up hatchet face. Nick tried to speak, but Burke started hitting him hard across the face and head. "You goddamn cock-sucking faggot—" Burke pushed Nick's head down, trying to force him to the floor.

Nick saw Burke's knee coming up. Burke kneed him hard in the balls. Nick gagged, dropping to the floor. Vomit burned the back of his throat. He felt the blood rush out of his head.

Burke kicked Nick in the small of the back. "You fucking queer!"

Nick pulled up his knees and rolled over on his side, facing the wall.

Burke kicked him hard in the butt. "Lay still!" he shouted.

Jeff pulled up the blanket to cover his body and watched the cops. He took in Rodríguez' scrunched-up baby face, his gun. Then he looked at Burke. Burke kicked Nick in the butt again. *Why?* This was completely insane!

"What the fuck are you doing?" Jeff said

Burke turned to Jeff. "Get up!"

Jeff got up off the bed. As if he thought Jeff was hiding a gun, Rodríguez yanked the blanket away. Jeff's body glistened with sweat. "What are you doing?"

"Stand over there." Burke indicated the wall by the bed. "Face the wall. Put your hands on your head." Burke shoved Jeff against the wall. "Spread your legs." Burke kicked Jeff's feet apart.

Nick moaned.

Rodríguez felt his ulcer burn. This sucked. He knew it was crap. So did Burke. They knew that *now*. Now was too late. They had to bust the fruits on *something* to justify their actions.

"Let's get some ID," Rodríguez said.

"Listen," Jeff said to Rodríguez, who sounded halfway sane. "You can't just come in here without a warrant, we haven't done anything."

Rodríguez glared at Jeff—at his smooth back and hairy little butt. Burke's ass was hairy, too. "Listen, you girlie piece of faggot shit," Rodríguez screamed in Jeff's ear, "we can do any fucking thing we want!" With an abruptness that startled even Burke, Rodríguez smashed Jeff's head against the wall. The thud shook a framed still of Ida Lupino in *Road House* off the wall; the glass shattered when the picture hit the floor.

"You'd better call for assistance," Burke said, barely suppressing a smile. To think he used to hate Mexicans.

Rodríguez glanced at his partner, knowing Burke was impressed. "Okay," he said cockily. "I'll be right back."

Nick heard Rodríguez clatter out the door. Nick felt his cock mashed against the floor. His balls throbbed. His heart was pounding like a rivet gun. He heard Burke step over to Jeff and say, in a fake confidential tone of voice, "So he was raping you?"

"He wasn't raping me." Jeff's head throbbed.

"Rape's a felony." Burke could smell Jeff's sweat. It provoked him on more than one level. "Forced sodomy. It's a felony. Even between two queers. Did you know that?"

Nick looked up at the wall. The movie poster for Hitchcock's *Rope* was dusty, covered with cobwebs. The overhead light was a sickly yellow. It made everything that had looked so pleasantly cluttered before seem cruddy. Nick scrunched up against the wall. He could see Burke now. He could see Burke standing right behind Jeff, who was facing the wall with his hands on his head. It was clear Burke was excited. On more than one level.

"I could have shot him," Burke said in Jeff's ear. "He was committing a felony. Did you know that?"

"Yeah."

"How would you have liked that? He's giving it to you one minute, the next minute you got his brains all over the back of your neck. That almost happened, you know that?"

"Yeah. I know."

Nick saw Burke glance at him. He stared at the floor.

"He's got a big dick," Burke said.

Jeff didn't say anything.

"I said, he's got a big dick."

"If that's what you're into—"

"What?"

"Nothing."

"What did you say?"

"Nothing."

Burke glanced down at Jeff's hairy butt. "It must have hurt. Did it hurt?"

"No."

"It didn't hurt?"

"No."

"Why not?"

"I don't know."

"You don't know?"

"No."

"You take it a lot?"

"Take what?"

"You know, take it. Up the ass."

"I don't know."

Burke snorted. "You don't know?" Burke laughed. And the way he laughed scared the shit out of Jeff.

"So you like to play the girl?"

"No."

"But you like to take it up the ass. Do you wish you were a girl?"

"No."

"It must fit real tight. He's got a big dick."

Right. And I'll bet you'd like to suck it, wouldn't you, you sick, latent geek? Jeff thought. "Yeah," he said.

"Did he make you bleed?"

"No."

"Did he slap you around first?"

"No."

"That's not what the manager said."

The manager? Doris?

"You like to get slapped around, don't you? You probably like to get beat up," Burke said. "You like to get beat up?"

"No."

"He didn't beat you up?"

"No."

"He just fucked you?"

"Yeah."

"You didn't put up a fight?"

"No."

"Why not? Weren't you afraid he'd tear you up? He's got a big dick."

"Listen," Jeff said, "we haven't done anything. It's not against the law. They changed the law."

"Let's see what he did."

Jeff didn't understand what Burke meant at first. Then Burke poked him in the butt with his gun.

"Look—"

"Spread your cheeks."

Jeff reached down.

Burke stood back and looked. "That's the most disgusting queer hole I've ever seen, you know that?"

Jeff didn't say anything. He saw Nick pulling himself up to his knees. Oh, Jesus, please don't do anything, please don't get yourself shot, Jeff thought. This couldn't be happening.

Burke looked down at his .38, an inch from Jeff's

butt. Burke's brain burned with speed and adrenaline.
He could do any fucking thing he wanted.

Jeff felt the cold barrel of Burke's gun against the
back of his balls. He wished he could will himself out
of his body.

"I've got a big gun," Burke said.

"Look, please—"

That's right, faggot, beg. You whimpering piece of
cock-sucking garbage. Lick my gun. Suck my cock,
faggot. I'll blow your fucking guts out, you fucking
piece of cock-sucking shit. *I'd like to fuck you!*

Burke looked at his gun—going into Jeff. He was so
transfixed it took him a second to react to the sound of
Nick getting up.

Burke whirled around just as Nick lunged at him.
He would have shot Nick in the chest, he would have
blown out Nick's heart, if Jeff hadn't grabbed his
arm, deflecting his aim. The gun went off with a
deafening blast, blowing a hole in the wall, as Nick
slammed into Burke full-force, knocking him down.

Jeff and Nick went down, too. Nick rolled on top of
Burke, trying to help keep him down long enough for
Jeff to waste him.

Jeff poked Burke in the eyes with his fingers. It
was the only cheap trick Jeff knew, one he'd memo-
rized to defend himself if he were ever attacked. This
was the first chance he'd ever had to use it. It worked.
Burke howled.

"Get the fuckin' gun!" Nick shouted.

Jeff twisted the .38 out of Burke's hand.

Nick rolled away from Burke and glanced up at
Jeff. Shaking like a palsy victim, he aimed the gun at
Burke.

"Okay," Nick shouted at Burke. "Don't even move,
man, or my buddy's gonna blow your fuckin' brains
out."

Burke didn't move. He lay there, palms pressed
against his eyes, barely able to see. He couldn't believe this had actually happened. This had never
happened; two unarmed men, one cuffed, both naked,

disarming an officer. He'd never live this down, never. He was almost tempted to try something, if only to avoid the humiliation later. But he took one look at the fruit with the gun and stayed where he was, sweat soaking through his uniform as he tried to catch his breath.

Then Nick twisted around and said, "Unlock my cuffs, fuckhole." Burke took his palms away from his eyes and shakily dug out his keys.

Rodríguez had heard the shot. Outside the apartment door, he pressed against the wall, gun in hand. Assistance was on the way. "Hey, Joe," he called into the apartment. "Joe?"

His hands free, Nick took the gun from Jeff. Slapping one of the cuffs on Burke's left wrist, he attached the other to the bedframe.

"Hey, Joe—" Rodríguez called again.

"Don't say a fuckin' word," Nick told Burke.

A second later, they heard Rodríguez clatter back down the stairs.

Nick put the gun down on the dresser and looked at the gouge marks the cuffs had left on his wrists. Then, his balls still throbbing, he picked up his pants and pulled them on.

Jeff stood there, trembling and sweating like a junkie going through withdrawal. "You insane fucking idiot," he said, glaring at Burke. "You could've killed us. I'm going to report you to your superiors—" Even as he spoke, he knew it was too late for that.

"Jeff, we gotta get *outa* here, man," Nick said. "Put on your pants."

"This guy's fucking insane!" Jeff shouted. "He tried to stick his goddamn gun up my ass. This guy should be in a fucking straightjacket. I'm going to call somebody."

"Who?" Nick shouted. "*The cops?*" He threw Jeff his pants. "Put on your fuckin' pants, man!"

Jeff picked up his pants and shakily pulled them on. "There has to be somebody we can call."

"There ain't *nobody*. You try and tell the other

cops what he did, they're gonna fucking laugh in your face." Nick looked at Burke. "Ain't that right?"

Burke glared at Nick, breathing hard, his red hatchet face shiny with sweat. He didn't say a word. He didn't have to.

"Okay," Jeff said. His head spun. "All right. All right. Let's go."

Nick stuck the .38 in the waist of his Levi's. "Get your shoes."

They grabbed their shoes and shirts and had started down the stairs to the court when they heard what sounded like at least a dozen cop cars warbling up in front and in back. Nick thought about where his Camaro was parked, halfway up the block. He couldn't even remember where Jeff's car was.

They ducked back inside and slammed and locked the door.

"Fuckin' shit," Nick said. "Fuckin' shit!"

"What do we do now?"

They heard something rattling in the bedroom. Burke was trying to pull the bedframe apart.

Nick and Jeff looked at each other. It wasn't over yet. They had a hostage.

12

"**H**ow is everything in there?" said the cop on the phone.

The noise of the police chopper overhead almost drowned him out, but Jeff answered, "Fine. How's everything out there?"

Nick peered out the window. He could see the SWAT men on the roof of the apartment building next door; he could see them ducking up the stairs to Doris' place. He could hear them on the roof overhead.

"Jeff, we'd sure like you to surrender. We know there's been a misunderstanding. We'll do what we can to get to the bottom of it. But we need your cooperation."

"I don't think we're planning to surrender," Jeff said. "I don't think that's what we have in mind, to be quite frank."

"Well," said the cop, who was trained in cooling out hostage situations, "what *do* you have in mind? Let's talk about it."

Nick took the phone from Jeff. It had a long cord and he dragged it into the bedroom and put the receiver up to Burke's face. "Tell him," Nick said.

Burke spoke into the phone with a dry exhausted whisper. "This is Burke. They want to leave and take me with them. They want you to bring a car around back and they want your word that you won't try to follow us or stop us."

Burke listened while the other cop talked. Burke

looked bad, Nick thought. Way beyond the usual limits of normal cop derangement. Nick almost felt sorry for him.

"Yes, sir," Burke said to the cop on the line, glancing at Nick. "He's the one with the gun—"

Nick took the phone away from Burke. "So you got it?" he said to the cop on the line. "Bring the car around to the alley and leave the engine running. Then back off. I mean everything. I want all that SWAT bullshit out of here. I want that fucking chopper out of here. I don't want to see no fucking plainclothes cops or police bitches or anything!"

"Okay, *Nick*," the cop said, much too easily. "I'd like to change your mind, fella. But if that's what you want, that's what you'll get."

"And listen," Nick said, "it better be a good car. With a full tank of gas. If there's anything weird about it, the cop's gonna get it."

"Sure, Nick. Anything else?"

"Yeah. The same goes if you try to follow us with unmarked vehicles or any of that shit."

"Well, maybe if you told us where you want to go, Nick, we could make sure no one else interferes with your plans—"

"I figured we might fly to Cuba. You think that's a good idea?" Nick winked at Jeff.

"We'll have to clear it with the Cubans, Nick. That'll take some time."

Nick snorted. "I was kidding. They hate fags in Cuba. I thought even dumb cops knew that."

"Nick, it would be a whole lot easier if you'd just release Officer Burke. If you feel he somehow overstepped his authority—"

"Would you call kicking me in the nuts and trying to stick his gun up Jeff's ass overstepping his authority?"

"Now, Nick." The cop laughed good-naturedly. "I can assure you we have appropriate channels for investigating any officer's conduct—"

"Yeah, I know. Your channels suck."

"Well, I can certainly sympathize with your feelings of ... agitation. But wouldn't it be better to simply proceed on a rational basis and file a complaint?"

"I've got a feeling it's a wee bit too late for that."

"Not necessarily—"

"Okay, I'll tell you what. How about if I just go on home and Jeff here tidies up a little and maybe drinks himself back to sleep. Then we can mosey on down to Parker Center come Tuesday and file an official complaint. How's that sound?"

"That sounds fine, Nick."

Nick snorted. "You must think I'm a complete moron. Have the car out back in ten minutes." Nick banged down the phone.

Nick watched the SWAT men climb down off the roof of the building next door. After they left Doris' apartment, he heard them climb down off the roof overhead. From the bay window, he watched the black-and-whites pull away out front.

From the kitchen window, Jeff watched the black-and-whites pull away out back as the sound of the chopper faded.

"Here it comes," Jeff said.

Nick came over and they both watched a dark-green Plymouth turn the corner and come up the alley. It stopped directly below and a plainclothes cop with a red beard got out, leaving the engine running. They watched him jog back up the alley to where an unmarked cop car picked him up and sped off.

Except for the idling Plymouth below, everything was quiet.

"What do you think?" Jeff said.

Nick didn't say anything for a moment. Looking at him, Jeff realized again how fucking beautiful Nick was, his clear brown eyes, in spite of everything, filled with a gentleness that was almost painful.

"Look, Jeff," Nick said softly, so Burke wouldn't hear. "Are you sure you want to go ahead with this?"

"What are you talking about?"

"It's just that, I don't know, I've got a history of stuff."

"What do you mean? What stuff?"

"Just bullshit mainly. I mean, I got busted out of the marine corps for being gay and stuff—"

"So what?"

"And I stuck up a few stores."

"You stuck up a few stores?"

"Yeah. A few Seven–elevens. About six years ago. But I don't know. The cops have a way of figuring out if you've done other stuff, you know, once they arrest you and everything."

"But if it was six years ago—"

"I know, I know. It's just a feeling I've got. It's different for you. I mean, you obviously come from a good background."

"It won't help. My mom's a terminal alcoholic and my dad hates my guts."

"Yeah, but maybe you could get yourself some hotshot lawyer or something. You could probably talk your way out of it. You could say you didn't know what was happening, that I brainwashed you. I don't know. Say you just met me and you didn't know I was a hardened criminal. I don't care if you blame it on me. I really don't give a shit, because I'm going to get away."

Jeff looked at Burke in the bedroom, the cop's face red and shiny as if it was about to pop. He had a strong feeling the things that would happen to him if he gave up now would make Burke's behavior seem like friendly horseplay. "I don't want any more cops looking up my ass for a while," Jeff said. "I'm going with you." He laughed giddily, scared and euphoric at the same time. "I'm having too much fun to stop now."

Nick smiled faintly, thinking about all the cops outside. Where were they now?

Nick leaned over and kissed Jeff deeply, and it felt so good. Everything but this was completely insane.

"We'd better get our traveling companion," Nick said finally.

13

Nick and Jeff weren't going anywhere. Not if Special Weapons and Tactics had anything to say about it. The LAPD SWAT team had handled over four hundred incidents since its formation in 1967; and as the chief enjoyed pointing out, they'd never lost a hostage. Their record wasn't just good, it was perfect.

And they weren't about to spoil it. Which was why Phil Cowell, the star shooter of the SWAT team, got the job of taking out Nick and Jeff. With thin blond hair, gaunt features, and acne-scarred skin, Phil was a scuzzy Aryan in green coveralls. He had blank blue eyes, a blank personality, and very little on his mind except the thing he did best: hit targets. He could pick off a gook at four hundred meters at night in the middle of a monsoon, and he had a record of 103 confirmed sniper kills in Vietnam to prove it. And from where he was positioned on the roof of the two-story building across the alley from Jeff's, he could also hit Nick in the head with a special hollow-point bullet.

The special hollow-point bullet would cause Nick's head to explode, Phil knew, and explode in such a way—Phil had learned from his Southeast Asia research—that Nick would drop the gun he was certain to have aimed at Officer Burke. If all went according to plan, Nick's head would still be exploding as Phil shot Jeff.

Phil had little doubt about his ability to accomplish either task. Yet he was inordinately nervous as he sprawled on the gritty roof and watched the slate gate for Nick and Jeff to appear. He was nervous for several reasons. If, by any berserk stretch of the imagination, he botched it and Nick shot Burke, Phil would not only have shattered the impeccable SWAT record, he would be indirectly responsible for the death of a fellow officer: a double fuck-up that could devastate his sense of smooth self-confidence, leaving him permanently uncertain and fidgety, and therefore useless as a shooter.

He was also edgy because he'd drunk too much coffee and had to piss so bad he could feel it in his teeth. Hurry up, you faggot crud, Phil thought, watching the gate through the scope on his high-power rifle. Come on out, so I can do my job and go take a leak.

Jeff opened the front door a crack and looked down at the court. It was empty. A faint breeze scattered dead leaves and cellophane across the concrete. The windows of the downstairs apartments were shaded tightly, like the fake windows of a movie set. Jeff bet there was a very good chance those shades were going to snap up, just like in a movie, rifles flashing in the sun as a spray of lead blew them away.

Would it hurt? Jeff wondered. Probably not for long. If they hit him in the head, would he die instantly? What was it like to die instantly? He opened the door wide for Nick and Burke, almost with a sense of adventure, feeling his death was only seconds away. At least now I'll find out what happens after you die, he thought.

Nick held on to Burke's wrists, both of which were cuffed behind his back, and jammed the .38 behind Burke's left ear. "Okay," he said to the cop. "You first. Take it real slow."

They started down the stairs. Burke's foot had gone numb while he was cuffed to the bed; he wobbled slightly and almost fell. Jeff hung in close behind

Nick and Burke, instinctively using the cop as a shield against the fusillade he was sure was imminent.

They had just reached the bottom of the stairs when a blast of laughter ripped through the air. Jeff flinched. Nick yanked Burke's cuffs, pressing the gun harder into Burke's neck. A blast of sitcom music followed, along with the distorted voices of David Cassidy and Shirley Jones. Somebody in a neighboring apartment was watching a rerun of *The Partridge Family*.

Jeff giggled. Nick glanced at Jeff. And Burke broke away.

Burke scrambled around the corner toward the slate gate. Nick went after him. He aimed the .38 at Burke just as Burke slammed through the gate. "You goddamn fuck," Nick shouted.

Nick could have shot Officer Burke—he had had maybe two or three seconds to do it—but something in him wouldn't let him pull the trigger.

Dead or alive, it didn't matter—they'd lost their hostage.

But Nick was still pointing the .38 at Burke when Burke slammed through the gate and a shot cracked. In a manner totally unlike anything Nick had ever seen in movies, unlike anything he had ever believed possible, Burke's head exploded against the pale-blue morning sky.

Up on the roof across the alley, Phil Cowell saw the dark-blue LAPD uniform below the spray of blood and urinated in his green coveralls.

"Fuck!" Nick ducked back to Jeff, blood misting the walkway behind him.

Jeff was too stunned to react. Nick grabbed his arm. "Through the front." They took off.

They ran down the front steps. The street, as always, was lined with parked cars, but there was no traffic and there weren't any cops they could see. Nick was thinking of only one thing: the Camaro. He didn't even know if it was still there, he couldn't see it. Maybe the cops had found it and towed it away. He dug in his pocket for the keys. "Come on!" he shouted to Jeff.

They ran up the street. Jeff ducked as he ran, like a man approaching a helicopter, expecting what had happened to Burke to happen to him any second.

Nick spotted the Camaro. "There!" He jumped behind the wheel, popping the other door for Jeff. The engine was cold and wouldn't start right away. Nick goosed the gas and tried it again.

"Come on, *Jesus!*" Jeff said, looking back, expecting bullets to shatter the windows at any second.

Finally it caught and Nick tore out, roaring up Catalina to Franklin, where he took a skidding right. He couldn't believe they were actually getting away.

They weren't. When they passed Berendo, the next street over, they saw at least twenty cop cars, double-parked, their sirens starting to scream.

14

Nick roared up Franklin, and took a hard turn through traffic when he reached Vermont, almost mowing down two gay men in shorts in the crosswalk. He knew where they were coming from. He was going there. Fast.

Jeff looked back and saw the first cop cars making the same turn. "Oh, man, we've had it. We've really fucking had it!"

"Just hold on!" Nick's face was glazed with sweat, his eyes flashing, the muscles of his arms flexing as he twisted the wheel, taking a sharp left up the winding road that led deep into Griffith Park.

The cop cars roared up the road behind them, their sirens vomiting terror over the brown scrub hills. But Jeff began to feel a strange sense of calm.

If I'm going to die, he thought, I'd rather go out like this, with a guy like Nick, than end up accidentally OD'ing as some fifty-year-old kiss-ass Hollywood nonentity.

But Nick had no intention of dying. It was the farthest thing from his mind as he roared around the bend toward the gay cruising section of the park.

He was getting off on the whole thing.

It was actually a relief that the shit had finally hit the fan. All the polite repression, the guilt trips, and the psychological terrorism—everything society could throw at him had failed. They'd finally had to send the police in the flesh. At last the fight was physical, the enemy clearly seen.

And he wasn't alone. He was with Jeff. But how much more could Jeff take? What would happen when the adrenaline rush wore off? When Jeff realized that what he was caught up in was going to waste all his plans for the future? Nick had always known something like this was coming. But Jeff was a nice guy with safe, conventional dreams.

Nick and Jeff shot along the ridge road, high above the San Fernando Valley. They squealed around the turn where the cruisers waited on hot afternoons, then up the road on the other side of the turn. The road was straight for several hundred yards, then it curved abruptly again, following the ridge deep into the park.

Nick floored it and checked his rearview mirror. The red-and-blue lights flashing through the eucalyptus trees told him the cops were just approaching the turn. He had about twenty seconds.

"Let's get the fuck out of here," Nick shouted at Jeff.

"What?"

"Down there." Nick indicated a deep ravine on the interior side of the road.

Nick floored the accelerator and jumped. Jeff saw where the car was headed and jumped too.

They scrambled into the brush just as the first cop car screamed around the turn. A second later, they heard the Camaro crash and explode at the bottom of the ridge.

Looking up, they saw cop cars screeching to a halt on the road. Jeff wanted to keep scrambling away through the brush, but Nick grabbed his arm. "Lay flat. Don't move."

Two cops came over and looked down at the brush where they were hiding. The rest of the cop cars were pulling up now. A cloud of black smoke rose from the opposite side of the road.

Two more cops came over and looked down at the

brush. Nick watched them study the landscape and talk. Did they already know the suspects weren't in the burning Camaro?

Finally, one of the cops laughed. Then they all went back across the road to watch the Camaro burn. But they'd be back once the fire was out.

"Okay," Nick whispered to Jeff, "we're going to have to crawl till we reach those pine trees down there. Try not to raise any dust."

Jeff snorted. The ground was like powder. "Then what do we do?"

"I don't know. It's Saturday. What do you feel like? A little antique-browsing? Maybe a light lunch at the Garden District?"

"I don't think I'm dressed right."

Nick jammed the .38 deeper into his belt so it wouldn't slip out. "You're right," he said. "You're not."

They started crawling.

15

I t was twenty minutes before the fire was put out and the cops saw that the charred bucket seats were empty.

By that time, Nick and Jeff had reached the pine trees, which they followed down through the ravine. The trees were thick and provided cover from the cop chopper that periodically passed overhead.

Finally they reached a sheltered glen near a road, an automatic sprinkler fanning across their path. Jeff bent down and gobbled water, washing the dust from his face.

"We've got to get you another shirt." Nick drank too.

"What's wrong with my shirt?" Jeff fingered the dirt-caked, sweaty rayon.

"It's too conspicuous. 'Suspect: male Caucasian, blond hair, medium build, cute butt, wearing bright Hawaiian shirt.' "

Jeff sighed. "Yeah, you're right." He took off the shirt. It was too hot to wear one anyway.

Nick sat down on the pine needles, exhausted. "By the way, I'm sorry about all this."

"It's okay." Jeff sat down, too, leaning back on his elbows, the sunlight catching the blond hair on his chest. He was beat. "Hey, you got any cigarettes?"

Nick shook his head. "Left 'em at your place."

Jeff stared off through the trees. "I can't believe this is happening to me."

"I can't believe that cop. How could he be that stupid?"

"Which one?"

"All of 'em, man. All of 'em."

"They had a sniper on the roof."

"Yeah, SWAT. Had to be SWAT. Shit, I could have gone a whole lifetime without seeing that. That guy's head just blew up, man. Like a fuckin' piñata full of brains. It still makes me sick just thinking about it."

Jeff was trying hard *not* to think about it. Christ, he wanted a cigarette. Then he heard a noise and froze.

Something was moving in the bushes. Breaking twigs. Panting. A dog. A German shepherd.

Nick sat up.

A man emerged a few hundred feet away, in a splotch of sunlight in the trees.

He was a tall man, attractive, wearing boots, shorts, a khaki shirt. Gay.

"It's okay," Nick said. "This area starts to get real cruisy about this time of day. That's why we're here."

"Oh, yeah?"

"Yeah. Give me your shirt."

"My shirt? What for?"

Nick picked up the Hawaiian shirt and began tearing it with his teeth.

"Jesus Chihuahua! My ex-wife paid two hundred dollars for that shirt."

"You gotta be shitting me," Nick said, using strips of the fabric to tie the gun to his leg. "This thing's gotta be thirty years old."

"That's the point." Jeff sighed.

16

The leather queen was leaning against a tree, black leather chaps over faded Levi's, black leather vest open to reveal the gray thatch on his chest. Steel-frame dark glasses hid his eyes, and his ears and tits were pierced and studded.

Nick had spotted him earlier but decided to pass. The guy was too outrageous. A hardcore veteran sadist, probably up all night, on a run. Trouble. Nick needed a normal cruiser.

Several had come and gone, all staying too near the road for Nick to try an approach. Periodically, he saw a cop car flash up the road beyond the trees. Choppers still whomped over the park.

Then a cop car pulled up below the trees and parked.

"Okay, pal," Nick said to Jeff. "Looks like you're going to have to be my slave."

Jeff didn't understand at first.

The leather queen was called Hatch. His real name was Myron Gillet, but everybody at the Backfire called him Hatch. The Backfire was the Hollywood leather bar where he spent a lot of time. He had been there till four that morning. For some after-hours play. Hatch and two younger masters had been working on a young slave. Giving Discipline, Verbal Abuse, and Humiliation. When he Tried to Escape, they took him into the Back Room and Restrained him. They put him in a Sling and attached Weighted Clamps.

Finally in the wee hours of the morning, they Pissed down His Throat.

Hatch had a headache. Too much amyl. But he hadn't come yet and he still felt hot. Griffith Park was a long shot. Sometimes he ran into other leather guys who were also on a run and didn't want to sleep yet. Or more likely, a normal kissy-face gay with latent S&M tendencies who could really get into Worshiping a Master.

During the week, Hatch was a claims adjuster for a major insurance company. A fifty-one-year-old confirmed bachelor, he wore a three-piece suit, drove a Buick Riviera, and had dinner at his mother's twice a week.

Hatch perked up as Nick swaggered from the bushes, striking an arrogant pose by a tree. Hatch liked what he saw, but he wasn't interested. He wished he was looking in a mirror, because Nick had everything it took to make one hell of a Master. The muscles, not extreme or gym-built, but powerful, macho, tough, butch-looking. The jet-black hair: on Nick's head, face, arms, chest, everywhere. The freshness of youth offset by extreme narcissistic arrogance. The Attitude.

Then Jeff stepped from the bushes, approaching Nick timidly. Without warning, Nick grabbed Jeff by the hair and pushed him to his knees.

When Jeff pulled back, Nick slapped him hard and forced Jeff's face to his bulging denim crotch.

Now Hatch was interested. He stepped over for a better look. He saw that Nick's cock was getting hard. But Nick's face remained grim, butch, devoid of excitement or pleasure.

Hatch was riveted.

Nick pulled Jeff's head back so Hatch could see his face: a contorted, quivering mask of handsome submission.

"He needs to be taught a lesson," Nick said.

Hatch stepped closer. He ran the back of his rough hand over Jeff's smooth shoulder. Jeff tried not to cringe.

*   *   *

Two cops got out of their car and started up through
the trees. They passed the sprinklers just as Nick and
Jeff reached Hatch's beat-up Ford pickup.

The empty cop car was parked several hundred
feet behind the pickup. As they got in, Hatch said,
"Lotta heat today."

Nick grunted.

When they reached the golf course, Nick felt his
guts turn over. There was a police roadblock up ahead
by the Greek Theatre.

"What's this shit?" Hatch said.

Nick was about to reach for the .38 when Hatch
made an abrupt right turn up a narrow road that led
back into the park. "Don't need *that* shit, right?"
Hatch said.

Jeff looked back as they shot up the winding road.
No one was following them.

Hatch knew the roads, and a short time later they
were out of the park. "What are your preferences?"
Hatch said to Nick as they got on the freeway.

"We're into everything, man."

Hatch tried not to show excitement. "Limits?"

"*No* limits," Nick said.

Hatch felt a terrible rush, but remained expression-
less. He glanced at Jeff, who was staring straight
ahead. "Novice."

Nick grunted.

Hatch pinched Jeff's tit approvingly. "Choice."

"Prime," Nick said.

"Piercing?"

"Have to see your toys."

"I've got everything."

For a moment Jeff thought he was going to giggle.
"Fistwork?" Hatch barked.

Jeff looked at Hatch's huge hands on the steering
wheel and felt ill.

"No problem," Nick said.

Hatch got over for the next exit. "Glendale."

"That's where Mildred Pierce lived," Jeff said

nervously. "You know, Joan Crawford, when she was still baking pies. Remember that stucco—"

Nick slapped Jeff across the face. "Silence, Slave." Nick winked, but Jeff was still stunned.

17

H atch's Glendale tract house looked like the set of a Doris Day movie, circa 1963. The French Provincial living room was perfect, seldom used. Nick stood at the window in the rumpus room. The backyard was overgrown, hiding them from the other houses.

Hatch brought a vial of Biphetamine capsules and two bottles of Bud. "It should take about twenty minutes," he said. "Relax. I've got to set up."

Hatch left, going down a flight of stairs. Nick grinned at Jeff. "He's got a real dungeon."

They each washed down several capsules with the beer.

"Nick, I've been thinking." Jeff watched for Hatch. "About getting a lawyer. For both of us, I mean."

"For both of us?"

"Yeah. I know this guy who represents a lot of top show-business people. He knows everybody. I used to trick with him. He gets people off who are incredibly guilty. And he's gay."

"I figured if you tricked with him, he probably was."

"We should call him, Nick. I know he can get us out of this. I don't know how, but if anybody can, he's the guy."

They could hear Hatch coming up from the basement.

Nick pulled up his pants leg and started to untie

the .38. But he'd tied it too well. He was digging at
the knot when Hatch stepped through the door, a
double-barrel shotgun in his hands.

"All right, boys. Just hold it right there."

Nick froze. So did Jeff.

"Get that gun and hand it to me by the barrel,"
Hatch said to Jeff.

Jeff did as he was told. Hatch took the .38 and
stuck it in his belt, keeping Nick and Jeff covered
with the shotgun.

Hatch had a set of handcuffs and a thick studded
collar device hooked to his belt. He unhooked the
collar device and tossed it to Jeff. "Put it around his
neck."

Jeff did as he was told. There was a steel bit attached to the collar.

"Put the bit in his mouth before you tighten it,"
Hatch said.

Jeff put the bit in Nick's mouth. It dug into Nick's
cheeks till he looked like a tortured chipmunk.

"Now tighten it."

Jeff tightened the collar till it dug into Nick's throat
and he gagged. "It's too tight," Jeff said.

"Ain't no good unless it's tight." Hatch chuckled.

Hatch unhooked a length of chain from his belt
and strung it through a clasp on the back of Nick's
collar. Then he tossed the chain over a two-by-four in
the rumpus-room ceiling, yanked it hard, and pad-
locked it to the collar in a way that left Nick dangling,
his feet barely touching the floor, like a crippled
marionette.

Hatch gave Nick a violent twist and laughed dryly
when the bit dug into Nick's mouth and the collar
choked his throat.

Jeff made a move to help Nick, but stopped when
Hatch shoved the shotgun under his chin.

"I know who you assholes are," Hatch said. "I
went through that roadblock on my way in. The cops
said they were looking for the two guys that shot the
officer. I knew it was you two from the word go. You

pussies couldn't fool anyone with your phony leather talk."

Jeff saw that even in the bright light Hatch's eyes were like tunnels. He'd taken enough speed to keep the Luftwaffe up for a week.

Hatch chuckled. "Now we're going to have ourselves a *real* party."

Several hours later, Hatch climbed the dungeon stairs, sweaty and exhausted. Break time. He chuga-lugged beer at the refrigerator, letting it trickle down his chin and chest, then went back into the rumpus room, where Nick still hung from the two-by-four. All that black hair on Nick's chest! Hatch imagined it sputtering like cellophane when he applied the poker now heating up in the hibachi downstairs.

Time for that later. He still wasn't finished with Jeff. He thought about the sweet curve of Jeff's surfer chest. *Too* sweet, like vanilla ice cream. Hatch made a face and got a razor blade from the bathroom medicine cabinet.

He went back downstairs, where Jeff lay hand-cuffed to the commode. He bent down, unwrapping the razor blade.

"Oh, Jesus," Jeff said. "Oh, hey, look—"

Hatch was holding the razor blade to one of Jeff's nipples when he heard wood splinter upstairs, fol-lowed by a heavy thump. What the hell? He got up and went around the corner to the stairs.

Nick was waiting on the steps. He jumped Hatch, wrapped the chain around Hatch's neck and pulled as hard as he could. Hatch gurgled and his face turned red. Nick pulled the .38 out of Hatch's belt, yanked him down by the chain, and kneed him hard in the face. Hatch collapsed on the floor.

Nick took the keys from Hatch's belt and unlocked Jeff's cuffs. Then he pulled Hatch into the toilet and cuffed him to the bowl in Jeff's place.

Nick tugged at his bit and collar. "Help me get this thing off," he said to Jeff.

Still trembling, Jeff undid the clasp and the collar snapped off.

"Look, you guys," Hatch said. "I was only joshing. I wasn't going to turn you in."

"We know you weren't," Nick said. "You were just gonna mutilate the fuck out of us for the next week and then dump our bodies in some canyon somewhere."

"Aw, no," Hatch said. "It was just part of the game. I was going to let you guys overpower me. Not right away. But eventually."

"This guy's too twisted for me," Nick said. "I can't follow his logic, can you?"

Jeff shook his head. He should be more upset, he thought; and on some level he was. But the speed was making him euphoric. "I just don't understand why all this came down. I'm not a bad person. It's Saturday afternoon. I should be down at Venice Beach right now, trying to find a place to park."

"I guess you ought to be more careful who you trick with, huh?" Nick winced as he touched the corners of his mouth where the bit had dug in.

"I think you're right. Maybe I should start dating more."

"I'll bring you a corsage next time."

Jeff closed the toilet door so Hatch wouldn't hear what he was about to say. "Look, let me call my lawyer friend. Did you hear what he said—about us being the two guys who 'shot the officer'? We didn't shoot anybody, did we?"

"Not yet," Nick said. It didn't work as a joke.

"But it sounds like that's what they're saying."

"I'm sure it is."

"Jesus, Nick, that's cop-killing. That's practically the worst thing there is. Especially to other cops. They're going to be trying to get us extra hard."

"I'm sure. Especially queer cop-killers."

"Maybe the SWAT guy'll tell 'em it was an accident."

Nick sighed. "I wouldn't hold my breath. The cops always lie. They always protect each other."

"Let me call this guy, okay? It can't do any harm."

Nick stared blankly at the fake brick wall. "What's this turkey's name anyway?"

"Harvey Berringer."

"Never heard of him."

"He's the best. He's a genius, a complete genius."

"What about money?"

"I'm telling you, he's a personal friend. And he knows everybody, Nick, the mayor and the governor and everybody. He can probably work something out so we don't have to surrender to the LAPD, or at least so we can do it where they don't have a chance to fuck us over in jail. That's what you're worried about, isn't it?"

"It's crossed my mind. But actually, surrendering is not very high on my checklist of must-dos this week. Even a hotshot lawyer can't go to jail with you. Anyway, I'm not going to jail, period."

"Maybe we can get out of the state."

"I was thinking more like out of the country."

"I've always dreamed of living in Greece. The islands are supposed to be incredible. Of course, we'd need passports . . ."

Nick grinned and stuck a finger in Jeff's torn pants. "Right now I think we need some fresh clothes."

While Nick got some clothes from Hatch's bedroom closet, Jeff called Harvey's home in Beverly Hills. His wife answered, telling Jeff in a slurred voice that Harvey was gone for the weekend. Would Jeff like to leave a number where he could be reached on Tuesday?

Jeff sighed. "No. Just tell him Jeff Gifford called." He searched the house for some cigarettes. Then he remembered seeing a pack of Camels in Hatch's vest.

Jeff went back downstairs, where Hatch was resting against the toilet bowl. Jeff dug the cigarettes out of Hatch's vest pocket.

"I would have respected your limits," Hatch said.
Jeff didn't know what to say.

"Come on," Hatch said. "It's your turn now. You
can do anything to me you want. Humiliate me.
Treat me like garbage. Put a brush in my mouth and
make me clean the latrine."

Jeff lit a cigarette. "You know, it sounds to me like
you've got a real self-esteem problem. Have you ever
considered therapy?"

"For God sake, do something!" Hatch begged. "I'm
at your mercy, damn it, can't you see?"

Nick came down the stairs, tossing Jeff a white
shirt and a pair of slacks. "Here. Put these on."

Jeff slipped out of his ripped pants and pulled on
the slacks.

"So?" Nick said.

"His wife says he's out of town. But I have a pretty
good idea where he'll be tonight. It *is* Saturday."

Nick stuck the .38 in his belt, checking to see if it
showed under the sport coat he'd put on.

"What about him?" Jeff indicated Hatch. "He wants
us to do something." Jeff laughed nervously.

"Oh, yeah? Like what?"

"Come on, you guys," Hatch said. "Let's get down
to some heavy-duty *scat*."

"So you're into scat?" Jeff said. "Okay, pal. I know
what you want. Stand back, Nick. This is going to be
extra heavy-duty." Jeff scat-sang a few bars of "Just
One of Those Things."

Nick just looked at Hatch and shook his head
disgustedly. "You are real fucked up, you know that?
It's guys like you who've given homosexuality a bad
name."

Hatch snorted. "Shit. You guys are no fun at all."

Nick sighed. "Is somebody going to find you eventually?"

"Yeah. My sister-in-law's coming by tomorrow. Her
and her kids." Hatch laughed sharply. "Leave me
like I am. I want 'em to find me like this."

"Your wish is my command, sport." Nick left the door open.

They took Hatch's Buick. With the stodgy car and Hatch's conservative clothes, they figured they could pass for a couple of ordinary young dads.

18

They passed a cop car on Cahuenga without incident.

"Where did you say this place was?" Nick asked as they glided through Hollywood.

"The Eighty-six-o-three? Are you kidding?"

"I told you, I don't go to the baths."

"I just thought everybody knew where the Eighty-six-o-three was. Granted, it was hotter a few years ago. Now all the light switches are greasy with Crisco."

"Sounds romantic."

"It's okay for what it is. I've had some good times there."

Nick glanced at Jeff. His lips were crusty, but the worst part was his eyes: they were glassy with fear, the pupils dilated from the speed. "Too bad you didn't bring your dark glasses. Your eyes don't look exactly sane."

"Can't think of everything." Jeff checked the glove compartment for cigarettes. There weren't any.

"Hey, you got some more speed?" he said.

"In my right-hand pants pocket. Help yourself."

Jeff reached into Nick's pocket. He found the pills. He also found something else. Nick's cock. He played with it a little. It started to get hard.

"That feels good." Nick reached over and squeezed Jeff's leg. "You know something? If none of this had happened, I was planning to stay in bed with you for about a week straight." A flicker of shyness cut through Nick's voice. "I mean, if you'd wanted to."

"I could probably have gotten into it."

Nick grinned. "I mean, if you'd had nothing better to do—"

Jeff dug some pills out of Nick's pocket and swallowed them. "I wouldn't have." A languid Roxy Music song played softly on the radio.

The sunset flooded the boulevard, drenching everything—the pawnshops, the adult bookstores, and porno theaters, and hustlers—with a dirty orange light.

The hustlers were out in force, more daring than usual. More blatant. It was, after all, Saturday night. Shiny vests over chrome pectorals gleaming in the sunset. Schlongs like cucumbers stuffed down their pant legs. Thumbs hitched in belts with buckles as big as fists. Thirty dollars, maybe forty. The streets were for Hoosier kids who blew into town with James Dean fantasies and scars from Dad's last beating. The prime grade worked through the message ads in the gay papers, or the "escort services" for rich queens who could pay hundreds of dollars a night for immaculate perfection. There would be a lot of that going on tonight. There would be a lot of everything going on tonight.

"Ever hustled?" Jeff said.

"No." Nick turned on La Cienega. "I thought about it once when I was broke. But I don't think I could take it. What about you?"

"Me?" Jeff thought about all the guys he'd gone to bed with, trying to make it in Hollywood. "Yeah, in a way," he said.

"In a way?"

"Yeah, but I wasn't very good at it. I forgot about the first rule of being a successful whore. You should always get paid up front."

"Yeah." Nick smiled. "I think I know what you mean, pal."

"There it is," Jeff said, indicating a battered red door in the side of a two-story stucco building. Delib-

erately low-key. Nothing to indicate what it was except perhaps the *Advocate* rack in front. Nick pulled
over.

"Tell you what," Jeff said. "I'll find out if he's
reserved a room. People stop in all day Saturday and
reserve rooms for later. If he's got a room, he'll be
here. Probably sometime after nine or ten."

"Nine or ten? Wait a minute—"

"Don't wory. This'll only take a second. I know one
of the attendants."

Nick grabbed Jeff's arm. "That means he knows
you. I really don't like this."

"Nick, look. This is a completely separate world.
This guy's probably been in here since early this
morning. I really doubt if he's had a chance to hear
anything."

"Man, don't you think this bullshit's been all over
the news? A cop gets taken hostage and shot, that's a
big deal. I don't like this at all."

"Just let me go up the stairs and check. It'll only
take a second. I know it's okay. I just have that
feeling."

"Okay. But I'm keeping the engine running. If the
guy seems the slightest bit weird, get your ass right
back down those fuckin' stairs, okay?"

Jeff got out. "I'll be right back."

Nick watched Jeff go in the door. Another guy was
coming out, whistling, his hair still wet. He glanced
over. Nick turned away to hide his face.

Jeff leaned against the wall, trying to act as non-
chalant as possible. There were at least a dozen
guys ahead of him on the stairs. He'd have to wait
his turn. He heard the door open behind him.

"Well, well, well. Hello, Jeff."

Jeff turned to see a familiar smiling face. Arnold
was fit and fifty, with gray hair and a Bain de Soleil
tan. He produced sitcom pilots that were seldom
picked up, and had smiled the same way one night

several years ago as he'd pumped Jeff's butt in his lighted Encino swimming pool.

"Hello, Arnold. Long time no see."

Arnold obviously hadn't heard the news. "You're telling me. The last time I saw you, you were just starting at ICM."

"I'm kind of operating on my own now."

"Well." Arnold grinned suggestively. "You're certainly *looking* good. You must be doing *something* right."

"Yeah, I use a moisturizer." Jeff smiled. Get away from me, you puke, he thought.

Jeff reached the top of the stairs. "Are you going in now?" Arnold whispered.

"No. I'm just going to reserve a room."

"When will you be back? I've got some Thai sticks. We could—"

"I'm just going to play things by ear tonight."

Arnold wasn't giving up that easily. Hugging Jeff from behind, he half-whispered, half-blew in his ear. "I want you, Jeffy. You know that, don't you?"

Cringing, Jeff pulled away. He tried to smile. "I've got to check in."

The attendant at the window was a sharp-featured man Jeff had never seen before. "Locker or room?" he said sharply.

Jeff strained to see back inside. His friend Gary was back there, folding towels. "Could I talk to Gary a second?"

"Gary!" the attendant called sharply, irritated that Jeff was holding things up.

Gary came over. He was a cute blond fantasy, with a lithe teenage torso and the sweetest little buns Jeff had ever seen. They'd dated for a while, but Jeff had been upset when Gary got the job at the 8603. Bath attendants somehow always ended up harsh and jaded. Though Gary hadn't reached that point yet, his innocence was rapidly becoming self-conscious.

"Hi, Jeff." Gary smiled his freshest ball-game smile. Obviously the news hadn't reached him, either.

Actually, Gary had fallen in love with Jeff, but pulled away because he thought Jeff regarded him as little more than a trick. Jeff, who'd had a crush on Gary that wouldn't stop, had been so sure Gary considered him just a trick that he'd treated him as casually as he could.

"Hi, Gary. Listen, I was wondering if a friend of mine was going to be here later. Can you tell me if he's reserved a room?"

"Sure. What's his name?"

"Harvey. Harvey Berringer."

"How *is* Harvey?" Arnold said over Jeff's shoulder. "I haven't seen him in *ages*."

"He's fine," Jeff said.

Gary checked the slips. "Yeah. I think you just missed him. Dark curly hair?"

"Yeah."

"Uh huh." Gary pulled the slip. "Room Forty-eight. He was just here."

"How long does he have it for?"

"Twelve hours."

"Thanks, Gary." Jeff started to leave.

"You want to reserve a room?" Gary said.

"Oh. Sure."

Jeff paid for the room. As Gary counted out the change, he said, "By the way, I'm off in half an hour. But I thought I might hang around. Maybe I'll see you later."

Jeff felt a pang. "That would be nice," he said, his voice unsteady.

"Jeff, are you all right?"

Before Jeff could answer, the other attendant stepped up and took the next patron's card.

Jeff pulled himself together. "Sure," he said to Gary. "Everything's great. Maybe I'll see you later, okay?"

Jeff went down the stairs, aware that Arnold was still watching him.

* * *

"What the fuck were you doing in there?" Nick said.

"Lotta hunky guys."

"Very funny. About two minutes more, I would've split."

"He's got Room Forty-eight."

Nick pulled the car out. "Man, this is total insanity. About fifty guys walked by here and checked me out with a microscope."

"They probably just thought you were hot."

"They don't know the fuckin' half of it."

"I reserved a room."

"You what?"

"How do you think we'll get in later if we don't have a room? The place is gonna be packed."

"Shit."

"Don't worry, it's cool."

"Fuck. You're talking about going in there with fifty million guys. This is fuckin' crazy."

"What do you want to do?" Jeff said as Nick took a left on Robertson. "We've got a few hours to kill."

"*Well*"—Nick did a hissy West Hollywood queen voice—"we can always go shopping. Beverly Center's just around the corner. Of course, all the really chi-chi shops are down on Melrose. Shall we?"

Jeff laughed. "You need anything special? By the way, you do that voice very well."

"Oh, let's see," Nick continued feyly. "Maybe just some satin lounging pajamas. You know, something to loll around in on Death Row."

Jeff quit laughing. "Nick, it's going to be okay, believe me. Harvey knows everybody. He plays squash with the DA. He can work something out. He can do a plea-bargaining number or something."

"Sure," Nick said, back to his normal voice. "Misdemeanor detaining of a cop. Petty armed hostage-taking."

"Resisting an unlawful arrest."

"That's got a nice ring to it. Too bad it doesn't exist."

"He can get that Latino cop to tell what happened."

"Fat chance."

"Look, I don't know what he can do. I'm just throwing out possibilities. He's a lawyer, we're not."

"Lawyers are assholes," Nick said, thinking of Randy. "They're all a bunch of fuckin' liars."

Nick took a right on Pico. He was quiet for a long time. Finally he said, "Jeff, I'm not gonna give up. I don't care what your friend says."

"It's quite possible that he'll advise us *not* to give up," Jeff said, but he didn't believe it. "He doesn't pull any punches. If he thinks our legal situation is fucked, he'll come right out and say so."

Nick laughed, more at life in general than the situation at hand.

Jeff watched him. Nick looked so good when he laughed. If only he could be laughing about something else, say in a restaurant or at a movie. Would that have happened? Would they have seen each other again? Would they have gone out, keeping it light at first, but gradually coming to know and love each other, and eventually shared an apartment? That had always been Jeff's basic romantic fantasy. Now it seemed hopelessly conventional and boring.

Nick reached across the seat to squeeze Jeff's hand, smiling. "So where do you want to go, if we've got a few hours?"

Jeff grinned. "I don't care." He looked up ahead. There was a rundown revival theater playing *Taxi Driver* and *Mean Streets*.

"What about that?" Jeff said. "You seen those?"

"Yeah, but so what?"

19

The theater smelled like rancid-butter popcorn and stale piss. The *Mean Streets* print was so scratched it was barely watchable. The tinny speaker was turned up too high. On the screen the actors screeched unintelligibly. Most of the patrons were black men. They commented on the action and talked to the screen.

Nick and Jeff sat in the back on the side. A white guy who'd been sitting farther down walked up the aisle, looking disgusted. When he spotted Nick and Jeff—two white faces—he sat down in the row in front of them. In a second he turned around and said, in a fake confidential tone of voice he intended the blacks to hear, "Boy, it's gettin' so you can't even go to a movie without a bunch of fuckin' *niggers* mouthin' off all the time."

Nick and Jeff ignored him, staring straight ahead at the screen where Harvey Keitel was spitting static at Robert DeNiro.

The white guy kept looking at them. Finally, though, not getting any moral support, he snorted and turned back to the screen.

"I'll be right back," Nick said after a minute.

The lobby was empty except for the Chicano usher kid at the concession stand, who had his girlfriend pressed against the wall. They ignored Nick completely as he climbed the battered Art Deco staircase to the johns. Nick glanced back down from the top, watching the couple fuck. He guessed straights got off on taking chances, too.

Nick went into the john. A toilet was running. The walls were pink, covered with Latino gang graffiti.

Nick went over to the urinal and unzipped his pants. Although at the time Burke kneed him, Nick was sure both his nuts had been crushed flat, they seemed okay now. Of course, the speed euphoria was canceling out any pain or soreness.

Nick was just starting to take a leak when he heard something. Somebody in the stall was beating off.

The stall was right next to him. Nick looked down and saw, about a foot away from his cock, a glory-hole about the size of a fist, and a pair of wet lips.

Nick felt his cock getting hard. Without thinking, he pushed his cock into the eager mouth. *Ooo yeah!*

He just let it happen for a few minutes, enjoying the incredible sensations. Then the guy stopped and Nick leaned down to see the most beautiful black guy he'd ever seen in his life.

The guy had a luscious glossy chocolate-brown body, tight and muscular, proportioned like an illustration in a gay jack-off book. His white undershirt was pulled up to reveal a washboard stomach and a shiny erection that knocked Nick's breath out.

The black guy stood, stepping to the glory-hole, and Nick got down on his knees. A minute later, they were making so much noise, Nick didn't hear the usher kid come in.

Then he saw the kid's shadow and turned to look. The usher kid was watching with appalled fascination. Just then, the black guy came, and Nick turned defiantly back to him.

Then Nick got up and wiped off his face with a paper towel. While the usher kid watched, too stunned to speak, Nick strolled past him and out the door.

"What took you so long?" Jeff said as Nick sat back down.

Nick shrugged. "I blew a black guy in the john."

"I figured it was something like that," Jeff said. He thought Nick was joking.

"Look," Nick said, "it's almost eight-thirty. Maybe we ought to get over there—"

"It's pointless till at least ten."

"Well, I'm getting itchy. And this theater is driving me nuts."

"I just think if we have to wait, it's safer to wait here. Just another forty minutes, okay?" Jeff started to get up. "I'm gonna get a Pepsi, you want anything?"

"Yeah, get me a Pepsi, too. I could use the sugar."

Jeff went out. Nick saw the beautiful black guy he'd just blown come in and sit down on the far side in the back. All the other black guys were sitting down in front in the center section. "Hit him, man! Hit him again!" one of them shouted at Robert DeNiro.

The white guy in front of Nick had been cool for a while but now he started to think out loud: "Fuckin' *niggers*."

Three black guys turned around and glared at the white guy. "What's this jive?" one of them said.

"Goddamn *coons*. Why don't you just *shut up*!"

Oh, shit, Nick thought.

Jeff got the Pepsis from the usher kid, who still looked rattled from what he'd seen upstairs. His girlfriend was smoking and looking for an ashtray.

Jeff was about to go back into the theater when he saw a flashing red light reflected in the foyer display window. He glanced outside and saw a cop car parked in the parking-lot entrance. Oh, *fuck*.

Jeff rushed in to Nick. "There's cops outside. I think they're checking out the car."

The black guys were closing in on the white guy.

"Fuck." Nick indicated the EXIT. "Let's go."

Nick and Jeff cut down the aisle and pushed through the exit door. Behind them, they could hear the white guy yelling as the black guys started beating the shit out of him. "Fucking niggers!"

The alley behind the theater was empty. Nick and

Jeff cut over to the next street and headed north toward Melrose.

"How far are we from the baths?" Nick said.

"A mile or two."

"I guess we'll have to walk it."

Suddenly a barrage of warbling cop sirens lacerated the hot night air. They seemed to be coming from all directions. The cops obviously knew who they were after.

"Our leather buddy must have got loose," Jeff said, "and reported his car stolen. He must've been lying about his sister-in-law finding him."

"Maybe she came a day early."

They were walking fast toward Melrose. The sirens were getting louder as the cops converged on the theater. "Man, this walking isn't gonna get it. They're gonna be combing this entire area in about half a minute," Nick said.

Nick checked the street ahead, a typical Hollywood side street: old Spanish-style stucco houses and new natural-wood condo buildings. Lots of parked cars. Nick saw a pair of headlights switching off. A woman got out of a Dodge Dart, slamming the door, and headed up the sidewalk toward home. Her keys jingled.

20

"Okay, lady," Nick said, wrapping his arm around the woman's neck. "I hate to tell you this, but if you start screaming or acting up, I'll snap your neck like a stalk of celery. It's an old trick I learned in the marines. Now get in your car real quiet and you won't get hurt."

Claudia Shenley, twenty-three, had just come out from St. Louis and landed a job with a swank interior designer, and she didn't want to get hurt. She got in the car very quietly.

Jeff drove. Nick kept his arm locked around Claudia's neck. From a distance they looked like passionate lovers.

"You guys don't want to rape me."

"You're right," Nick said, "we don't."

They crossed Melrose. "I've got an infection," Claudia said. "Plus I've got warts. It takes years to get rid of them. Years of painful treatment. Burning."

"Save it, lady," Nick said. "You're not gonna get raped."

They could still hear the sirens and Jeff saw cop lights flashing along Melrose in the rearview mirror.

"What now?" Jeff said.

Nick was thinking hard. "What do you mean, what now? The hospital, man."

Jeff hesitated but went along. "Yeah, right. Okay."

Claudia tried to hide her panic. Nick relaxed his

grip slightly. "We're not gonna hurt you," he said. "We just had to get out of that neighborhood. The cops are after us for something we didn't do."

Jeff glanced at Nick. "That's not completely true—"

Suddenly Claudia remembered something. "You're the two guys who took that cop hostage and killed him," she said. She'd just watched the news at a friend's house.

"Here we go again," Jeff said.

"Where did you hear that? On the news?" Nick said.

Claudia nodded.

"What did they say?"

"I don't know, I don't remember. I wasn't paying any attention." But she remembered vividly: the mini-cam shots of Burke's covered body in the alley, blood smeared across the asphalt. "Please," she said, "don't kill me now. My career's just starting to take off."

"Don't worry," Jeff said. "You've got success written all over you."

In spite of the circumstances, Claudia enjoyed the remark, hoping Jeff was right.

Nick let go of her when they reached the hospital. "We're gonna let you go now," he said. "You're okay. Your car's okay. You're a little shaken up, but we didn't really hurt you." Nick paused. "Now we're gonna visit Jeff's mom in the hospital here. She's dying of leukemia. This is the last chance he's ever gonna have to see her before she checks out. Now you can do one of two things when we let you go. You can pull out and stop the first cop car you see and tell 'em where we are. If you do that, there's gonna be at least fifty cops swarming into the hospital within five minutes. You can imagine the effect something like that would have on Jeff's mom. Plus, it'll be the beginning of a legal nightmare for you. You'll be dragged into court for the next two years, assuming they catch us. They'll ask all kinds of personal questions. You'll wish you'd forgotten the whole thing. That's your second choice. Just drive on home and forget you ever saw us. Will you at least consider doing that?"

Claudia nodded vehemently.

Nick and Jeff got out of the Dart. They watched Claudia drive off as they headed toward the hospital entrance.

"What do you think she'll do?" Jeff said.

"I don't know," Nick said. They cut past the hospital and headed toward the 8603. "But I hope there ain't no old lady at the hospital named Gifford."

"I just hope they buy it," Jeff said. "I don't think the cops are exactly unaware of the Eighty-six-o-three being practically next door."

He was right about that. But as it turned out, Claudia, who was a lesbian, never called the police.

21

"Do you want to go in as my guest or do you want to wait for me?" Jeff said at the door of the 8603. Two honey-blond lumberjacks came out, looking like incestuous macho twins, eyes flitting over Nick and Jeff, checking their faces and crotches.

"Wait where?"

"You could go over to the hospital lobby and read a magazine or something."

"Very funny."

"There's that bar across the street. A lot of industry people, especially agents. You might get discovered."

"I think I'll go in with you. I don't feel much like Lana Turner tonight."

They had to wait on the stairs for a long time. It also took a long time to fill out the guest forms for Nick and to persuade the sharp-featured attendant to let Nick share Jeff's room.

"No sharing," he said sharply.

But the sharp-featured attendant backed down when Jeff mentioned the owner. "I don't think *Chris* would mind." Actually, Jeff barely knew Chris, a good-looking young businessman who had come out from Kansas and made millions of dollars with the 8603 and a disco in Garden Grove. Jeff had seen Chris at a couple of parties, one at the home of a TV variety star's

manager, another at a rich fag hag's estate in Monte-
cito. Both times Chris had flashed in coked to the
gills, wearing steel-framed shades that made him
look chicly S&M, two macho Italian guys flanking
him, both looking like jet-set designers from the pages
of Andy Warhol's *Interview*.

The sharp-featured attendant shoved the key under
the window. "Get your towels inside." He buzzed
them through the steel doors.

Donna Summer was wailing over the sound system and the place was jammed with beautiful young
men. Most had towels on but many were deliberately
showing off their buns and cocks. Lots of cocks. Lots
of big cocks. Lots of real big cocks.

Rock Hudson and Jane Wyman were on the Video-
Beam in *Magnificent Obsession*. The Video-Beam Room
was a time-out area. Nobody fucked there, but everybody looked. The lights were low and red and everybody looked so good. Like *Blue Boy* models: short
hair, trim mustaches, muscular builds but nothing
extreme. Some guys wore items of clothing: 501s, a
blue plastic visor maybe, but nothing elaborate. A
guy in a jockstrap. Another guy in red nylon trunks.
A cute guy in baggy boxer shorts that looked like
they came from Sears. They smoked cigarettes and
joints and watched the arrivals, gathering their
strength to get up and do it again.

Nick and Jeff made their way up the central
corridor. The walls were covered with exaggerated
cartoons of hyper-realistic amyl-nitrite sex. The vi-
sual equivalent of the way it *felt*—at least the way
everyone hoped it would feel.

"Harvey's room is downstairs," Jeff said, leading
the way.

Nick was neither shocked nor turned on. Seeing so
many good-looking young men standing around waiting to get their rocks off, practically standing in line
like tourists at Disneyland, made him remember why
he didn't like the baths. There was no real adventure.

It was like a crowded Alpha Beta on a Friday night.
Your milk could turn sour while you were waiting in
the checkout line.

Nick and Jeff went down the crowded stairs past
the showers, which were also jammed. A dozen guys
watched as one guy got fucked under the running
water. Usually, the showers were a time-out area.
But it was, after all, Saturday night.

"Here it is," Jeff said, reaching Harvey's room. He
knocked. "Harvey?"

Nick glanced into the room next door. A guy with a
muscular little butt was stretched out on his stomach.
He looked at Nick and wriggled and squirmed his
butt around, a big container of Lube on the bed
between his legs.

"Harvey?" Jeff knocked again and tried the knob.
"Shit."

"You think he still isn't here yet?" Nick absently
stared at the guy in the next room; he was squirm-
ing like crazy. "It's got to be at least ten by now,"
Nick said, turning back to Jeff.

Jeff glanced around. "We'd better go to our room
and take our clothes off. We're attracting attention."

"Look, I don't especially want to hang out here,
you know what I mean? This may be your forte, but
it sure ain't mine."

"Okay, but let's at least take our shirts off, so we
can blend in a little better. Then we can look around."

"Look around?"

"Yeah. I have a feeling he's already here. He's
probably either up in the orgy room or the tea-room
room. Of course there's another possibility that's a
little grimmer."

"What's that, the sling room?"

"No. That he's met somebody."

The cute young man rolled over and looked at
Harvey Berringer. He had to make up his mind fast
whether to get rid of this number or ask him to stay.

He noticed the expensive gold chain around Harvey's neck. "Wanna smoke some dope?" he said.

At the same moment Harvey smiled and locked the cubicle door, the sharp-featured attendant was speaking on the phone back by the vending machines. "Hello, Chris?" he said. "This is Felix. There's something I think you should know."

Chris was irritated. He hated when the phong rang in his silver Jaguar on the way to a big party. He wasn't in the mood for business. The Clash was blasting from his tape system. He gestured to his driver to turn it down.

"So what is it?" he said into the phone.

"Well," Felix said, "you know those two guys on the news who took that cop hostage last night? They're here. I thought I recognized the one guy this afternoon when he came in to reserve a room for this evening. Then when he came back with the other guy, I checked his name. Jeff Gifford?" Felix paused. "He *said* he knew you. Anyway, it's them. The Gifford guy is blond. The other one's dark. I saw their pictures on the new tonight right before I came on. Just thought you'd like to know."

Chris didn't say anything for a long time. This could ruin his evening if he didn't come up with something fast.

"Chris? Are you still there, Chris?"

"Yes, Felix. Tell me, how long have they been there?"

"Twenty minutes maybe."

"Okay, listen, Felix. Do absolutely nothing. I'll be over in a little while. Don't mention this to anyone else. You haven't, have you?"

"No. As soon as I realized, I called you."

"I'm glad you did." Chris hung up. "Go to the baths," he told his Italian driver.

"What about the party?"

"We'll still make it." Chris punched information, got a number, and punched the number on the phone. When a gruff voice answered, he said, "Hello, Mr.

Gertin. Chris Dryer, Eighty-six-o-three. Listen I'm sorry to disturb you at this hour but I'll come right to the point. I'd like to discuss a price break on the Glory-hole insurance."

Willis Gertin didn't like to take these call at home. Willis didn't like to use words like *insurance*, that was gangster talk. And Willis didn't like to talk about *price breaks*. He was a master of the oblique when it came to negotiating the payments gay clubs and baths made so they wouldn't have trouble. And Willis found the idea of a deputy chief of police discussing an establishment called the Glory-hole with a drug-addled wealthy fairy in the presence of his wife and grand-children totally distasteful.

"Perhaps we'd better discuss this next week, Mr. Dryer."

"Those two guys that killed that cop," Chris said. "I know where they are. Right now."

Willis got up. He was a husky white-haired man who stayed in shape at the gym. "Let me get on another phone, Chris."

Willis agreed to a price break on the Glory-hole, a club Chris was planning to open within the month. He also agreed to have plainclothes officers wait as discreetly as possible outside the 8603, where they would be able to pick up Nick and Jeff when they tried to leave. Chris didn't want any trouble inside. He certainly didn't want armed cops streaming into the mass of naked men searching for the fugitives. He bet the police would just as soon avoid that, too.

Maybe Willis didn't really understand the crowded nature of the baths. Maybe he thought there were only a few dozen fairies cavorting around in a steam room. Or maybe he just wanted to take credit for something highly dramatic, a response appropriate to the offense. Whatever his reasoning, Willis Gertin had no intention of having some plainclothes cops wait discreetly by the entrance of the 8603 until Nick and Jeff just happened to come out.

He planned to have the LAPD take the 8603 by storm.

In their room, Nick and Jeff took off their jackets and shirts. Nick took out the .38. "This fuckin' thing's too big for its own good. I sure wish I had one of them stubby little guns like the detectives got."

He rolled up his pants leg and was about to tear up his shirt when Jeff said, "Why don't you leave it here? You can't go around with a goddamn gun tied to your leg. Besides"—Jeff looked at himself in the smudged mirror—"we oughta take off our pants, too. Nobody goes around in a pair of double-knit slacks, for Christ sake."

Nick hesitated. Jeff had a point. "Okay," he said. "But I'm telling you, we're going over this place once, and if the guy isn't here, we're splitting. I mean, fuck, you can call him next week or something. We can lay low for a while."

"Oh, yeah? Where?"

Nick took off his pants. "Actually we could stay here. Renew the room for the whole weekend. They'd just think we're in here fuckin' our brains out. You could moan every once in a while." Nick put on his towel.

"Maybe we should just do that for real. If we get caught, at least we'll have got in some good fucking."

"If we get caught, you're in for a *lot* of fuckin', man, good or otherwise. With your butt, you'll be the premier punk of Cellblock B."

Jeff tried to pinch Nick's butt. "Oh, yeah? What about you?" Nick pushed Jeff's hand away, but Jeff persisted. They struggled playfully.

"Okay, knock it off," Nick said finally. He shoved the .38 under the mattress. "Let's find this guy."

On their way to the orgy room, Jeff gave Nick a description of Harvey. "I already seen about fifteen guys that look like that," Nick said.

"Then look for a gold chain. Or *feel* for it. You know, it's just a thin tasteful gold chain. If you feel a gold chain and the guy's real hairy, just ask if it's him. You check the orgy room, I'll check the tea-room room."

"Ten minutes."

There were a number of men hanging out in the tea-room room, waiting for other men to vacate the stalls. A Prince song was pulsing through the air as Jeff caught a man leaving a stall and pushed in ahead of another guy.

Jeff hooked the door and sat down, peering through the glory-hole on his left. It wasn't Harvey. It was a college jock-type guy wearing a baseball cap, stroking himself and peering back at Jeff.

Jeff turned to the glory-hole on his right and gasped. The buns pressed against it like a hairy biscuit were strangely familiar. Suddenly Jeff realized: Gary.

Jeff felt his cock leap into a full erection. Before he knew what he was doing, he was standing up and pushing his cock through the hole. He'd never fucked anybody through a glory-hole before and he was getting off on it. Especially since it was Gary.

Gary groaned. Jeff wished he could reach through the partition and grab Gary around his smooth chest and run his hands down his hard little stomach and grab his hard cock and jack him off.

Jeff fucked Gary with everything he had. All the terror and anxiety, the speed and confusion—everything went into it.

He groaned and pounded his fists against the partition and came for what seemed like hours. When he finished, he was a sweaty mess. Slowly, he pulled his cock out, wishing he could drop down to kiss and hold Gary. Instead, he leaned against the partition and felt the sweat trickle down his stomach. When his head began to spin with exhaustion, he sat down and leaned back against the wall. Finally he leaned over and glanced through the glory-hole, with a tired smile, prepared to say, "Thanks, Gary."

It was Arnold. He stared at Jeff and stood up

abruptly, shoving his ejaculating cock through the glory-hole.

Jeff grabbed his towel and lunged from the stall, the door slamming shut behind him.

Nick was in the orgy room. The place was packed and it was hard to see in the dim blue light. He couldn't pick out the hairy chests. One by one, he approached the men and ran his hand across their chests, ostensibly admiring their pecs, but really feeling for a thin tasteful gold chain. He found one. The guy dropped down to his knees and started sucking on Nick's cock.

"Harvey?"

The guy didn't respond, he just kept sucking.

"Harvey?" Nick tapped the guy's shoulder and the guy quit sucking. Nick edged across the room toward another guy with a hairy chest.

Jeff was getting panicky. The thing with Arnold was the last straw. He pushed into the orgy room, half-crazed. "Harvey!" he called. "Harvey Berringer!"

Everybody stopped to squint at Jeff in the dim light. Nick pushed his way over and grabbed Jeff's arm, pulling him through the door, into the mirror maze.

"What are you *doing*?" Nick said.

"We gotta find him, it's getting late." Jeff was exhausted and glassy with sweat.

"Jeff, don't freak out now. *Please*. Look, let's just get out of here, okay? This is hopeless. I mean it, we can hole up somewhere. You gotta get some sleep."

"I'm okay," Jeff said. But he was clearly coming unglued. "Let's check his room one more time, okay?"

Harvey was dressed and at the checkout window. He drew a few stares in his baggy Bermudas and loud Bad Taste fifties sports shirt. Fuck 'em if they couldn't take a joke. He signed for his wallet.

The cute young man signed for his. He was dressed

for nostalgia, too, Harvey mused, though the kid didn't know it. Someone should tell him those LaCoste shirts were *out*, as dead as a disco songbird.

"I just can't believe you're really taking me to this party," gushed the cute young man. "I've heard so much about his fabulous house. And that there's always just jillions of hot young guys around." Oops. Had he already said the wrong thing?

But Harvey smiled. "There are. You'll fit right in." His eyes dropped to the cute young man's crotch. "Come on."

Felix buzzed them through the steel doors. They went down the crowded stairs, the cute young man really excited. Like every other waiter, he was studying acting, and a party at the home of the outrageous Southern producer could well lead to something profound.

They pushed through the battered door, ducking traffic on Robertson as they crossed to Harvey's Rolls Royce in a restaurant parking lot.

Busy checking his car for scratches, Harvey didn't notice the five unmarked cop cars that slid up to the door of the 8603.

Detective Lieutenant Max Brundl got out of his Plymouth, other plainclothes cops crowding around him. Lieutenant Brundl was thirty-nine. He had a flabby quarterback's body and the debauched good looks of a paranoid boy-next-door. Juries always believed him, ignoring the intensity of his eyes, the same way they'd ignore the hint of violent insanity in the eyes of a butcher at Safeway. Lieutenant Brundl came from Indiana, where four farmboys had butt-fucked him in a barn when he was eleven. He hated queers.

Brundl took out his .38. "Come on." He kicked open the battered red door of the 8603.

The gay men on the stairs cringed and flattened against the wall as Brundl led the charge to the top. This couldn't be happening. Not in the eighties, not in Los Angeles. But it was happening.

Brundl shoved a man aside and flashed his badge at Felix. "Open the doors."

Felix was flabbergasted. Surely Chris would never agree to anything like this. "Not unless I see a warrant—"

"We don't need a warrant," Lieutenant Brundl said. "We're in pursuit of felony suspects. Open the fucking doors!"

"I'll have to call my boss," Felix said. "I can't assume responsibility—"

Lieutenant Brundl was not about to stand around and argue the law with some simpering pansy. Grabbing a billy club from one of the other cops, he struck the window. The club connected with a dull thud, and Felix flinched, but to Lieutenant Brundl's astonishment, the glass didn't break. It was bulletproof.

Lieutenant Brundl could see the buzzer that opened the double set of steel doors, maddeningly out of reach on the other side of the glass.

"You fucking faggot, open the doors."

But Felix ducked back behind the dryers, grabbing the phone and frantically dialing Chris' number.

Lieutenant Brundl was enraged. He kicked the steel door in frustration. "Downstairs," he ordered his men.

Inside the baths, men near the towel cage had heard the thud of the billy club. "What was *that*?" some of them said, picking up the mood of fear in the cage.

"Police!" Word traveled fast along the clogged corridors and through the thin walls of the cubicles. "It's a raid!"

Men ran to their lockers, and rushed to their rooms. They banged into each other in the corridors. An Oriental kid got tramped in the tea-room room. It was total panic.

"Oh, man," Jeff said to Nick, still in the mirror maze. "This is it. This is really it."

A guy without a towel ran past them, smacking into a mirror and shattering it.

"We gotta get our stuff," Nick said.

"Through here." Jeff indicated the orgy room.

The orgy room was empty—except for one guy on a large mattress in the center of the room as Nick and Jeff dashed through. Pulling himself out of a trance, he said, "Hey, where'd everybody go?"

"Stay loose, man," Nick called. "They just stepped out for more Crisco."

Outside, the cops pried back the bars on the first-floor window. Busting the black-painted glass, they crawled through the window into the video room, smashing through the flimsy plywood partitions.

Nick and Jeff fought their way through the mass of panicking men in the central corridor. As everybody shoved toward the front, Nick and Jeff shoved toward the back. They both lost their towels.

Stark-naked, Nick and Jeff charged down the empty stairs into the seemingly deserted bottom floor.

They came into the hallway by the showers just as the first cops came around the corner at the other end.

A young man who looked like—and actually was—a lifeguard, stepped out of the steam room halfway up the hall. The steam room was soundproof—it even had its own music channel—and the lifeguard had no idea what was going on. He had just finished fucking another young man and his cock jutted out in front of him.

When Lieutenant Brundl aimed his .38 at Nick and Jeff and squeezed the trigger, he shot off the lifeguard's cock.

The lifeguard couldn't believe it when he looked down to see his beautiful cock gone, blood gushing everywhere.

Neither could Nick. "Holy Jesus."

Jeff was stunned. Vomit burned the back of his

throat. Nick yanked him back to the stairs a split second before Lieutenant Brundl squeezed off his next shot.

Nick and Jeff dashed back up around the stairs.

The cops charged past the lifeguard as he deliriously scrambled around on the floor, blood gushing everywhere.

Nick and Jeff banged their way through the mirror maze and came out by a black shuttered window.

"Here," Jeff said. "This goes to the sundeck."

Nick yanked the shutter off its hinges and they scrambled up the steps to the sundeck.

Stars twinkled in the clear night sky as Nick and Jeff ran across the roof. They jumped down to the lower roof of the adjoining building. It had a huge skylight. They could see guys working out on the Nautilus equipment in the posh, bright interior below.

They kept going, to the edge of the building, but there were no stairs, no fire escapes, and it was too far to jump. Looking back, they saw the cops climbing out to the sundeck.

"Through the gym," Nick said. He was drenched with sweat, his genitals shriveled with terror. Jeff was white as a corpse and streaked with puke in the moonlight.

Nick tried to lift the skylight. It was too heavy. When he dropped it, it shattered.

Glass fell like snowflakes on a young man attached to a Nautilus machine below. Noticing that his smooth pecs were flecked with blood, he looked up just as Nick and Jeff leapt through the skylight, tumbling on the carpet below.

Nick and Jeff got up and scrambled down the stairs to the street level. They shot past the shiny equipment and the half-dozen young men with lithe seductive bodies. They pushed through the smoked-glass doors and came out on Robertson.

Chris' Jaguar was idling at the curb with the lights on. Both doors were open. Chris and his driver were up at the corner getting the story from one of the patrons. Several men in towels were dodging traffic on Robertson. One guy lost his towel and was picking it up in the middle of the street when a Mercedes plowed into him.

The man screamed in agony.

The Mercedes kept going.

Busy watching the man who had been hit, Chris didn't see two other naked men jump into the Jaguar and pull out.

22

Twenty minutes later Nick pulled into an ARCO station in Studio City. The station was closed and dark, which was why Nick and Jeff chose it. Nick pulled up close to the phone booth. Jeff went through Chris' Gucci accessory bag. There were two hundred-dollar bills, credit cards, two grams of cocaine in a platinum vial, thirty ludes, ten Desoxyn, and some loose change.

Jeff ducked quickly into the phone booth. He left the door ajar so the light would stay off, making it less obvious to passersby that a naked man was making a call.

Jeff dialed the number he knew by heart. "Hello, Victor?"

Victor was stunned and immediately paranoid. He punched off the stereo that was blasting a Go-Gos song, and whispered into the phone. "Jeff. Jesus Christ, man. What the fuck did you do?"

"Victor, you're not going to believe what's happened." Jeff cringed when a car passed. "We were just at the Eighty-six-o-three and the cops came and almost caught us and they shot this guy's dick off and a guy got hit by a car in the street, but we got away."

"Jesus."

"Victor, I'm at the end of my rope, I don't know what to do, I'm scared shitless. We stole this Jaguar and we don't have any clothes. I'm here at this fucking phone booth and I'm totally naked. You gotta help us, Victor."

"Where are you?"

"We're at that ARCO off Ventura Boulevard."

Victor was starting to sweat, but he said, "Well, come on over."

"Victor, we're *naked.*"

"You mean, *completely* naked?" Victor laughed nervously.

"Yeah. I told you, we were at the baths."

"What the hell were you doing there?"

"Looking for Harvey." Jeff was trying not to cry. "Victor, I'm really scared. They shot this guy's cock off." Jeff could feel tears in his throat.

"Jeff—"

"What?"

"Listen. I better meet you in the alley. I'll bring some clothes out. A bunch of my neighbors are sitting around on the front steps drinking and stuff. I don't think it would be too cool for you to flash in here naked."

"You mean those guys with their cars?" Victor had had trouble with his neighbors before, when they were drunk and sitting around on the steps at night. One of the guys in particular liked to affect a lisp when Victor passed by.

"Yeah, but fuck 'em," Victor said. "I'll meet you in the back in five minutes."

Jeff got back in the Jaguar. Nick was checking out the drugs. "Well, this is something," he said. "And two hundred bucks. Enough to buy us breakfast."

Jeff leaned back. "He'll meet us in back of his place in five minutes." Jeff rubbed his eyes. "Oh, man."

"Are you okay?"

"Yeah, I'm fine. Why shouldn't I be? This is great fun. Riding around in a Jaguar naked. Nothing quite like the feel of a fine hot leather scalding my bare sweaty thighs." Jeft felt something on the seat under his leg. A card. He picked it up. An invitation.

"Knock off the sardonic crap, will ya?"

"Sardonic? I thought I was being droll." Jeff read the invitation and suddenly realized what it meant. "Fuck. Of course!"

"What?"

"*This* is where Harvey is. This is where *everybody's* going to be. Saturday night, Labor Day weekend—"

Nick looked at the invitation. "Malibu?"

"It's going to be *the* end-of-the-summer party. I don't know why I didn't remember it sooner—"

" 'Dress: Fifties Barbecue,' " Nick read. "What the fuck does that mean?"

"Like the barbecue scene in *Summer and Sweat.* Everybody's going to wear toreador pants and pedal pushers and shit like that."

"The guys, too, huh?" Nick snorted and tossed the invitation on the dash. "So where's this guy with *our* clothes? Let's hope he's got something besides pedal pushers. I don't feel much like Doris Day tonight."

23

Victor stuffed old cords and shirts into a shopping bag in his apartment on the second floor of the Woodview Manor, a building he liked to describe as "the architectural equivalent of Peter Pan collars." There was a knock.

Victor opened the door. "Heeeyyy, *vato!*" his brother Rudi said. His straight brother Rudi. His straight brother Rudi who owned a beer bar in Pico Rivera. "We thought we'd surprise you, man!"

We? Victor looked down the stairs, where he saw his sister-in-law, Negra, helping his mother up the steps. His mother was ancient and she'd had a stroke. "Just a few more steps," Negra said to her.

Victor's mother broke into a radiant smile when she saw her son at the top of the stairs. Victor broke into a sweat.

He could smell tequila on Rudi's breath. "We had dinner at a Hollywood restaurant," Rudi said, fingering his flashy suit. "And I said, 'Hey, Victor lives only a few minutes from here.' "

Victor felt weak. "Come on in," he said.

Suddenly Victor realized there was a *Playguy* magazine on the coffee table with a picture of a bearded cowboy unzipping his Levi's on the front. He quickly shoved it under a *Gentleman's Quarterly.*

Negra helped Victor's mother through the door. Rudi said, "Hey, I gotta use the, ah—"

"Up the hall."

111

Rudi went up the hall to the john, whistling. Negra helped Victor's mother to the sofa.

Suddenly Victor's insides turned over. There was a Colt calendar over the toilet in the bathroom. A construction worker with a fistful of engorged bulging-veined cock.

In the bathroom Rudi quit whistling.

Nick idled the Jaguar in the alley behind the Woodview Manor. "Are you sure we can trust this guy?"

"Victor's my best friend."

"So where is he?"

"Just relax. He'll be down." Jeff looked at the invitation again. "Nick, I *know* Harvey's at this party."

"You *knew* he was at the baths, man. Look where that got us."

"He was there. He *was* there. We just missed him, that's all."

"That's all? Tell that to that guy who got his dick shot off."

"Shit," Jeff said. "That poor fucking guy." The image throbbed in his mind: the guy's shiny cock, the blast, then the blood. The cock, the blast, the blood. The cock—

"Fuck this," Nick said. He started to pull out.

"Wait. Look, let me go up. Let me check it out."

"What about the neighbors?"

"Maybe they've gone inside. I just wanna see." Jeff started to get out.

Nick shut off the engine. "I'm goin' with you," he said.

Nick and Jeff ducked up the walkway to the court. The neighbors, still sitting on the front steps drinking, sounded extremely wasted. One of the guys was telling a story and making drag-race sounds as Nick and Jeff peered around the corner.

The mood in Victor's apartment had taken a grim turn. Rudi had come out of the bathroom and he was staring at Victor with a look of sullen drunken hatred. His brother, a queer.

Victor's mother, oblivious, smiled radiantly. She was so glad to see Victor. She didn't say much. The stroke had affected her speech.

Negra smiled compulsively. "This is a really nice place," she said. This whole thing had been Rudi's idea. Negra, realizing long ago that Victor was gay, had been afraid something just like this might happen.

"Let's go," Rudi barked.

Nick and Jeff ducked across the court when they thought none of the neighbors were watching.

But a girl nuzzling her boyfriend saw them dart up the stairs. "Hey," she said, "I swear to God, I just saw two naked men run up the stairs."

Negra was helping Victor's mother to her feet when there was a knock on the door. Shakily, Victor opened it.

"Hey, what's going on, why didn't you come down?" Jeff blurted as he and Nick burst in.

For a few seconds everybody just froze. Victor closed his eyes. Rudi's mouth dropped. Negra's smile crumbled. Victor's mother crossed herself. Nick made a perfunctory attempt to cover his cock with his hand. Jeff involuntarily said, "Ooops."

Victor handed Jeff the bag of clothes.

Nick and Jeff quickly put on the clothes while Victor and his relatives watched. Nick caught some pube hair in the zipper of the cords. "Ouch."

Rudi broke into a sweat.

When they were dressed, Nick said, "Let's go."

Jeff looked at Victor, glanced at the others, and said, "Thanks. Sorry." He and Nick took off down the stairs.

They dashed through the court without looking back to see if the neighbors were watching.

24

"We can take this to the freeway," Jeff said when they reached Mulholland Drive. "Then cut down Sunset to PCH, and shoot straight out to Malibu."

"We can also take this to the freeway, heading north and just keep going," Nick said.

"Going where?"

"I dunno. 'Frisco, maybe. *I* know a lawyer in 'Frisco, man. Used to trick with him." He was thinking of Randy. "A real shark. Maybe he knows a weight clinic doctor who does plastic surgery on the side. We could get new faces—"

"Yeah. I could dye my hair black. Burn off my fingerprints with acid."

"Actually, we're going in the wrong direction. What we oughta be doing is heading for Mexico. Look, do you think this attorney guy'll loan us some money?"

"For what?"

"To get the fuck outa the country, what do you think?"

Jeff was afraid to tell Nick what he really thought. "I'm sure he will, if he thinks that's what we should do."

But Jeff wasn't sure at all. And being on Mulholland Drive brought it all back. He didn't really know where he stood with Harvey; they weren't really *friends*. They certainly didn't hang out together.

Jeff had met Harvey at a party for a faded TV star over a year ago. Jeff had known from the start that Harvey was one of the three or four most powerful attorneys in Hollywood. He was also attractive, in his own way. But Harvey was married. And Jeff's place was "out of the way."

So they'd gone for a moonlight drive in Harvey's Corniche. Jeff blew Harvey as they snaked along Mulholland Drive. Harvey did a popper and nearly drove off a cliff when he came.

A few weeks later, Harvey invited Jeff to have lunch with him at Ma Maison. Jeff got dressed up and went to Harvey's Century City office at noon, where he sucked Harvey off at his desk while Harvey's secretary held his calls. After he came, Harvey made a long call to Hong Kong and told Jeff he'd have to take a rain check on lunch.

Since then, Jeff had seen Harvey at the dance clubs and bars, at parties here and there. Harvey was always friendly, even warm. He and Jeff might have a drink and talk about show business. Then Harvey would get bored and move on. He had no further interest in Jeff sexually. But he was friendly, even warm.

"Want to know something fucked?" Nick said.

"How fucked?"

"We're outa gas."

The Jaguar was in fact sputtering and dying and grinding to a halt.

Nick steered the Jaguar over to the side of the road, and he and Jeff got out.

"This is *truly* fucked," Jeff said. "We're miles from everything."

"So come on," Nick said.

They started walking.

It was still warm and the sky was clear. They could smell a brush fire and see its orange glow off to the northeast, but it was too far away to worry about here. The black hills around them were speckled with lights but the road itself was dark unless a car roared by. Nick and Jeff cringed when that happened, the headlights blinding them: two good-looking young men on foot. Several cars slowed as they passed.

"This is *too* fucked," Nick said. "We gotta get off this road."

"Over there." Jeff pointed to a clot of black trees and houses. "We can cut down through there back toward town."

"Town, huh?"

"You got a better idea?"

"Don't you know anybody that lives around here? I thought you knew a bunch of movie stars. Maybe we could work out a deal. Sell 'em the rights to our story."

"I don't think we're sympathetic enough. Stars always worry about stuff like that."

Another car passed. Nick cringed.

They hurried on toward the clot of black trees and houses.

After consulting with his attorney, Chris reported his Jaguar stolen. The cops hadn't had much trouble figuring out who'd taken it, and when the highway patrol found the Jaguar on Mulholland Drive, they radioed in that it looked like the suspects were still in the area on foot.

Lieutenant Brundl was still at the baths, watching the ambulance crew load up the lifeguard, when he heard the call. He and his men turned on their sirens and took off heading north toward the Hollywood Hills.

Lieutenant Brundl was sweating like a crazed hog. His heart was pounding like a red fist. "These fucking queers," he said.

Nick and Jeff reached the clot of black trees and houses. Suddenly Nick saw a peripheral flash of red-and-blue light back on Mulholland Drive.

"Fuck."

"Down there." Jeff indicated a dirt road that ran behind the houses. He and Nick took off running.

The flashing cop lights snaked up Mulholland Drive. A couple of cars veered off down the dirt road. They slowed and used their search beams to scan the chaparral.

Chuck MacDonald was thirty-four. He had short brown hair, a trim mustache, and a husky body he kept in exceptionally good shape. Chuck lived in a condo in the Hollywood Hills and every night he ran along the dirt roads in the hills behind his condo. He liked to run at night because it was cooler. It also helped him get to sleep. Sometimes he had trouble sleeping because of his job.

Chuck was jogging at a moderate pace, wondering what was going on with all the cops in the area, when Nick and Jeff flew around the corner and Nick smashed into him. Nick and Chuck both fell.

Jeff doubled back. "Come on," he shouted to Nick.

Nick got up and looked at Chuck. Chuck was stunned. He could see Nick's face clearly in the moonlight. He recognized Nick—and then Jeff—with a jolt. He knew they were the "homosexual fugitives."

"You guys, look," Chuck said as he got up, the red-and-blue lights flashing over the black hills, the search beams slicing through the chaparral. "I know who you are. Come on. I live right up there." Chuck indicated a dark rectangular shape on the horizon.

Nick and Jeff hesitated. They were breathing hard.

"It's all right," Chuck said. "It's all right, I'm gay, come on."

Nick glanced at Jeff. Jeff nodded feverishly.

They all took off.

25

Chuck led the way up the hill and up the back steps of the condominium complex. Nick glanced back at the lights combing the chaparral as Chuck unlocked the door.

It was a one-bedroom place, cheaply furnished, a little cluttered, but the atmosphere was warm and appealing. So was Chuck.

Jeff had a special weakness for jocks like Chuck, and he couldn't help thinking about what might occur under different circumstances. But Nick was extremely uneasy. To him, short-haired, straight-looking jocks looked like cops. He avoided them when he cruised, and Chuck was especially disturbing because he was so *convincingly* straight-looking. Whatever he did for a living, passing was obviously vital.

Chuck peered out the window. The lights were still crisscrossing the chaparral, and a chopper passed overhead, but it looked like the search was fanning out and moving down toward the canyon.

"They'll probably do a door-to-door before the night's over," Chuck said. Then he looked at Nick, checking him out very closely, and said, almost casually, "So, you really shoot that cop?"

"Which cop?" Nick said.

"You know. The cop."

"No," Nick said, exhausted, exasperated. "Another fucking cop shot him!"

One side of Chuck's mouth smiled. "Don't get overwrought," he said. "I'm on your side."

"Sorry," Nick said. "It's been a rather stressful weekend. Of course, it's not over yet."

"What you guys ought to do is get a real good lawyer and turn yourselves in to the mayor or something. With lots of press around. Otherwise, they'll waste you."

"Yeah, we already reached that conclusion," Nick said. "They've been trying their best to do just that."

Chuck sat down and started taking off his Nikes. "You guys might as well relax. If I was you, I wouldn't try going anywhere till tomorrow. They'll probably be around here all night, but if they don't find you in the morning, they'll figure you got away." Chuck got up and peeled off his shorts. "I gotta take a shower," he said.

Chuck peeled off his sweaty jock and tossed it in a wicker hamper on his way into the bathroom. Jeff looked at Chuck's hairy butt and half-wished Chuck would turn around, but he didn't. He turned on the shower and stepped in, steam wafting through the open bathroom door.

Jeff looked at Nick. "Nice guy."

"Yeah. *Real* nice." Nick peered out the window again. "This is like one of those prison-break movies."

Jeff looked over Nick's shoulder. "It looks like they're moving on down toward the Valley, though. I think we lucked out."

Nick was about to express some reservations, but he didn't get a chance. Because there was suddenly a brutal pounding on the door.

Chuck heard it, too, and came dashing out of the shower. The cops pounded again. "Jesus, I didn't think they'd be here this soon," Chuck said. "Go in the bedroom. Get in the closet."

Nick hesitated, trying to read Chuck's intentions. Had this guy been planning to turn them in all along?

"Goddamm it, Nick, come on," Jeff said. He grabbed Nick's arm and pulled him into the bedroom.

Nick looked back at Chuck, who wrapped a towel around his waist and unlocked the door.

Nick and Jeff ducked into the closet and shut the door. It was pitch-black. Jeff's heart was pounding. So was Nick's.

Momentarily, they heard voices in the living room. Low cop voices. Nick's head brushed something hard hanging in the closet. He touched it.

Nick almost crapped in his pants. It was a gun.

He felt it again. A gun in a holster. On a thick leather belt. He felt for the light cord and pulled it. The light came on.

"Oh, my God," Jeff said.

A collection of dark-blue LAPD uniforms hung under plastic on the rack. The holstered gun hung on the door. There was no doubt. Chuck MacDonald wasn't a uniform queen. The insignia on the uniforms was genuine. Chuck MacDonald was a cop, a real cop.

"Oh, fuck." Nick took the gun from the holster and checked it out. It was a six-inch Colt Python .357 and it was loaded.

Carefully, Nick opened the closet door.

Nick crossed the bedroom and peered out into the living room.

Chuck was leaning in the doorway, talking to the cops. One of them had a shotgun. The other one said something and Chuck laughed.

Nick cocked the Python.

But Jeff had a feeling. He put his hand on Nick's shoulder. "Wait,"

"It used to be," said the cop with the shotgun, "you bust a fruit, he breaks down and sobs and begs for mercy."

"Yeah," Chuck said. "I guess they think they're real hot shit now or something."

The cops started to leave. "They're probably back in town by now anyway. Sniffin' around some toilet

somewhere. That's the only way a lot of those fruits
can get a hard-on."

"Yeah, they're sick," Chuck said. "Hey, well, listen.
Good luck, okay?" He closed the door.

Chuck was feeling pretty good that he'd brought it
off, but when he started toward the bedroom, Nick
threw the door open and shoved the .357 in Chuck's
face.

"Okay, man. What the fuck kind of cop are you?"

Jeff tried to intercede. "Nick, come on. Please.
Really. Wait a second."

Chuck looked at the gun and remembered the uniforms in the closet. He smiled faintly and made a
helpless openhanded gesture. "I'm not a cop," he
said.

"Then what the fuck's that shit in the closet?"
Nick indicated the gun in his hand. "Then what the
fuck's this? A nickel-plated dildo?"

Chuck sighed, strangely resigned and sad. "Come
in here," he said. "In the bedroom. I wanna show
you something."

Nick glanced at Jeff. Cautiously, Jeff nodded. Nick
kept Chuck covered as they went into the bedroom,
but Chuck's persistent calm was already deflating
Nick's anger.

Chuck switched on a lamp and indicated the dresser.
It was clogged with trophies and citations that revealed Chuck's occupation. He was a P.E. teacher at
a West Los Angeles high school. But what Chuck
wanted to show them was a framed photograph stuck
behind the trophies. It was a photograph of a smiling
fresh-faced young man. In a cop uniform.

Chuck indicated a large red vinyl album on the
chair beside the dresser.

Jeff picked up the album and took it over to the
lamp and opened it. It was full of snapshots of Chuck
and the smiling cop. Together. Hunting. On camping
trips. In Mexico. Playing football with other guys
who looked like cops. In a staged drunken fight with
one big cop who was built like a hog. At parties with

their arms around trashy-looking gals. At the beach.
At the marina, posing beside a marlin. All regular
buddy poses. Except for a series toward the back. Of
Chuck and the smiling cop with their arms around
each other in front of a modest Christmas tree. In the
last of which Chuck was planting a kiss firmly on the
smiling cop's cheek.

There were loose newspaper clippings, too. Nick
looked over Jeff's shoulder. One of the clippings fea-
tured the smiling cop's portrait. "Policeman Honored,"
it said. And the paragraph that followed cited several
instances of bravery in the brief career of Officer
Kenneth J. Gregory, dead at age twenty-six of acute
gastrointestinal disorders.

Chuck sat down on one of the twin beds. "This is
where we were going to live," he said. "We were
going to be . . . roommates. We might have brought
it off." He smiled sadly. "At least for a while."

Nick took the bullets from the gun and put them in
his pocket. He put the gun down on the dresser—
beside the photograph of the late Kenneth J. Gregory.
"I'm sorry," he said to Chuck.

Chuck didn't look up. He just sat there. It was
clear he wanted to be alone. Nick and Jeff went into
the other room.

Finally Chuck got up and went to the dresser. He
opened a drawer and took out a pair of cutoffs and
put them on. Then he looked at Ken's photograph.
He picked it up, stuck it in the drawer, and closed
the drawer hard.

Chuck agreed to take Nick and Jeff to Malibu in
the morning. Michael Reed's parties being what they
were, Jeff was fairly sure Harvey would still be there.
Nick had reservations, but he was too tired to argue.

Chuck brought out some blankets and pillows, and
Nick and Jeff slept on the living-room floor. They
didn't undress. At first they slept separately, but Jeff
finally rolled over and hugged Nick. He was glad
when Nick hugged him back and kissed him gently.

They were so exhausted that, in spite of all the amphetamine they'd taken, they soon fell asleep.

Chuck lay in bed and stared out the window at the clear star-filled sky. Nick and Jeff were snoring in the other room. Every once in a while a police chopper whomped and blinked across the sky. Chuck was awake all night.

26

It almost felt like an ordinary, relaxed Sunday morning. Nick drank coffee, looking out the window. It was warm and exceptionally clear; he could see all the way across the city out to the ocean and Catalina. This was the way you imagined L.A. before you got here, when you still thought it was a place where dreams come true, he thought.

Jeff sat on the bed, lacing up the Adidas Chuck had given him. "So is it pretty tough being a coach?" he asked Chuck. "Being gay and everything?"

Chuck smiled. There was something unaffectedly fresh and clean-cut about Chuck that knocked Jeff out. He was a dream coach: a handsome young jock who grew up into someone the guys in P.E. probably had crushes on right and left.

"I keep my sexual preference to myself," Chuck said. "It's nobody's business what you do in the privacy of your own bedroom."

Jeff had to smile. "That's what I told the cops who busted in on us."

"But you guys were fighting. That's what the paper said."

"We weren't fighting," Jeff said. "We were fucking."

"You're gonna need a real good lawyer."

"That's why we were going to Malibu."

"Well . . ." Chuck sighed. "I don't know what to tell you." He sounded wistful. "Good luck."

"Thanks."

They were standing close. Jeff wanted to kiss Chuck badly, but instead he just smiled. Then he picked up the old pair of sandals Chuck had dug out of the closet and took them out to Nick.

Nick had taken some speed with his coffee and he was getting edgy again. "Let's get out of here before this guy gets fucky with us," he whispered to Jeff.

"Fucky? What do you mean?"

"Man, I don't care if he's gay or not. Didn't you see those pictures? Half his friends are cops! What if he has second thoughts or something?"

Chuck came into the living room before Jeff could respond. He had his car keys. "Ready?"

"Yeah," Jeff said.

"Okay, I'm gonna go down and get the car out and look around a little. But I'm sure everything's okay now." Chuck went out.

"I gotta use the can," Nick said.

But instead Nick went into Chuck's bedroom. The Python was still on the dresser. Nick took a few bullets from his pocket and stuck them in the gun. Then he stuck the gun in his belt. His shirttail hid it.

"Nick!" Jeff called.

Nick hurried back into the living room, where Jeff was peering out the window.

"Oh, shit," Nick said.

There was a cop car in the driveway below. And Chuck was talking to the cop behind the wheel.

"That goddamn fuck," Nick said, "I told you."

But Jeff was sure they could trust Chuck. "Easy," he said.

In a minute Chuck smiled, waving. The cops pulled out.

They heard Chuck open the garage door below and start his car. He backed out in an old Pacer. They figured he was about to get out and come up and get them.

Instead he threw it into drive and tore out.

"What the fuck! What's he doing?" Nick said.

The Pacer barreled up the road toward Mulholland
Drive.

Chuck MacDonald was scared. The cops had told
him about the roadblocks on Mulholland and in the
canyons. They were sure Nick and Jeff were still in
the hills after all, and there was no way out. Chuck
didn't know what to do. His nerves were raw from
lack of sleep. His mind was filled with visions of
ruin. Why had he helped them?

It had seemed like the right thing to do last night.
An impulsive act of courage that seemed to make up
for all the sneaking around he'd done with Ken. But
now he felt like an idiot. With one stupid gesture, he
had irrevocably gutted his neatly ordered life. He
had to put as much space between himself and the
fugitives as possible. Maybe they'd just leave. If they
were caught there, he'd just tell the police they broke
in after he left. Oh, Jesus, they'd never believe that.
He was screwed. He'd be arrested for harboring
criminals. Everybody'd find out he was gay. Ken's
cover would be posthumously blown, their affair dis-
sected in court. He'd lose his job. He'd never coach
again.

Chuck careened along Mulholland Drive. Maybe I
should just drive over the edge, he thought. Maybe I
should, maybe I will.

"I told you," Nick said. He and Jeff clattered down
the stairs from Chuck's condo. "That guy's as squirrely
as a brain-damaged wombat."

"We gotta get a car," Jeff said as they came out by
the garage.

Nobody saw them leave the condo complex.

Nobody saw them cut down to the dirt road and
cross the chaparral and head toward the dark-green
residential area.

A cop chopper veered over the horizon just as they
reached the trees—but the cops in the chopper didn't
see them either.

A few minutes later, Nick and Jeff came up to a

huge ersatz Tudor mansion with a three-car garage. The garage doors were open. There was a shiny black Bentley inside.

A Great Dane came to the leaded-glass window above the garage and barked at Nick and Jeff as they ran up to the Bentley.

"It's got the keys," Jeff said.

They jumped in and backed out.

Jeff drove. Nick looked back at the barking Great Dane. Nobody came to the window to see what the dog was barking at.

Lieutenant Brundl leaned against his Plymouth at the roadblock on Mulholland Drive. It was almost two and he had to admit it: it looked like the queers had got away again.

It was hot and he was exhausted. He wiped sweat off his face with the rolled-up sleeve of his white Sears shirt. Then he got back into the Plymouth and started the engine.

Before his partner got in, he quickly reached down and pushed something back under the seat, something red and squishy in a plastic zip-lock bag.

27

Nick and Jeff got out of the hills. Jeff took a series of residential streets and dirt roads, eventually cutting back to Mulholland Drive on the far side of the roadblock. West of the San Diego Freeway, Mulholland became a dirt road, too. Several dusty hours later they reached asphalt again at Topanga Canyon and headed south toward the beach. Toward Harvey, the miracle worker.

"That black singer a couple of years ago," Jeff said. "Shot his girlfriend point-blank in the face at a shopping mall in Florida. Hundreds of witnesses. Harvey got him off. You want to know how?"

"What I want to know about is this chichi producer," Nick replied.

"Michael? He produced *Summer and Sweat*—he's hot now. What about him?"

"This is his place we're going to, right?"

"I'm sure he doesn't know anything about what's happened, Nick. It's a holiday weekend—"

"You said the same thing at the baths. Don't you think this decadent queen ever watches TV?"

"Not over Labor Day weekend."

"So what does he do?"

"He goes crazy. Michael's Labor Day bashes are legendary. He throws these horrendous Southern barbecues, like the scene at Twelve Oaks in *Gone With the Wind*. I mean, if you didn't know better, you'd think an era was ending."

"I think one is," Nick said darkly.

"You may have a point." Jeff took a right on Pacific Coast Highway.

"But the invitation said: Fifties Barbecue. Maybe we ought to stop somewhere and get some Bermuda shorts. And one of those campy aprons with a bunch of wieners on it."

"I'm sure Michael has all the wieners he needs."

"Yeah, that's what I've heard."

They drove in silence for a while, Nick looking at the pretty tanned men and women along the beach. He took deep breaths of the fresh ocean air. It was a great day for the beach.

Jeff couldn't help admiring the posh restored interior of the Bentley, and wishing the car were his. His heart ached, his guts churned with envy, when he saw expensive cars. He'd always dreamed of owning a Rolls. If Jennifer's first album had taken off, he would've had one. A Silver Shadow. He'd been planning to pay cash in Beverly Hills. A few weeks after the album stiffed, his Porsche Speedster was gone, and he was taking the bus—in L.A., the epitome of utter defeat.

Then there'd been the humiliation of seeing rich show-business people from his Jennifer days when he was driving around in his crummy little Honda. Cringing at a stoplight beside a rock star in a Lamborghini.

"So *Summer and Sweat*," Nick said, "that's a pretty big hit."

"Are you kidding? It's threatening to make *E.T.* look like a flop."

"Are you shitting me?"

"A little, but not much. It's a blockbuster."

"I hear it's a piece of shit, though."

"It's good clean family entertainment."

"That's what I mean. It's like one of those Southern hothouse pictures they used to make in the fifties, where everybody was always all sexed-up with nowhere to go. Only he took out all the sex."

"You're right. It's essentially a neo-*Tammy* picture,

extremely sanitized and vapid. I guess it had to be to appeal to everybody from junior to grandma. The guys *do* take off their shirts a lot, though."

"Yeah, I'm sure. I guess even grandma likes that."

"Junior might not mind it, either."

"But the music—that *really* sucks. All these fuckin' horns and screechy voices. It's like some fuckin' Broadway soundtrack from thirty years ago."

"What else would you expect, given Michael's background? Anyway, they still love that stuff in Des Moines."

"What do you mean, his background?"

"Jesus, don't you know? Michael Reed was a Broadway child star back in the forties. A musical-comedy prodigy. I mean, he was *adored*. He'd just come to Hollywood and was all set to star in a big musical with Judy Garland when disaster struck."

"His voice changed."

"No."

"Judy tried to kill herself."

"Worse. Apparently, he'd been having an affair for some time with his stepfather. And one day his mother caught them in the act. She shot and killed Michael's stepdad, then turned the gun on herself. It was hushed up at the time, because of Michael's tender age, but the studio moguls all knew. Michael was finished, a has-been at sixteen. Supposedly, he drifted through the South working as a male hustler through most of the fifties and early sixties. Very butch, rough trade, called himself Dean, you know the syndrome. Then his looks went and he came back to L.A. and turned to drag with a vengeance. I saw him once, about six years ago, lip-synching 'People' in a *My Name Is Barbra* wig in a grungy little beer bar in Pico Rivera. Pathetic. Then a miracle. A rich chicken hawk who'd doted on him as a child star passed away and left him twenty million dollars. The next thing anyone knew he was back on the scene as a major producer. Times change. Money talks."

"But he only looks about thirty. How could he go through all that and still—"

"Plastic surgery. Ever see *Seconds* with Rock Hudson? The change was almost that dramatic. You can say what you want about his life-style, but in my opinion, he's a hell of a guy. A survivor."

"Yeah. I guess anyone who's been through all that has earned the right to be a pig."

"Well, right now he's one pig we need on our side. So be cool, okay?"

"Don't worry. I'm as cool today as I've ever been. How'd *you* meet him, anyway?"

"Gee, I don't remember exactly." But Jeff remembered. "I see him around a lot. If it's *in*, he'll be there. Just like me. I tend to run with a pretty chic crowd, Nick."

Nick laughed. "Yeah, I know. I guess this weekend's an exception."

Jeff grinned and squeezed Nick's leg, but he was becoming apprehensive. He remembered only too well the night he'd met Michael Reed. Though it had been nearly four years and Michael had been cordial the few times Jeff had run into him since, he doubted that Michael had ever really forgiven him.

It had been one of those odyssey Saturday nights, Jeff dancing and bar-hopping all over town until he found himself on his way to a "Hollywood party" with several hot young men he'd just met at the Motherlode.

A very exclusive Hollywood party, it turned out, at the Bel-Air home of one of America's favorite neutered gay celebrities, an innocuously fey game-show clown. Many of the other guests were of the same closeted generation: faded CinemaScope stars, sitcom dads, and romantic Vegas crooners, men who changed the genders when they chatted with Johnny and Merv.

There were also a number of hot young men, dancing shirtless, dripping sweat, included—like Jeff and his acquaintances—simply because of their youth and looks and, Jeff soon realized, their availability.

But Jeff had no intention of trying to cheaply advance himself that night—until he saw Michael Reed.

He couldn't believe his eyes at first. When he first
spotted the husky, handsome man across the room,
he thought it was somebody who looked *like* a young
Michael Reed. He was flabbergasted when he realized it *was* Michael Reed. Michael's restoration was
still fresh: he looked about twenty-six, his smooth
skin glowing. Jeff found it difficult to reconcile this
image with the baggy-eyed Baby Jane Hudson gargoyle he'd seen staggering around in drag a few years
before. Of course, Jeff was aware that Michael was
the hot producer of the moment; although he had yet
to make a picture, he'd just closed one of the biggest
production deals in Hollywood history. He was also
extremely charming. There was something a bit dated
about him—he had a kind of fifties physique-magazine
look: get out the sailor suits and posing briefs. But
his Southern voice was gentle and beguiling. There
was also a rather disturbing undercurrent to his boyish
appearance, an unavoidably Dorian Gray connotation:
he was, after all, not twenty-six but fifty. But the
alcohol and the heady aura of power overrode Jeff's
reservations. When Michael invited him back to
Malibu, he accepted.

They went in Michael's car, a pristinely restored
'58 Cadillac convertible, soaring along PCH with the
top down. Jeff thought more than once of Paul
Newman in *Sweet Bird of Youth*. Of course, Jeff should
have been the one at the wheel, Michael should have
been curled up with the bottle. If either of them was
the Geraldine Page figure, it was Michael. But, as it
turned out, Michael had already selected another
Great Lady to portray.

Jeff was sipping a mint julep on the veranda swing
at Michael's Tara-themed Point Dume house when
he heard his host returning. But when he looked up,
he saw Liz.

Jeff spilled his drink, he couldn't believe it. It was
the worst Liz he'd ever seen—laughable, demented—
but he could tell Michael didn't mean it as a joke.
Michael was too tall, for one thing, and those jutting

bazooms looked like footballs under his top. The tons of stiff black hair were late-sixties Liz, circa *Reflections in a Golden Eye*. The lipstick was smeary, the beauty mark on the wrong cheek. Destroying what illusion there was, Michael's dong hung below the hem of his trashy miniskirt. He approached, coaxing, beckoning, like a vixen in heat.

Jeff was horrified. He'd never been into drag queens—he considered the phenomena decadent, the result of rancid gender definitions—and he found the idea of having sex with one totally repellent. When Michael took him into a smothering perfumed embrace, Jeff slipped from his arms and ran.

Laughing incredulously, but scared, Jeff dashed through the house, pursued by a hulking sex-kitten banshee intent on assault. Jeff ducked into the hothouse, where Michael cornered him.

"Come on, little man. Let's see what you're made of," Michael spit in an evil-bitch voice straight from *Virginia Woolf* as he closed in.

When Michael smashed his cherry-red mouth to Jeff's, Jeff pulled back and without warning threw up.

"Oh, my God!" Michael yelled, holding his soiled top away from his fake bazooms. "You disgusting animal! You've ruined it! You've ruined it, *get out!*"

Jeff could still see Michael chasing him up the driveway—wig lopsided, melons askew, dong swinging—as he and Nick reached the top of the hill and saw the house on the bluff below.

"I guess that's it, huh?" Nick said.

Cypress trees rustled in the ocean breeze before the columned plantation house. Although it was less than five years old, it had been aged, like a movie location, so that it appeared as if it had been there since before the Civil War.

Jeff started down the road to the electric gate. "Yeah, this is it. It looks less gothic in the daylight."

28

It was naptime in Michael Reed's Southern beachfront paradise. The only sounds were the slapping of waves and the buzzing of flies.

The waves broke against the sand on the beach below the gutted living room, with its barbecue-sauce-smeared furniture, with its tap and scuff-marked hardwood floors, with its smashed once-belonged-to-David-Selznick gold-leaf coffee table, with its left-behind hula-hoop party favors (one labeled: King Kong's cock ring), with its used-as-coasters Polaroids of the *Summer and Sweat* "kids" in the act of destroying the floors, (drunk, luded, ablaze in the pink-and-lemon-yellow costumes they'd worn in the film, stomping, shrieking every show tune Michael could throw at them, until they collapsed on the sofas dripping sweat).

The flies buzzed on the buffet tables, feasting on the ravaged grits and beans and corn bread, the sodomized soufflés, flat Dom Pérignon, and thousands of dollars' worth of fetid caviar. They hung in the air above a torn, stained pair of pedal pushers tossed over a life-size statue of David.

The hunky young caterers were gone, the obese Mafia financier had absconded with them. Everybody else was gone, too. Except Harvey. Even the boys had taken off, they were exhausted. Except Tim and Robbie. Not that they weren't exhausted, too, but somebody had to take care of Michael. And

Harvey—the only thing Harvey couldn't do was stop.

A sharp laugh broke the tranquillity.

It was Tim, in the kitchen, laughing at something Robbie had just said. "Well, maybe *this time* you can finish him off," Tim said.

"I've been *trying* to finish him off for the last sixteen hours," said Robbie, an extremely good-looking young man with a smooth suntanned body and a semierection in his sheer blue Speedo swim trunks. "My buns are achin', honey," he said with a voice that unconsciously mimicked Bette Midler.

Tim broke up again and opened a bottle of Perrier for Robbie. Tim was also extremely good-looking, a *Blue Boy* magazine archetype with a trim cop mustache, short jock hair, and a slightly ill-proportioned torso stretching the weave of his Diana Ross T-shirt. He and Robbie had both been working for Michael for several months now, part of Michael's frequently replenished stable of hunky young men; they considered themselves veterans and, privately, "sisters". Although Michael himself had an affinity for fifties camp talk ("Here comes Miss Walter. She's *such* a bitch"), he insisted that his boys be as genuinely butch as possible. As a result, Tim and Robbie indulged in exaggerated nelliness, hissing their *s*'s and cultivating semiparodic bitchy-queen attitudes, only when they were alone.

"So, is it very big?" Tim said.

"Seven inches." Robbie shrugged. "But this is about the fourteenth time he's come, I shit you not. I don't know *when* he's gonna get tired. This girl is pooped."

"Douche with this." Tim handed Robbie the Perrier. "You want some ice and a squeeze?"

"No," Robbie said, even now looking too good, too perfect—so flawless he barely had a soul. "I'm sure he'd prefer to drink it straight from the bottle. He's a real animal. Well, *ciao*."

"*Ciao*."

Robbie padded out past the hothouse and the swimming pool, past the overturned brunch table, tiptoe-ing through the smashed glass and sausages and scrambled eggs and vodka and tomato juice, down to the striped cabana where Harvey lay playing with his cock.

Harvey reached up and pulled down Robbie's Speedos.

"Here's your Perrier." Robbie tried to look hot and emotionless.

Harvey didn't take the bottle. His hands were busy, parting Robbie's perfect cheeks.

Robbie saw a sailboat far out at sea. He wished he was on it.

Upstairs, Michael Reed snored on his blue-velvet-canopied bed. Though fifty-four, he had the tucked-and-lifted, gym-pumped body of a brawny VistaVision leading man. Beneath the lime-green cosmetic mask now covering his face, his features were smoothly youthful—a bit too smooth now, a little doll-like and ceramic from last year's chemical peel. His gray hair was dyed a metallic blond, fixed in a greasy jelly-roll style considered chicly rockabilly; he'd been wearing it that way since he turned his first trick in '52. His renovated eyelids fluttered. He was dreaming, perhaps, of an age when men were men, queers were queers, and Southern ladies suffered. His dream stopped when the intercom buzzed.

He felt for the switch. "*Buona sera*, darling," he said in his soft Southern accent, like an aging belle on the Spanish Steps.

Jeff's heart sank when he recognized Michael's voice. He'd been hoping for one of the boys who could call Harvey to the phone. Despite what he'd told Nick, Jeff believed there was a distinct possibility Michael had heard by now. A feverish retelling of the police-hostage story involving "two homosexual men" would have been prime material for Michael's gossipy Sunday-brunch crowd. "Oh, my God," Jeff imagined Michael shouting with mock horror as the names of the criminals were mentioned. "I know him! He's actually been a *guest* in this *house!*"

If he knew, Jeff was convinced, Michael was exactly the kind of guy who would turn them in.

"Hello, Michael. This is Jeff, Jeff Gifford."

"Jeff, darling, how are you?" Michael said blandly. He didn't know.

"Fine, fine. Look, I'm sorry if I'm disturbing you, but I was wondering, is Harvey there? It's really kind of important that I speak with him."

"Let's,see." Michael glanced at the clock. His lime-green mask was cracking, flakes of it dusting his bronzed chest. "Dear God, is it two-thirty already? Harvey?"

"Harvey Berringer."

"Oh, yes, Harvey. What about him? Oh, my God, out like a light."

"Is he there?"

"Yes. That is, he was. For brunch, as I recall."

"Well, is he still there? I thought he might still be there."

"Let me check, Jeff." Michael buzzed Tim.

Michael was nearly asleep again by the time Tim came in.

"Nap's over," Tim said, parodying a fussy nurse.

Michael cringed. He was going to have to let Tim go; the kid was becoming way too chummy, way too sardonic.

Michael sat up. "Timothy, darling, be an angel, would you, and bring me the cocaine."

Timothy stopped opening the drapes and went to the antique dresser.

Michael suddenly remembered that Jeff was at the gate. "Where's Harvey?"

"In the cabana." Tim brought Michael the elaborate silver coke service.

"Still? *God*, what a *stud!*" Michael said, thinking it sounded like something Tallulah might say. He switched on the intercom. "Jeff? Berringer's indisposed at the moment. Can I give him a message?"

"It's an emergency, Michael. I've come all the way from Hollywood. Could you tell him that—"

"Oh, hell, Jeff," Michael said blandly. "As long as you're here, you may as well tell him yourself."

Jeff got back in the Bentley. The electric gate hummed open.

"He's there," Jeff said to Nick as they drove in.

Nick looked uneasy. He checked the Python tied to his leg.

"Nick, please. We're almost home free."

Nick looked back—at the electric gate humming shut. "Are we?"

Michael did his coke, using a petite spoon that had supposedly belonged to Robespierre or somebody. But he also inhaled some lime-green mask residue and began coughing. "Oh, God."

Tim brought him a handkerchief. Michael blew his nose and looked at the handkerchief. "What a waste." He sniffled. "Oh, well." Michael rose from the bed. "Timothy, be an angel, would you, and draw my bath. And then, let's see, I'll wear the white cotton double-breasted tonight. With the Monty Clift Hawaiian. Then see if you can find my sable cock ring, I'll wear that too. Then call Tris in London, I'll take it in the bath. And let's shake Harvey if it looks like Jeff Gifford's going to hang around. Then kick them both out as soon as I've gone."

Down in the cabana Harvey was giving it to Robbie as if there was no tomorrow. At least he was trying to. But it wasn't any good anymore. He might as well have been plowing air.

Finally he gave up, rolled over, and lit a cigarette.

Robbie stayed where he was, his back slick with Harvey's sweat. He felt Harvey glaring at him. "I'm sorry. I guess my butt's seen better days."

"Right," Harvey said sharply, glaring at his cigarette.

Robbie was exhausted and he was so sick of Harvey he wanted to scream. "I gotta hit the john. Back in a sec." He pulled on his Speedos and went back up to the house.

Harvey stubbed out his cigarette and picked up his counterfeit Cartier tank watch and strapped it on. God, was it two-forty-five already? What was he doing here? When was all this going to end? Harvey squeezed his greasy genitals, gritting his teeth in frustrated rage.

The party last night had been something else. Harvey had flashed in with the cute young man from the baths with that aren't-we-hot-we-just-fucked-our-brains-out look stamped all over them. He'd hit his stride with a lot of coke and wine, and astonished everybody for hours on end until, before he knew it, it was dawn. By that time, the gorgeous if all too classically moronic young star of *Summer and Sweat* had impulsively taken off in his red Lamborghini with the cute young man Harvey had met at the baths, streaming up the coast, as Michael put it, "like Ava Gardner and Rossano Brazzi in *The Barefoot Contessa*, toward a doomed honeymoon." Which was fine with Harvey. Because by then he'd met Robbie. Robbie had literally followed him around all night with an ashtray, wearing nothing but an Oldie 45 (Percy Faith's "Theme from A Summer Place") over his magnificent uncut spindle. How could you resist a bit like that?

First they'd done it in the sauna. About seven in the morning, they'd done it in the dining room, which was littered with debris from the party. Harvey had Robbie hang from the chandelier, a zany idea he'd never actually tried before. The chandelier came down with a crash. Nobody was cut. But Michael had still been pissed about it at brunch; although, of course, that would pass.

Brunch had been poorly attended. The director of Michael's next picture had been there with his succulent Colombian lover. There'd been everybody's favorite TV mom, with her gruff one-eyed lesbian lover

of thirty years. They'd left early, when too many
Bloody Marys led to too much raunchy male talk.
The young married studio vice-president had fretted
endlessly over the threat of blackmail: he'd inadvertently blown a studio grip at a private club, and now
the kid wanted a break or else. Michael had ex-
pounded at great length on the future of movies.
"People are sick of realism! They want fantasy! They
want magic! They want Gidget and Tammy again!"

Around noon the young *Summer and Sweat* star
had called from Carmel. He was hysterical. The cute
young man had taken off with his Lamborghini and
his wallet. Michael arranged a rescue.

After that, Harvey had retired to the cabana, requesting Robbie's presence. There he'd fucked the
kid. Once, twice, three times, Harvey lost count. Each
time lousier than the time before.

Goddamn that mindless plastic doll, Harvey thought.
He hates me, I can tell. He's deliberately trying to
spoil it.

Why? 'Cause the kid knows I've got it made and
he's a flea.

Harvey looked down at his hairy body and thought
about a shower. He liked his body. He didn't work
out at a gym but the squash seemed to keep the flab
off. He was sinewy, brown, oversexed. Jesus Christ,
was he oversexed. No matter how many times he
came, he got hard again—just like now. He squeezed
his cock, twisting his wrist so he could look at his
watch. Goddammit, where was the no-good bum-
fuck punk anyway? What the hell was taking him so
long?

Jeff parked next to Harvey's olive-green Corniche.
"That's his car," Jeff said. "I told you, this guy's on
top of it. But he's totally unpretentious. You're going
to like Harvey. He's really zany. But he's also a
genius."

"Maybe I'll just wait here," Nick said.

"We should both talk to him, Nick. Look, it's okay.

Don't ask me why, but for the first time I feel safe. These are the people who *control* things, Nick, and they're my friends."

"I think you're full of shit," Nick said. But he got out of the Bentley.

Robbie showed them through the foyer. "He's in the cabana."

Robbie watched Nick and Jeff head down to the beach. Then he padded down the cool tile steps to the basement, where, at last, he was alone in a quiet, safe place. Away from Harvey. Away from Michael. From everyone.

Robbie went to the Art Deco bar and poured himself a stiff drink. Then he slipped a cassette in the VCR and settled back in a plush red velvet chair, watching the big screen TV as the cassette began.

Robbie always loved this moment. Especially now, when his ass was aching and it wasn't fun anymore, when the promise of love and stardom that had caused him to venture west from Nebraska seemed so remote, he wanted to abandon himself to the spiritual warmth of this ultimate fantasy, this allegory of his life.

Robbie buried his face in his hands and sobbed uncontrollably as—for what? the hundredth, the thousandth time?—little Judy Garland wailed "Over the Rainbow" with all her tender, doomed heart.

Robbie looked up when a sudden shaft of white light threw a long shadow aross the room, across the big screen TV, across Judy.

Harvey was standing in the door. He popped the plastic lid off a can of Crisco.

"Fuck. He's gotta be here somewhere," Jeff said to Nick in the cabana. "Here's all his Gucci stuff. Let's check the beach. Maybe he went for a dip."

Michael was soaking in the tub of his posh antebellum bathroom, scanning a screenplay as he spoke on the phone to Tris, his London business partner. "Tell me something vicious and gossipy, Tris. I'm wading through an excruciatingly dull script by a major writer and I'm literally numb with boredom."

Tris was a handsome twenty-seven-year-old financial genius who had, among other accomplishments, sodomized Jeff in the basement of the Thalberg Building during a screening of *The Goodbye Girl*. And the news item he now relayed caused Michael to understand, to *feel*, as he never had before, exactly what Scarlett must have felt when a grungy Yankee soldier violated her beloved home.

"No." Michael steadied himself against the rim of the tub. "Oh, my God!" The script slipped into the water."Are you sure? Are you *absolutely* sure? Jeff Gifford? *The* Jeff Gifford? *Our* Jeff Gifford? Oh, my God." Michael stood abruptly, sudsy water splashing. "Timothy," he shouted. "The towel!"

Jeff looked up and down the beach. There were a lot of people out, heads bobbing in the ocean. "Let's just wait. He's obviously got to come back for his stuff."

"What about the house?" Nick said.

A logical question. But Jeff still wanted to avoid Michael if possible. It didn't seem possible. They went back up to the house.

Tim tried to dry Michael off, but it wasn't easy. Michael was extremely agitated, the towel getting tangled in the telephone cord as he moved from window to window, watching Nick and Jeff as they approached below.

"Oh, God, Tris. They're coming up to the house. What should I do, Tris? Should I call the police? Oh, my God, the other one's horrible. A killer. It's *In Cold Blood* and I'm the Clutters. Oh, my God." He strained to see below. "They're coming into the house. They're *inside* the house. Oh, God, Tris, what should I do? Oh, Tris, there are a couple of *killers* in my *house*! God only knows what they're *on*. I know what's coming. It's Cielo Drive! I'm Sharon Tate! Now I know *exactly* how she felt! What should I do, Tris. *Tell me!*"

But it was too late to do anything. Michael looked through the bathroom door and saw Jeff and Nick in the hall.

"Hello, Michael. I'm sorry to disturb you, but—"

Before Jeff could say more, Michael started screaming, "Get out of my house! Get out! Timothy, lock the door! I'm calling the police!"

Tim tried to slam the bathroom door, but Nick pushed his way in.

Michael was punching numbers on the phone when Jeff amazed himself by grabbing the phone out of Michael's hand. "Don't do that, Michael!"

Michael was stunned and livid, and a second later he attacked. He flailed at Jeff and gouged him in the eye. That made Jeff mad. Jeff slammed his palm against Michael's nose, breaking it. Blood spurted.

Tim came at Nick with a hair dryer, trying to bash him with it. Nick slugged Tim in the face and shoved him into the tub. Then he went to help Jeff.

Nick and Jeff pushed Michael back against the bidet. He came down hard, banging his tailbone on the porcelain.

Nick finally dug out the Python and stuck it in Michael's face. "That's enough."

Michael rested on the bidet, fighting for his breath, rivulets of blood crisscrossing his bronzed physique.

Tim sloshed in the tub, making no attempt to climb out.

Jeff tossed Michael a wad of toilet paper. Michael dabbed his nose and glared at Jeff, catching his breath enough to say, "Small circles, Jeffrey. Word travels fast. You'll never work in this town again. I'll see to that, I promise you."

Some other time it would have been funny. "Where's Harvey?" Jeff said.

"He's in the cabana."

"He's *not* in the cabana."

"Then let me find out." Michael reached for the intercom.

Nick poked Michael's taut stomach with the Python. "Be real careful, okay?"

Michael punched buttons on the intercom, saying repeatedly, "Robert? Hello, Robert?" Finally he punched the basement.

Judy Garland wailed over the intercom. Somebody else was moaning. "Robert?" No response. "Robert, are you there?" Still no response.

Then Harvey answered, sounding far from the intercom. "Michael, is that you? Hey, I'm in a meeting, heh heh. Let me get back to you, okay? Heh heh heh."

Nick and Jeff took Michael and Tim down to the basement. As they reached the door, they saw a tornado taking Judy away to Oz, and caught a sharp reek of amyl nitrite. As they stepped through the door they gasped.

Robbie lay naked on his stomach on the billiard table, Harvey's arm pressed between his cheeks— where it vanished, just below the elbow.

"Dear Lord," Nick said.

Harvey jerked around to see who it was, and Robbie cried out, "Oh, no! No, no!"

Robbie's eyes were glazed with terror. Harvey's eyes were shot with demented awe.

"Oh, Jesus, Harvey," Jeff said weakly. "Oh, Jesus, what are you doing?"

"So this is your genius attorney," Nick whistled through his teeth.

Even Michael was appalled. "Really, Harvey. This time you've gone too far."

Tim was more than appalled; he was infuriated. "Stop it!" he screamed at Harvey. "For God sake, you're going to kill him!"

"It's okay," Harvey said with an embalmed monotone. "I know what I'm doing."

Nick realized the whole thing was a bust. But Jeff

ludicrously persisted. "Harvey, we need to talk to you about a legal situation. We're in trouble."

"Not now, Jeff. Call me at the office on Tuesday." He crushed a popper under his nose, reeling as it hit.

"But, Harvey," Jeff said, "you're our last hope."

Harvey's eyes rolled back in his head, showing the whites, as his tongue lopped out.

Tim couldn't stand it anymore. He blew up—at Michael. "Goddamn you, this is all your fault. You don't give a shit about any of us. We're just sex toys for all your rich, sleazy friends. I hate you!" He flailed at Michael, busting his lip.

Suddenly, Harvey got a stunned look. "Oh, crap. I forgot to take off my watch."

Robbie keened into hysteria.

"This is hopeless," Nick said to Jeff. "Let's get the fuck out of this squirrel cage."

Jeff took one last look at Harvey and knew Nick was right.

Tim shoved Michael into the big screen TV, then he dashed back to help Robbie. Michael went after him, smashing into him as he grabbed Harvey.

"Oh, no! No, no, no!" Robbie cried as he and Harvey hit the floor with a grisly thud.

Michael got Tim in a scissors hold, cutting off his breath. His face turning red, Tim bit Michael's ass. Michael howled and tried to shake Tim loose, but couldn't. Judy skipped up the yellow brick road.

Nick and Jeff made it out to the Bentley.

"Whew." Jeff got behind the wheel.

"Really."

Then Jeff looked up at the gate. "Oh, fuck."

Cops. Black-and-whites, lights flashing as they swooped down the hill, slamming on their brakes as they reached the gate.

Tris had called them.

Nick and Jeff took off on foot, cutting back through the house, down to the beach. Running through the sand was hard. Jeff felt like he was stuck in a slow-motion dream.

Beachgoers stared at them. It was clear they weren't joggers. They looked like criminals, propelled by fear, fleeing the scene of a crime.

By the time the cops surrounded Michael's house and demanded over a bullhorn that Nick and Jeff surrender, Nick and Jeff had scaled a cliff and cut back to Pacific Coast Highway.

And by the time the cops stormed Michael's house and discovered Michael and Tim and Harvey and Robbie clamped onto and plugged into one another in a writhing mound of blood and sweaty flesh, Nick and Jeff had stuck out their thumbs and been picked up by a beautiful young woman in a sparkling blue BMW 320i.

29

"**I** wouldn't normally pick up a guy, let alone two guys," said the beautiful young woman in the BMW— she was on her way home from Santa Barbara and didn't know anything about Nick and Jeff from the news—"but you guys are gay, aren't you?"

"How'd you figure that out?" Jeff said, Point Dume slipping away behind them.

The woman had curly sun-bleached hair, like Jeff's. She also had a supple-looking athlete's body, the kind of body, if you saw her from a distance or from behind, you could easily mistake for that of a teenage boy. All she had on was a pair of clogs and a yellow two-piece bikini. Her skin was flawless and tan.

"I have kind of a sixth sense about gay guys," she said, glancing at Nick, then at Jeff. "Not that you're obvious. You're not effeminate or anything. None of the usual stereotypes. But I can just tell."

Nick cleared his throat and glanced back up the highway. No cops, just lots of beach traffic.

"I like gay guys," she continued. "I have quite a few gay friends. That's one thing that's nice about it. It's still pretty rare for a woman to have male friends who are, you know, just friends. With straight guys, they come on like they want to be just friends sometimes, but when all is said and done, they still want sex. I think gays and women have a lot in common, don't you?"

"How's that?" Jeff said.

Nick grinned faintly. He'd heard all this before, back when he was hanging out with Randy, and Randy's gay political friends, in San Francisco.

"It's a similar kind of oppression. From straight, macho men. Not that I'm all that political anymore. Politics has its limitations." She smiled at Nick. "In fact, I must confess to a certain ambivalence about machismo. My boyfriend, for example, is fairly macho. At least on the outside. But he's really a very gentle, tender person on the inside. I guess that's what intrigues me about a lot of macho gay guys, too. That tough exterior mixed with a really shattering sweetness." She kept glancing at Nick. At all parts of his body. "So how far are you guys going?"

"Hermosa," Nick said.

That was news to Jeff.

"Well, look," the woman said. "I'll take you but I'd like to stop off at home first. Are you guys in a big hurry? You feel like getting high?"

Her name was Mirna. She lived in a converted brick auto-shop building a block from the beach in Venice. The buildings in the neighborhood looked seedy on the outside but burglar-alarm boxes indicated the influx of affluent young people who, like Mirna, now considered Venice a chicly bohemian place to live. She did sculpture, she told them, and her boyfriend was a video artist. He was in the Mojave Desert documenting a conceptual-art performance, she mentioned as they went into the studio. "Are you into conceptual art?" she said.

Jeff made the mistake of saying, "Sure."

A half-hour later, Mirna was boring Jeff blind with a cassette of one of her boyfriend's conceptual-art tapes on the set in the cozy alcove in the back of the studio. On the far side of the room Nick used a phone book to look up a number in Hermosa Beach. He was having trouble. He was extremely loaded.

Mirna lit yet another joint and passed it to Jeff. He was extremely loaded, too. He sat on the floor, leaning against the bed. Mirna sat on the bed. She accidentally brushed her leg against Jeff's cheek as she passed him the joint.

Jeff stared at the TV: a static shot of a dull industrial street and maybe once every five minutes, a truck would drive by the camera. Jeff still wasn't sure if it was the same truck each time or not.

With difficulty, Jeff got up. "I'll be right back," He handed Mirna the joint and went over to Nick. "What are we doing here?"

"I'm trying to find this guy's number," Nick said.

"What guy?"

"Dewey. Dewey Webster. Or was it Wexler? Let's see." Nick tried to remember the alphabet. "Man, I am obliterated."

"Who the fuck is Dewey Webster or Wexler?"

"He's this guy I know. He's kind of a surfer. Only he does other stuff, too. He goes down to Mexico a lot. He's real familiar with Mexico."

"What do you mean, he's a dope smuggler?"

"He does a lot of things."

"Oh, Jesus."

"Look, I feel the same way about this guy that you felt about your lawyer friend. I just want to discuss the situation with him and get his advice. I trust him. We had kind of a thing."

"It sounds like it. You don't even know his last name."

"Who knows anybody's last name? That doesn't mean anything. I'll bet you've been tight with lots of people where you never found out their last names till six months after you knew 'em. That doesn't mean shit. Dewey's okay. He's about the only person I've ever met in this shithole of a city who even treated me like a real human being." He found the number. "Here it is. Dewey Wexler. A *brother*. Which is more than I can say for most of the faggots I've met."

"So call him. It's fine with me."

Nick dialed the number, glancing over at Mirna. "You better get back to Mirna. We're gonna have to get her to give us a lift pretty quick."

"I think she's got something else in mind first."

"I know she does."

Jeff went back to her.

Mirna was becoming increasingly provoked by her own thoughts. She handed Jeff the joint again and watched Nick talking on the phone across the studio.

"He's hot," she said. "So are you, though. I'll bet you guys have a lot of fun together."

"Yeah, yeah. It's an endless party."

"Have you been together very long?"

"Oh, yeah. We've been lovers since junior high." Jeff instantly regretted being facetious. Mirna was a nice person. But it was too late.

"That's pretty rare. Most gay relationships are fairly short-lived. At least that's the stereotype. Of course, straight relationships are getting more and more like that, too. I've been with Ralph almost six months now. We have an open relationship."

"Really? That's great."

"It works out pretty well. Because, let's face it, everybody has fantasies. And you can't expect any one person to fulfill all your fantasies, can you?"

"No, I guess not."

Nick got Dewey on the phone.

Dewey was very serious and sober. He had heard about what had happened. Dewey had worked with people who were hot before—if not quite *this* hot. He was a careful, meticulous criminal who seldom took chances. When Nick was through explaining, Dewey said, "If you're going to go south, you're going to need some money, Nick."

"I know. That's why I called you."

"Why don't I meet you at the Hermosa pier at, say, seven? Can you make that?"

"Yeah, I think so."

"If everything's cool, we'll take it from there. I

know this has been an ordeal for you, Nick. I'll do whatever I can."

"Dewey—"

"Yeah?"

"Look, I don't want to have to do anything *really* heavy, if you know what I mean—"

Dewey didn't say anything for a moment. "Let's talk about it when I see you, okay?"

Nick hung up and went over to Jeff and Mirna. They were involved in a discussion of sexual fantasies. Jeff was being deliberately talkative, hoping to dissipate Mirna's intentions. "I used to want to fuck this assistant manager at Safeway, you know, right in the aisle with everybody watching. Just yank down his polyester pants and fuck the shit out of him in Frozen Foods."

"That's great, I love it." Mirna clapped. "What about you, Nick?"

"What about what?"

"Do you have any sexual fantasies you've never lived out?"

"Yeah. I'd like to butt-fuck a priest."

Mirna laughed softly. "I love it," she said.

But Nick suddenly thought about the handsome young priest in Detroit, Father Timothy, who'd blown him when he was fourteen, and who'd later committed suicide. He hadn't thought about Father Timothy in a long time. He wished he hadn't said what he said.

"I've got a fantasy," Mirna paused significantly, then continued in a low sultry voice. "I've always wondered what it would be likt to get it on with *two* hot gay guys . . . at the same time."

Jeff gulped. "No kidding—"

Mirna leaned back on her elbows and smiled. "What do you think about that?" Her nipples were clearly hard.

When Jeff craned his neck to look up at her, his face was level with her crotch. The yellow nylon was damp and sticky-looking.

Jeff was galvanized. Mirna was hot, so hot it almost transcended gender. Even Nick was beginning to wonder what it would be like: both Jeff and Mirna could see that his cock was getting hard.

There was a long charged pause, the kind of pause that could only end with someone making a move. Jeff was about to when they heard a key in the lock and the door swung open. It was Mirna's boyfriend, Ralph.

He had to duck to walk in the door. Nearly seven feet tall, he was a thin Scandinavian blond, severely sunburnt, with pale-blue eyes and a scowl that looked like a hatchet scar.

Nick and Jeff froze.

Mirna reached for her cigarettes. "Hi, babe," she said casually, "you're back early."

"Yeah."

Ralph unstrapped his portable VTR and set it down on the concrete floor with a thunk. The veins in his temples were throbbing. He started toward the bed. And he didn't look like he was interested in a four-way.

Jeff got up and smiled nervously. "Look, she just gave us a lift and we—"

Ralph grabbed Jeff's neck like a can of Coors and threw him across the room. Jeff fell clattering into one of Mirna's rusty metal assemblages, nearly impaled on its jagged fins and spikes.

Ralph didn't do anything to Nick; Nick wasn't in his way. He yanked Mirna up by the arm and hurled her against the wall.

She hit her shoulder hard. And it made her mad. "You shouldn't have done that, babe," she said.

"You fucking cunt." Ralph pinned Mirna against the wall with one hand and hauled off to slug her with the other.

Jeff and Nick cringed, expecting the sickening splat of bludgeoned flesh.

But it didn't happen. Instead, Ralph dropped to his knees and sobbed.

Nick and Jeff were stunned. It was a tremendous

jolt, seeing a giant like Ralph on the verge of murder suddenly crumble and start bawling his brains out.

"Why do you do this to me, baby?" Ralph sobbed.

Mirna stroked his hair. "Don't cry, baby. I'm sorry," she said. "I'm so sorry, baby." But her soothing gestures seemed mechanical, and her apology was cold and unconvincing.

Nick helped Jeff up. Mirna looked at them both and said, "Please leave."

Nick hesitated. He'd been counting on that lift to Hermosa. "Look, I hate to ask you this under the circumstances, but—"

Ralph sniffled and looked up at Nick and Jeff. His eyes were red, his cheeks glistening with tears.

Mirna gave him a Kleenex. "Here, babe, blow your nose," she said. But the *way* she said it gave Jeff chills. Mirna suddenly looked old and haggard, and disgusted, and capable of anything.

Ralph blew his nose. Jeff just wanted to get out of there, but Nick persisted. "So how about it? I mean, could we get that lift?"

"Get out," Mirna said. The look on her face convinced even Nick that further discussion was pointless.

"Okay," he said. "Okay. Hey, thanks anyway. Good luck. See you around."

Jeff hurried Nick out the door. They walked up the Speedway, the alley running parallel to the beach. It was clogged with cars, horns honking as roller skaters and skateboarders cut through the traffic. Kids screeched, rowdy teenagers hooted, creating a hectic carnival atmosphere.

"I didn't understand that scene at all, did you?" Nick said. They cut down an arched walkway toward the boardwalk.

"Yeah, I understood it," Jeff said. "I think she was just using us to make her boyfriend jealous. It's the oldest game in the world. Fight and fuck. They're probably back there right now smothering each other with kisses."

"I wouldn't bet on it."

The boardwalk was clogged, too. Swarms of roller skaters, winos, and Marina couples, musicians, blacks with congas, jugglers, gay guys in bikinis, packs of bodybuilders, joggers, dusted Chicanos, junkies with gray ponytails, jocks—*everybody* was out today, including the beach patrol, two members of which were working their way through the crowd by the pavilion, on the watch for dogs, liquor, fistfighting, and nudity.

Both cops were stocky, poured into their sporty blue Bermuda shorts and white blue-trimmed T-shirts: one black, the other white, steel-frame dark glasses hiding their eyes.

Nick and Jeff cut past a pack of oiled bodybuilders and ran right into them. Nick was cool, but Jeff saw the guns and the LAPD insignia on their T-shirts and cringed. Glancing quickly away, he followed Nick.

"Oh, man, oh, fuck," Jeff said under his breath. He was sure the black cop had looked right at him.

"Just keep going. Don't look back," Nick said. They walked briskly through the crowd.

Nick and Jeff meant nothing to the white cop. But the black cop did a double take, adrenaline drenching his brain like an amphetamine rush. He grabbed the white cop's arm.

Jeff looked back. "Oh, shit."

Nick looked back, too. The cops were drawing their .38s.

Nick and Jeff took off running. They cut through the crowd, the cops dashing after them.

Nick dug out his Python as he and Jeff dashed past a hot-dog stand, though it was much too crowded to get a clear shot. He was sure the cops wouldn't dare open fire either.

But when Nick and Jeff cut past the paddle-tennis courts, they were momentarily in the open. At least it looked that way to the cops. They took aim.

They didn't know about Vern and Kelly Martin. Vern was the husband and Kelly was the wife, although sometimes, people joked, it was difficult to tell them apart. They resembled each other more than anyone since Steve and Eydie, the host of the *Honeymoon Game* had joked only last week. "Do either or both of you sing?" he'd quipped. The roller-skating had been Vern's idea, a fun way to spend a Sunday afternoon. Kelly'd been nervous at first; she'd never skated before. But she was catching on fast and feeling fairly confident as she came around the blind corner by the paddle-tennis court. Now Vern had warned her about blind corners.

Kelly Martin screamed when she saw the guns aimed at her.

"Get down, you stupid bitch!" the white cop shouted as Kelly wobbled through his line of fire. "Get down!" He felt his finger squeeze the trigger.

He fired all six rounds a second after his partner threw Kelly Martin to the ground. Bystanders screamed and ducked for cover.

"You stupid fucking bitch!" the white cop yelled at Kelly Martin. "I almost shot you, you stupid cunt!"

Vern saw the blood where Kelly had scraped her arm when she hit the ground and thought she *had* been shot. "You shot her! You shot her! You shot her!" he screamed like a malfunctioning game-show buzzer, skating circles around his hysterical, sobbing bride.

By the time an ambulance and more cops arrived, the crowd was turning ugly. The way most people saw it, this was just one more instance of the LAPD shooting first and worrying later about who got hit.

By the time Lieutenant Brundl arrived and angrily surveyed the mobs of people up and down the beach, Nick and Jeff were several miles down the bike trail, on a couple of derailleurs they'd stolen, lost in the thick bicycle traffic.

They watched a spectacular orange and red sunset all the way into Hermosa Beach.

30

Nick and Jeff waited at the Hermosa pier for over an hour. They didn't know Dewey was in the blue van that had cruised by twice. There were still a lot of people out. Surfers, skateboarders, strolling couples, a few people drifting in and out of the jazz joint. A fog was rolling in.

Nick and Jeff were exhausted. The speed was wearing off, and although Nick had more, he decided not to take it. Hopefully, they could get some sleep at Dewey's.

"Maybe he got cold feet," Jeff said.

"He never got cold feet in his entire life. He's just careful."

"How well do you really know this guy anyway?"

"I told you, he's a friend."

"You said you had kind of a thing with him—"

"I met him at Studio a while back." Nick leaned against the rail and watched each new car as it approached the pier. "Last summer. We saw each other a lot for a while. At first it was just kind of a sex thing. Then we started hanging out, too. That's when I realized what he was into. That he was more or less a criminal, for lack of a better word. So I kind of backed off. Which wasn't easy. Because I was starting to like him a lot. I guess that in itself spooked me a little. But mostly, I just didn't want to get involved in any of his illegal activities."

"What kind of stuff does he do?"

"I told you. A little of everything. It changes. Coke. Grass. He's made a lot off grass. But he does other stuff, too. I guess mostly he sets things up. He's kind of like an agent, in a sense. He puts people in touch with each other. And takes a cut. That's the thing. He knows everybody."

"So what other stuff?"

"Let's just wait and talk to him, okay?"

The blue van pulled around again, this time idling at the foot of the pier.

"That's him," Nick said. "Come on."

Dewey opened the door for them. "Hey, Nick."

Dewey was twenty-seven with short blond hair and a bushy blond mustache. He kept his husky suntanned body in shape through almost daily surfing and with a strict vegetarian diet. He practiced Soto Zen meditation and didn't drink or smoke cigarettes or dope. He didn't seem especially gay and blended easily into the surfer population of the Southern California beach cities. The only thing that disturbed his archetypal surfer look was his glasses. They were thick and suggested a man capable of extreme and relentless obsession, the kind of man who might pour liquid Drāno in the punch bowl at his ten-year high-school reunion.

"Am I glad to see you," Nick said as he and Jeff got in. Nick introduced Jeff to Dewey. They limply shook hands.

"You guys look terrible," Dewey said, with a soft adolescent voice. He was right. Jeff's nose was blistered, and both he and Nick had a hollow-eyed, scared-shitless look.

"It's been a little hairy," Nick said.

Dewey pulled out, shooting Nick a half-amused, half-disparaging smirk. "So I've gathered."

Dewey adjusted the stereo separation on the Beach boys' "Don't Worry, Baby." Nobody said anything for a while, until Dewey turned up a narrow hillside street lined with bungalows. People were out on their porches, drinking beer.

"This heat's something else, huh?" Dewey said.

"Yeah." Nick checked out a group of laughing, shirtless young men.

"So what were you doing before all this happened?"

"Working," Nick said. "In a warehouse. Out by the airport."

"I wondered. I kept thinking I'd run into you somewhere. You quit going out?"

"No. But I got sick of the bars and all that shit, you know. Except for dancing."

"I thought maybe you'd met somebody." Dewey glanced at Jeff.

"Nope. Jeff and me just met the other night."

"No kidding. A real whirlwind romance." Dewey grinned. "I stopped by your place once. You'd moved. They didn't have your new address."

"Yeah. I moved last February."

Dewey pulled up and parked in front of a small house. "You're in real bad trouble, Nick. You should've called me sooner."

"Maybe I should have."

Dewey dug out a key and gave it to Nick. "Get some sleep." He indicated the house. "Some friends of mine live here, but they're out of town. Don't go out. I'll see you in the morning, okay?"

"Okay. Thanks, Dewey." Nick leaned over and gave Dewey an awkward hug.

"Don't worry, Nick. I'm already talking to people."

"You are?" *What* people? Nick thought.

"We'll talk in the morning, when you're rested."

"Hey, thanks," Jeff said as he and Nick got out.

"Sure thing." Dewey was still trying to size Jeff up.

Jeff had already decided about Dewey. Nobody who looked that good could be all bad. And it was a relief to finally find somebody who understood their situation and was calm and matter-of-fact—somebody who seemed to see a way out.

*   *   *

That night Nick and Jeff ate TV dinners in the breakfast nook. The house was sparsely furnished with rattan and wicker furniture. They could see that it belonged to an affluent young married couple. The woman did macramé. The man liked to fish. They both liked to sail down to Mexico.

Nick and Jeff watched the eleven-o'clock news on the TV in the bedroom. There was a report on the Malibu siege. The reporter at the scene did little to hide her frustration. Nobody was talking. Michael Reed and his attorney and two members of his staff had been hospitalized. But the police and the hospital wouldn't give details. In fact, the police wouldn't even confirm that the suspects had actually been there. "The situation's still very confused. Back to you, Jerry."

A report from Venice followed, "Kelly Martin, a beachgoer from La Mirada, emerged shaken but unharmed after inadvertently roller-skating through the crossfire between suspects and police." The reporter winced. "A lucky girl."

"Crossfire?" Jeff said. "There was no crossfire."

Several witnesses at the scene agreed with Jeff. "The cops did all the shooting," one of them told the reporter. But a red and sweaty Lieutenant Brundl squinted in the harsh sun and said, "The suspects opened fire. Officer Brown, at a considerable risk to his own life, secured Mrs. Martin's safety, and then and only then, did Officer Higgins return fire."

The reporter summed it up by saying there had been "a lot of shooting" and the truth would have to be sorted out in due course. "The manhunt continues, this tragic and violent Labor Day weekend."

"Jesus. A lucky girl, indeed. Fuck." Jeff looked at Nick. He was already asleep.

31

Nick and Jeff made love in the morning in the sun-drenched bedroom. Jeff woke up with a hard-on and ran his fingers down the crack of Nick's hairy butt.

"Be careful," Nick said as Jeff reached for a bottle of suntan lotion. "I'm practically a virgin."

He wasn't lying. It felt so good Jeff went a little crazy.

Later, Nick fried eggs while Jeff made coffee. They were eating when Dewey came in.

Dewey looked even better in daylight. His tanned skin seemed to glow from within from all the sunlight it had absorbed and Jeff definitely found him attractive. But Dewey still seemed unsure about Jeff. He focused on Nick as he spoke. "I've talked to some more people."

"And?" Nick lit a cigarette. He looked better, too. Rested and bright-eyed. A little too bright-eyed. He'd washed down a few Desoxyn tablets with his coffee.

"Well, there's one situation that could set you up for quite a while. You want to hear about it?"

"I told you on the phone," Nick said. "I want to stay away from that."

"Stay away from what?" Jeff said.

Dewey glanced at Jeff. Nick read Dewey's mind. "Jeff's okay, believe me. He's a little green, but he's come through in surprising ways."

Dewey went on cautiously. "Look, Nick. I know

what you said on the phone. I understand how you feel. But let me describe the package. A hundred grand up front. Another hundred when you complete the hit."

"The *what*?" Jeff said.

Nick whistled. "That's a lot of bread."

"I've already talked to the buyer," Dewey said. "He's been following you guys on the news and thinks you're ideal." Dewey hesitated. "There's really only one drawback as far as I can see." He looked at Jeff. "Your blond friend over here will probably have to be the one who does the actual killing."

Jeff laughed incredulously.

"Why's that?" Nick said.

"Well, to be blunt, because of the two of you, he's the more feminine."

"Hey, fuck *you*," Jeff said.

Dewey snorted. "You'd like to, wouldn't you?"

"*Fuck* you."

"You just said that."

"Jeff, calm down," Nick said, then turned back to Dewey. "Maybe you should explain—"

"Well, the situation is this. The target's in prison."

"Prison?" Jeff said.

"Yeah. He's due for release in about a year. But once he hits the streets, it'll be too late. He'll have bodyguards up the ass."

"So, who is it, some Mafia guy?" Nick said.

Dewey hesitated. "Let me just explain the logistics first. We'll save the good part for later." Dewey leaned across the table. "This is the plan. Now this guy is in a special unit, separated from the general prison population. Very maximum security. But once a week, every Friday, they take him to this low-security area so he can fuck his wife."

"You mean, for a conjugal visit," Jeff said.

"Right. That's what I said. So this is what happens. The two of you bust into his wife's house just as she's getting ready to leave. Now, this is no problem. She's got a place in town not far from the prison, so she can be near him. Okay, so while you, Nick, hold her hostage, Jeff, *you* will slip into her clothes—"

"Oh, come *on*," Jeff said.

"Then you drive out to the prison on her car. Okay, you're made up, you've got a wig, the whole bit. Now she comes out every Friday, so they see you in her car and wave you through the first gate. Now the second gate you gotta walk through, so you act real upset. You're crying, with a hankie up to your face, saying how your mother just died. So they don't bother you, right? And the hankie helps hide your face."

"I don't believe this," Jeff said.

"So you go through the metal detector. But that's fine, because you don't have a weapon. It's cyanide. A pellet in your purse. You get to the trailer in the minimum-security area, where you wait. You're looking out the window, your back to the door, as they show your hubbie in. He gets out a line, maybe 'Gee, honey, you've put on weight' when you grab him and shove the pellet in his mouth, smash his jaw shut, and that's it."

"What then?" Nick said.

Jeff was astonished. "Nick, for God sake. This is completely insane. This is the most fucked-up idea I've ever—"

"Jeff, let him finish."

Jeff shook his head as Dewey continued.

"Okay, so the target's *kaput*. There's nothing more to do . . . except walk out. See, you always leave first. It's already been timed. You'll be out the last door before the guards find his body. If by any chance there's a delay"—he looked at Nick—"you've got a hostage. They want to see the real missus alive, they let Jeff go."

"Oh, sure," Jeff said. "I'll explain all that to them as they blow me out of my high heels. Wait! Why am I even thinking about this? This is demented! I'm not going to do this."

Nick remained calm. "Who's the target?"

Dewey leaned back and grinned. "Let's play quiz show."

"Oh, Christ," Jeff said.

"I'll give you clues. You press the buzzer when you know."

Jeff got up. "I have to take a dump."

"Jeff, sit down," Nick said.

Sighing disgustedly, Jeff sat down.

"Clue Number One. This guy ... got away with murder."

Nick thought hard. Jeff just shook his head.

"He's a Nazi war criminal?" Nick said.

"No, no, no. Boy, you guys are slow. Okay, Clue Number Two. This guy likes junk food. I mean, he really, really goes for Twi—"

"Buzzz!" Nick said, and yelled the man's name.

"You got it!" Dewey yelled.

Jeff rubbed his brow and looked at the floor. "Oh, Jesus."

"Come on, come *on*, Jeff," Dewey said. "Tell me you don't want to see this fuck dead. What kind of a faggot are you?"

"Okay, yeah, *yeah*, I'd like to see him dead," Jeff said. "I'd like to rip his fuckin' guts out. I just don't want mine blown out a few seconds later."

"Jeff's got a point," Nick said.

"Oh, come on, not you too. Fuck, I'm giving you guys the chance of a lifetime. Shit, there's thousands of people who'd do this for nothing! This guy is the premier scumbag of recent memory. He shot two people in cold blood and they gave him a fucking slap on the wrist. You take him out, you'll be worshipped."

"It's tempting," Nick said. "You're right. I'd *love* to be alone with that fuck for about a minute. I'd show him what faggots are all about. But this scheme's just too fucked up. It sounds okay on paper but ..." He looked at Jeff. "I've seen pictures of that punk's wife, and frankly, there's just no resemblance."

"But Nick," Dewey said, "with makeup and a de-

mure little blouse, and maybe some tasteful Sarah
Coventry jewelry—"

Nick shook his head. "His hands are too big."

"He could wear a muff."

"A muff?" Jeff said. "Nobody wears a fuckin'
muff—"

"Dammit," Nick said. "I wish there was some other
approach. Man, I'd *really* like to take him out. But I
just don't think Jeff can bring it off." Nick sighed.
"I'm afraid we're gonna have to pass."

"Oh, heck, just when I was about to change my
mind," Jeff said. "Hey, I'll tell you what. Let me get
in drag right now. I'll run down to Zody's and get a
pantsuit. You guys can tell me what you think. Dewey,
you can give me pointers."

Dewey ignored Jeff. "You're making a big mistake,
Nick. Chances like this don't come along every day.
Two hundred grand for a few hours' work."

Nick waved his hand to clear the air. "Look, fuck
all this hitman shit. We've been through enough all-
ready. We don't need to put our asses on the line
anymore. All we need is something that'll keep us
going for a while in Mexico."

Dewey looked glum. "Famous last words, Nick.
What do you want to do, stick up a Pup 'n' Taco?
Even Mexico costs money if you want to be safe. I
don't understand you, Nick. I've offered you a place
in history, and you're talking chickenshit armed
robberies."

Nick stood. "Hey, give me a break. That hit sucks
and you know it. It's somebody's fantasy, that's all.
Whoever tries it is gonna get wasted." Nick came
around the table. "Dewey, come on. You've always
got some juicy little job in the works. How about it?"

Dewey sighed deeply. "Okay, Nick. Okay."

"Ten, twenty thousand. That's all we need for now."

Dewey drummed his fingers on the table. "I think
you can do better than that." He hesitated, on the
verge of an impulse. "Yeah, all right. I've got something for you." He looked at the clock. "Yeah, you'd

be right on time. And today being Labor Day might actually be a plus. Fuck it." Dewey stood. "Let's just do it. Come on, let's go."

"Do what?" Jeff said as Nick followed Dewey to the door.

"You'll see," Nick said. "Come on. It's cool. Jeff, *come on.*"

They got in Dewey's van, Nick in the middle, and took off. Dewey stopped at another house, running in for a second, leaving the engine on. When he came back and they took off again, Dewey reached under his shirt and pulled out a six-inch Trooper .357 and laid it across Nick's lap. "Sweet, huh?"

Nick picked up the gun and looked at Jeff. "I think this is gonna be yours, pal."

Jeff took the gun. "Is it loaded?"

Dewey snorted. "Just don't look down the barrel and pull the trigger." He snorted again. "Nick, I don't know about this guy—"

"Hey, fuck you." Jeff let Nick take the gun back. "I know how to fire a goddamn gun. Even an asshole can do that."

"You said it, not me."

Jeff stared out the window, pissed, scared.

32

Dewey explained the job on the San Diego Freeway. Nick listened attentively, nodding. Jeff opened the window. He needed air.

Nick's leg was pressing against Dewey's, and Dewey was getting a hard-on. Near Seal Beach, Nick opened Dewey's fly and pulled out his cock.

Dewey had known about the job for a long time. "It's a clean package," he said, "especially because it's never been done and consequently they're not expecting it. These two dykes from Pacoima were gonna do it about a month ago. But they got busted in a stolen Barracuda the night before. I promised I'd save it for 'em till they could get it together again, but—" Dewey moaned as Nick squeezed his cock. "I'm breaking all the rules, Nick, I want you to know that. I never go along on a job. I'm only doing it for you. Of course, this *is* a piece of cake."

"I appreciate it." Nick started to lean over.

Dewey shook his head. "I don't want to have a wreck."

With his free hand Nick rubbed Jeff's crotch until Jeff got hard too. Nick unzipped Jeff's pants as Jeff stared out the window. Nick had a cock in each hand and two guns in his lap. They got off the freeway in Orange County.

It was a church, at least it was now. A few years before it had been a discount drugstore. A section had been added to the top of the big red plastic T, turning it into a cross.

Dewey swerved through the vast empty parking lot, pulling up to the back of the building. There were two cars parked in the basin of the loading dock: a Honda Civic and a Mercedes 450 SL with the licence plate: PSALMS.

"Good," Dewey said. "They're still here."

He meant the associate pastor and his secretary; their presence was essential to the robbery plan. Without them the money would be locked in the safe, no way to get at it. The money was yesterday's donations: the regular service donations, and the special donations for Abundance Park, a multimillion-dollar planned Christian community.

On a normal Monday, Carl Hinds, the associate pastor, took the money to the bank around ten-thirty. He wouldn't be doing that today because of the holiday. He wouldn't be doing it tomorrow, either.

Carl Hinds was doing well for twenty-nine. He was wholesomely handsome, with short sandy hair and a ready smile. He was easygoing but aggressive, serene yet *Dy-namic*! Like the Reverend Pat himself.

Pat Haggart had founded his church in the banquet room of an Anaheim restaurant in 1971. The church had grown rapidly, making Pat a wealthy man. But that was all right, nobody minded his Rolls Royces and Newport Beach estate; that was his message. The Kingdom of Plenty! Jesus and Real Estate! Power and Abundance through Christ! At sixty-three, Pat had a special place in his heart for Carl, his connection to Young People. Carl was enormously popular with the Young People in the huge congregation. He Spoke Their Language. He galvanized fresh-faced Orange County teenagers in Bible-study classes that looked like pictures in a slick candidate's brochure. Carl had, everyone agreed, a Fantastic Future ahead of him.

He also had a wife, Julie, who was fresh and pretty and also worked at the church. She would ordinarily be in the office with Carl on a Monday morning, but today she was still home in bed. She was close to giving birth to their fourth child. Carl and Julie had two adorable girls, Heather, three, and Patricia, four. Their little boy, Carl, Jr., was five.

Carl also had a drawer in his desk at home that was locked. Carl carried the key on his Young Republicans key chain.

If Carl had been "rapping" with a group of young people—perhaps discussing the possibilities of what might happen if "Jesus were born today, in, say, Newport Beach or any modern American city"—and someone had shouted, "Hey, Carl, what about *Ramrod*?" Carl would probably have been puzzled at first. But several seconds later it would probably have hit him and knocked his breath out and made him start to sweat.

Ramrod was the name of a gay porno magazine in Carl's locked desk drawer. He bought it one night in a fit of lust and terror at a sleazy adult bookshop in downtown Los Angeles. That was several years ago. *Ramrod* was now dog-eared, the black-and-white photos of Carlos and Johnny splotched and stuck together. Sometimes, in the fading orange light of late afternoon, when Julie was out of the house, Carl would lock the door of his home office, unlock the drawer of his desk, take out *Ramrod*, and study the pictures of Carlos and Johnny—and toward the back, Frank, who had the biggest one of all—as they fucked and sucked and rimmed and licked with passionless detachment. Sometimes Carl would unzip his Dacron slacks and masturbate across the braided carpet. Most of the time that wasn't even necessary: he came in his pants just looking at the pictures. And thinking. Fantasizing.

That was all. Carl had never had a real gay experience, and he didn't intend to. He was a father, a husband, and most of all, a Christian. It was okay as long as he didn't actually *do* anything. To think was not the same as to do. He had no time for guilt.

Ramrod was simply medicine for a minor ailment, like taking a decongestant and blowing your nose.

Carl's secretary, Vicky, saw the men coming up to the door of the office, but she was determined to finish typing an address before she stopped to see what they wanted. She was on the zip code when she felt a cold steel ring pressing against her neck.

It was the sudden silence that made Carl Hinds step from his office to see what was going on. He froze when he saw the guns.

"All right," Nick said. "Just give us the fuckin' money and you won't get shot."

Carl was stunned. Sweat started seeping through his colorful sport shirt. The possibility of something like this happening had barely crossed his mind. Liquor stores and banks got held up. Not churches. Not in Orange County. Nobody would stoop that low.

"Look, guys," Carl said. "I think you've made a mistake. The bank's up at the mall. This is a church." He tried his boyish smile.

It didn't work. Nick grabbed Carl by the shirt, snapping buttons. "Look, fuckface, give us the goddamn money!"

Vicky screamed. Perky and virginal, she reminded Jeff of a Mormon girl he'd dated in high school. "Shut up," he said to her, putting the gun in her face, hoping it didn't accidentally go off.

Nick was right up in Carl's face, which was turning red, when a strange thing happened. They made blurry eye contact and for a split second they both wanted to kiss each other. And they both knew it. It made things more awkward.

"Where's the fuckin' bread?" Nick spit in Carl's face.

"In there." Carl glanced at his office.

The money was in bags on a table by the safe. Six large bags. Nick pushed Carl into the room while Jeff kept Vicky covered. "Is this all of it?" Nick said.

"Look, you guys can't take this. This money's going to take care of little amputee children in Africa. Babies, for heaven's sake. This money's going to *feed* them. If you take it, you're committing genocide."

Nick hesitated. Carl was very convincing. But Nick noticed the deposit slip for $43,234.75. Made out to the Abundance Park Development Fund.

"You lyin' sack of shit," Nick said, though the anger was draining from his voice. "Starving babies, shit. That money's going to build a bunch of condos."

"It was worth a try." Carl shrugged and smiled.

Again, Carl and Nick made a strange eye contact—a contact that seemed to transcend the situation.

Normally, Carl would have stifled his attraction to Nick. But suddenly—he had absolutely no idea why—it didn't seem to matter.

"You know," Nick said, almost gently. "It's kind of too bad you're a minister."

"Yeah, well, it's kind of too bad you're going to end up doing twenty years for this," Carl said.

Nick grinned. Carl didn't seem to connect them with whatever he might have heard about the cop-hostage incident in L.A..

"Is it there?" Jeff called from the outer office, where he kept Vicky covered.

"Yeah, it's here."

Jeff backed into Carl's office, breaking the contact between Nick and Carl. Jeff was jerking with adrenaline as he scooped up three of the bags. "Come on. Let's get the fuck out of here." Jeff cut back through the outer office.

Nick picked up the other three bags and then he did what he had to do. He went over to Carl and kissed him hard on the mouth. To Nick it was like kissing a virgin. To Carl, who ate it up, it was like the kiss of a vampire Christ.

Vicky could see into Carl's office. She could see Nick and Carl kissing, but she couldn't believe it. Her face turned into a grimacing mask and she bit her lip so hard it bled.

Carl was stunned. Nick looked at him one last time and shook his head, giving Carl a look of such poignant regret it made Carl's heart shatter like a window in a slammed door.

Nick and Jeff ran out to the van and Dewey took off. "See, I told you it was a piece of cake," Dewey said. They were only a few blocks from the freeway.

"Yeah," Jeff said, trembling. "With shit frosting."

"How much?" Dewey said.

"Forty-three thousand," Nick said.

Dewey whistled. "That's a lot of shit frosting."

"You wanna lick the bowel?" Jeff said.

Dewey did a fake laugh, indicating Jeff didn't know him well enough to get away with sarcasm. They swerved onto the freeway.

They didn't see the 450 SL cutting through traffic behind them.

Carl's mouth still tingled from Nick's rough kiss. Back at the church, seconds after Nick and Jeff took off, Vicky had started to call the police. But she couldn't look at Carl. That was the giveaway. He knew she'd seen the kiss. "There they go," Carl had said, running out to his car.

"'I'll tell you what," Dewey said. "I'm going to take you to Burt's place in Huntington. I think what we ought to do is let you kick back there for the next week or so. It's gonna take me that long to get you IDs and set everything up down south. I got a buddy with a house near Manzanillo. I'll call him tonight."

"Who's this Burt?" Nick said.

"Just a friend. Trust me, Nick. I haven't fucked you over yet, have I?" Dewey glanced in his rearview mirror. "Oh, Christ! I don't believe it!"

Nick and Jeff looked back, expecting to see flashing red lights. Instead they saw the 450 SL.

"It's PSALMS! It's that fucking preacher," Jeff said.

Nick looked sick. "Oh, my."

"What's this turkey trying to pull?" Dewey said.

*   *   *

Carl didn't know himself. But he had to follow the van. He couldn't stay at the church, not now. Not with Vicky. She'd never mention the kiss to the cops, of course, not in a million years. But she'd know. *Someone knew.*

But what could he do if he caught up with the van? It didn't make sense. Why am I doing this? Carl thought. But he couldn't go back. He'd follow them, that's what he'd do. Find out where they went, then tell the police. Oh God, would the kiss come out at the trial? Why had Nick kissed him? Why did he think he could do that?

Carl wiped sweat from his eyes.

In the van, Dewey was becoming unusually agitated. "Shit, man, I should never have come along on this. I should never have involved my own car in this." He looked in the rearview mirror. "What's this guy's story?"

"Closet case," Nick said. Then he added, "That's the vibes I got."

"What's he want, a blow-job?" Dewey said. "The guy's gotta be crazy. He's taking his life in his hands."

Dewey maintained a steady speed. He didn't want to attract any cops on the freeway. He got over for the Laguna Canyon turnoff. "We'll see if we can lose him in the canyon. If we can't, we may have to get radical."

Ramrod. The graphic sexual photos were all that Carl could see. Carlos, Johnny, and Frank! Carls mind caved in, the implications of *Ramrod* gushing into every other facet in his life. I'm not a father, I'm a queer. *Queer queer queer queer queer queer,* oh, God.

He thought about the crush he had on Reverend Pat. Then he thought about *Ramrod.* No, it wasn't right, it wasn't holy. Carl suddenly remembered Glenn, his best friend in high school. He'd loved him so dearly, so hopelessly. *Ramrod.* Glenn's hairy butt.

Jacking off alone. The smell of Glenn's jacket. Glenn's soft smile. Glenn, killed in Vietnam. Glenn, the love of his life. Julie couldn't even hold a candle! *Ramrod*! Glenn, I love you, so very very . . . Look out!

Carl smashed into the center divider, slashing along the concrete several hundred feet before he came to a skidding stop.

The left side of the Mercedes was mangled. Carl was all right, and would have stayed that way if he'd remained in the car. He was climbing out the right side door when a Seatrain semi ripped him off like a mailbag at a whistle-stop.

"Oh, sweet Jesus," Jeff said when he saw it happen.

Nick and Dewey looked back too. Traffic screeched. Several cars ran over something that looked like a mangled side of beef. There were several rear-end collisions.

Dewey kept going, slowing down as he took the Laguna Canyon exit turn. He and Jeff were both stunned and shaken, and so, especially, was Nick.

They said very little the rest of the way to Huntington Beach. Jeff was startled when he glanced at Nick at one point. There were tears in Nick's eyes.

33

Dewey pulled into the driveway of a cheap Huntington Beach tract house and parked behind a tricked-up VW bug with a surfboard rack.

Nick didn't place the VW, but he recognized Burt when he opened the door, rubbing sleep from his eyes. Burt was the guy Nick had dumped in favor of Jeff a couple of nights before in Ocean Park. A couple of nights. Shit, it seemed more like a couple of years.

Burt recognized Nick, too, and although he didn't know what the hell was going on, he knew and trusted Dewey enough to let them all in.

The house was run-down, utilitarian—dirty clothes everywhere, scuffed furniture—a pit stop more than a home. Burt, wearing only a pair of faded green gym trunks, led the way into the living room and plopped down in a chair.

In the sunlight streaming through the dirty picture window, Burt still looked about twenty, but he had a tough edge that wasn't a pose. Wrinkles and bags were forming under his eyes; he was glowing with youthful vitality and prematurely debauched at the same time. His body was lithe, smooth, and hairless, except for his blond pubes, which were visible when he put his foot up on the chair. Everything else was visible, too, and he seemed to enjoy the way Jeff kept trying not to look.

Burt listened to Dewey with an air of respect, one

businessman to another. Dewey and Burt were the kind of guys, Nick thought, who could have made a fortune selling stereos or gym franchises if they had been so inclined.

Burt allowed himself a smirk when Dewey got to the part that revealed who Nick and Jeff were.

"So," Dewey concluded, "is it cool?"

"Sure. They can stay here. I'll have to call off the party. That's the only thing that was coming down."

"Good. I'll be in touch." Dewey stood.

Nick stood too. The money was still in the van. "Better bring in the loot," he said.

"Look, Nick. You're not going south with six bags of small bills. I'm going to have to change the money for you."

Nick hesitated, but he had no reason not to trust Dewey. "How long will that take?"

"A day. Maybe two. Look, don't worry about anything, you're going to be okay. Burt's a great host. The next time you see me, I'll have a whole bunch of goodies for you, okay?"

"All right."

Nick gave Dewey a hug. Then he stood in the door and watched Dewey drive off down the elm-lined street—with all the money. It seemed cool.

Burt stubbed out his cigarette and got up and stretched. "Fuck." He went into the kitchen. It was a mess.

"Well, it looks like I'm gonna have to get some food. Do either of you guys cook?" he called.

Nick looked at Jeff.

"Not really. I can sew, though."

"Too bad." Burt came back through the living room, smiling at Nick. "I don't either. I guess we'll have to get stuff that cooks itself." Burt disappeared into the bedroom.

"It's too bad Victor isn't here," Jeff said. "He's a great cook. He has about three dozen cookbooks. You know, meals of the world. He can do anything. He does this Yugoslavian goulash that's really insane."

Nick didn't feel much like talking about food. He was still thinking about Carl. "That guy really got mangled," he said.

"It was an accident," Jeff said. "I mean, it was stupid. It looked like he got out of his car and stepped right into the fast lane. They always tell you, if your car breaks down on the freeway, stay in your car, don't get out."

"Yeah. I don't know. He seemed like a nice guy in kind of a twisted way. Maybe I shouldn't have messed with him."

"Messed with him? What do you mean?"

"I kissed him. In the office. I got the feeling he wanted something like that to happen. And I just did it."

"You *kissed* him?"

"Yeah. You know. A kiss. On the mouth."

"Why?"

"Why anything? I don't know. I just did."

"Jesus."

Burt came back. He had put on sandals and a T-shirt. "You guys really shoot that cop?" he said as he stuck his wallet in his butt pocket and looked around for his keys.

Nick and Jeff were both so sick of the question neither one of them responded.

"I saw the whole thing on the news yesterday," Burt continued. "They didn't know what the fuck was going on! Were you guys really out at that guy's place in Malibu?"

"Yeah, we were there," Jeff said.

"I guess they figure you've left the county by now. I guess they're right, aren't they? This is Orange County."

"Yeah." Jeff didn't much care for Burt's glib attitude.

"So you want anything? I'm gonna hit the market."

"Yeah," Nick said. "How about a fifth of Jack Daniel's and a couple six packs of Coors. Jeff?"

"I don't care. Maybe a good dry white wine. Chilled, of course. Get the gallon bottle."

"Sure thing," Burt said, smiling at Nick. He seemed to want to finish what they'd started the other night.

After Burt left, Nick told Jeff about meeting Burt in the beach lot two nights ago.

"That's odd," Jeff said. "I guess that used to happen a lot more in the past. I've heard guys tell about running into the same people at gay bars and cruising spots all over the world. You know, back in the fifties and sixties. But now, there's so many gay guys you're lucky if you ever see the same person more than once. Or unlucky. Whatever."

"Yeah." Nick kicked off his sandals. "The wonders of gay life."

Nick and Jeff stepped through the sliding glass door to the patio. The backyard grass was dead, and a scrawny lemon tree was dying. Beyond the cinder-block walls, the complex of deteriorating tract homes stretched out through puffs of elm.

"So you ever been to Mexico?" Nick said.

"Yeah. My wife and I went to Acapulco on our honeymoon."

"No kidding." They walked across the yellow grass. "I guess there's a lot we don't know about each other."

"Yeah. All the usual boring-type shit."

"I guess Mexico's okay." Nick smiled. "You ever see *The Wild Bunch?*"

"Yeah."

"They all went to Mexico, William Holden and all those guys. And in the end they were all laughing their butts off, remember?"

"Yeah, I remember. But that was a flashback, Nick. They were all dead."

"I know *that*," Nick said, but he'd clearly forgotten. "But that was just a fuckin' movie. What does Hollywood know? The point is, this time next week, you and me are gonna be kicked back on a white beach suckin' on an ice-cold Mexican beer, the smell of hot bean dip wafting through the air.''

Jeff laughed. "I don't think they call it bean dip down there, Nick.''

Sherri Moran was cleaning her windows next door and saw Jeff laugh. She was hurrying to finish in time for *All My Children*; the TV was already on.

Sherri was used to seeing young men in the backyard next door, she never knew if they were gay or what. They didn't seem gay, they usually seemed like typical surfers. But there were never any girls around. She wondered about that. She also wondered how Burt made a living. He didn't seem to have a steady job, coming and going at odd hours, day and night.

Sherri thought Burt was cute. He was always pleasant, always said hello. Her husband didn't like him, though, referring to Burt as a "surfpunk.''

Sherri thought Jeff was cute, too. He was blond, like a surfer. But the other one was dark, dark and rough-looking. Like a criminal. Oh, Jesus. Like that guy's picture on the *Mid-Day News* a minute ago.

Frozen at her window, Sherri watched Nick hug Jeff.

"I'm sorry about all this," Nick said. "I mean, fucking up your life and everything.''

Jeff shrugged. "It was already fucked up. I was living a cliché. It's hard not to be when you come to Hollywood with dreams of being rich and famous and loved.''

Nick smiled. "Well, we've got money. We've got our pictures all over the TV. And I love you. So I guess all your dreams came true.''

"Yeah." Jeff kissed Nick. "One of 'em did, anyway.''

Jeff felt so good holding Nick. He didn't know shit about love anymore, but he knew how he felt right now. Being with Nick was the difference between terror and acceptance.

Nick felt the same way about Jeff. He couldn't

imagine going through all this alone. He believed
enough in fate to think that meeting Jeff had been
inevitable. And he believed that their getting away
together was just as inevitable.

Nick kissed Jeff, burning Jeff's face with his whiskers.

But Sherri Moran didn't see it. She was already on
the phone to the cops.

There were a couple of cop cars in the lot of the
Boys Market when Burt pulled up. There frequently
were. The cops stopped there for coffee and donuts
from the market bake shop. They were leaning against
their cars, their radios sputtering, as Burt got out
and headed toward the market. He wasn't worried.
He was clean.

Burt was about to go through the automatic doors
when he heard a call on the cop radio. He didn't
recognize the code, but when he heard the address,
"—20768 Getty Lane—," he calmly continued on into
the store, using the pay phone in the back to call
Nick and Jeff and tell them the cops were on their
way.

Jeff was in the bathroom taking a crap, leafing
through a Soldier of Fortune, when he heard the
phone ring. A few seconds later Nick burst through
the bathroom door. "Jeff, the cops are coming!"

Jeff didn't bother to wipe his ass.

They ran out the back door and jumped the cinder-
block wall. There was nothing for at least a half-mile
except clumpy fields of brown grass. A line of cop
lights blinked along the highway off to the left, the
first cars just entering the housing tract.

34

Nick and Jeff started running, Nick indicating the red-and-white Boys sign in the distance, the plastic letters reflecting the sun. "Over there!"

They ran across the fields like revved-up track stars, propelled by the fear of being shot in the back.

Jeff cried out as the first shots cracked. Nick anticipated a sting in the shoulder or a flash of white light as a bullet hit his brain. He and Jeff sprinted as more shots cracked. Then it stopped. They were out of range.

The cops at the house holstered their guns and radioed other cops, telling them Nick and Jeff were headed for the Boys.

Their lungs burning, Nick and Jeff reached the market seconds ahead of the cops.

They rushed inside and tried to act normal. But that wasn't possible. They were sweating and hyperventilating like maniacs and the cute young assistant manager quit bagging and stared at them.

Burt was still on the pay phone in the back of the market, trying to reach Dewey. He was jolted when he looked up and saw Nick and Jeff hurrying past the meat section. Cop cars were warbling up out front.

Burt had to make up his mind: he could either stay where he was and hope the cops didn't know about him, then slip out later, after it was all over. Or he could do what he did: he intercepted Nick and Jeff by the stockroom.

They were startled to see him, but glad when he said, "Go out back and jump the wall. I'll come around and get you."

Nick and Jeff ran through the stockroom and out to the loading dock. On the far side of the loading dock was a low cinder-block wall. They jumped it—a second before a cop car screeched up to the loading dock.

Whistling to the Muzak, Burt strolled from the market, gawking at the cops as they clattered through the doors and fanned out along the aisles. Everyone else was gawking too.

Burt got into his VW, slowly pulling from the lot as the Orange County Sheriff's SWAT team squealed in. He drove up the side street, past the back of the market, past the loading dock, where the cops were covering the rear door, past the low cinder-block wall.

Nick and Jeff were crouching and trembling behind it.

Burt slowed down long enough for them to crawl out and climb into the car.

A police chopper whirled across the clear blue sky, veering down toward the market as Burt moved out at a conservative clip, cruising through the shady residential streets, whistling the *Leave It to Beaver* theme under his breath. Whatever else might be said about him, Burt had balls.

35

The piano-bar singer crooned a wavering rendition of "Have You Ever Been Mellow," over the din of talk.

Dewey hated the Purple Lantern Lounge, but the sleazy Italian owner was the only person he knew who could handle the cash transaction on such short notice. The owner was supposedly en route from Laguna Nigel, but it was going on an hour. Dewey sipped his third Perrier and stared at the singer's linty blue blazer. The guy had deep crow's-feet and a gray Caligula haircut. He struck Dewey as obviously gay, a gay eunuch singing alcoholic love songs for rude straight couples. Dewey looked at his watch and thought about the money stashed out in the van. Maybe he should go check it. It would be just his luck that somebody'd try and rip off the tape deck—or the van itself—and find the money in the back.

Dewey was about to get up when he saw Nick, Jeff, and Burt coming in. They spotted him and started over, turning heads. Three sweaty, crazed men disrupting the oily Vegasoid atmosphere. If they'd ever been mellow, they weren't now.

"This is very uncool," Dewey said. "What the hell's going on?"

Burt told him.

"Oh, shit," Dewey said. "This is fucked. That's *my*

house. I mean, I *own* that house. Now they're gonna be after *me.*"

"Did you change the money yet?" Nick said.

"If I'd changed the money, would I be sitting here? I'm waiting for the guy now. God, this is fucked."

It was even worse than Dewey imagined. There was already an APB on his van, and two cops in a black-and-white had just spotted it out front. They were calling for assistance.

"I'm sorry," Nick said. He felt responsible for bringing all this down on Dewey.

Dewey sighed, suddenly looking very tired. "I'll let you in on a little secret, Nick. My days were numbered anyway. One of my ex-partners is testifying before the grand jury right now. It was just a matter of time." Dewey gulped down his Perrier. "Fuck this changing the money," he said. "Let's get out of here."

Dewey tossed some change on the table. They were all heading for the front door when Nick said, "I gotta take a leak. Be right back." Nick went up the hall to the men's room.

"We'll be out front," Dewey called.

There were two loud obnoxious guys in the small men's room. Rather than wait, Nick peeked into the ladies' room and, finding it empty, went in and locked the door.

A couple was coming in just as Dewey, Burt, and Jeff reached the front door, and Dewey caught a glimpse of the cops out by the van.

"Looks like we don't get to keep the money," Dewey said.

By the time Jeff pushed past the two loud obnoxious guys coming out of the men's room, sirens were warbling out front.

Jeff burst into the men's room. "Nick!"

When Nick wasn't there, Jeff figured he had already taken off through the kitchen. Dewey and Burt caught up to Jeff.

"Where is he?" Dewey said.

"I don't know. He's gone."

They saw cops coming through the front door.

"Come on." Dewey led the way back through the kitchen.

They ran up the alley, bashed through a gate, cut past a swimming pool, and reached the next street.

A few minutes later they pulled a Roto-Rooter man from his truck behind a Burger King and drove off.

Not long after that, the cops bashed into the ladies' room at the Purple Lantern Lounge. It was empty, but they noticed glass on the floor. Looking up, they saw the skylight Nick had smashed through to get away.

Nick ran up the wide Orange County boulevard. It wasn't very cool to run, but Nick was way beyond being cool. He had no idea where he was going or what he was going to do. He was just trying to get away.

He ran for blocks, past the gaudy plastic tropical motels and chain restaurants that lined the boulevard across from the Americanaland theme park. Cars rushed by, there weren't any sidewalks. He tripped on a curb, got up, and kept going.

First he heard the chopper, then he looked back and saw it: coming straight at him up the center of the boulevard. Winded, he ducked into the next building, a pancake house. A bad move.

"He was a saint," Vicky, the late Carl Hinds' secretary, said at the table for twelve in the back. Then, once again, she wept uncontrollably.

Her boyfriend, Dale, comforted her. Several other young women at the table also began to weep, and their boyfriends comforted them too. All the coffees were cold, nobody was eating. "There, there," said Dale, a clean-cut young man in a tight Qiana shirt. "I know he's sitting at the right hand of Jesus right now. I believe that with all my heart."

Vicky was exhausted from talking to the police about the robbery. She had told them everything. Except about seeing Carl and the robber kiss. She couldn't tell them about that, she just couldn't. Not now. But she could still see it; in fact, she could think of little else. She sobbed, trying to push the picture from her mind, a picture she would never understand.

"He was so alive," cried one of the other fresh-faced girls. "Damn them to hell. Just damn them to hell!"

"I can't imagine the Holy Land this year without Carl," said a young man with red hair and freckles. "His lectures, his . . . everything . . ."

Vicky blotted her eyes and saw something that made her blood run cold: a man, rushing into the restaurant, pushing past the hostess—a crazed, sweaty man, cutting through the tables crowded with families.

"That's him," Vicky shrieked. "That's the man who kissed Carl!"

Nick heard Vicky shriek, he saw her point at him. He saw the guys at the table getting up, their faces contorted with rage. He saw them leap across the table.

Nick cut through the tables, bumping a waitress, spilling pancakes on a man and his wife. They shouted.

Nick pushed past a mother with a baby, trying to cut behind the counter.

Dale and his fellow Christians scrambled after Nick. They knocked over a table, Dale bumping the mother with the baby, knocking her down. She screamed.

"You goddamn queer!" Dale shouted at Nick. "I'm gonna *kill* you."

Dale and two of his pals climbed over the counter, cutting off Nick's escape through the kitchen. They started closing in. Dale picked up a knife and came at Nick.

Nick picked up a glass coffeepot and hurled its contents in Dale's face. Dale howled, dropping the knife.

The redhead came at Nick with his fists. Nick slugged him in the stomach. He doubled over, gagging.

Another Christian grabbed Nick from behind. Nick

threw him into a family just coming through the door. They all went sprawling, dad cracking the colonial-style door with his plaid butt.

Several other dads had had enough. They picked up knives and chairs and started toward Nick while their wives cringed.

Nick slugged another Christian and kicked a knife-wielding dad in the nuts. Nick broke a colonial chair and used the leg as a club. He whacked an attacking dad across the face with it. He knocked a fork from Vicky's hand as she tried to jab him.

A woman threw a plate of French toast at Nick. It broke against his head, leaving a gash. Blood trickled down Nick's forehead and got in his eyes. Somebody else threw a pitcher of maple syrup at him. He deflected it and ducked back, trying to wipe the blood from his eyes. They were forcing him back against the plate-glass window.

"He's a goddamn queer," somebody shouted. "He's one of those dirty queers!"

"Kill him," Vicky shrieked, her face a mask of red hate. "*Kill him!*"

Everybody charged at once.

When the cops pulled up, they saw Nick with his back against the plate-glass window, the polyester mob obliterating him, turning his flesh into hamburger. The only thing that saved him was that the glass finally broke and his bludgeoned body fell into the parking lot.

37

Dewey, Jeff, and Burt ditched the Roto-Rooter truck in Laguna Canyon and hiked down through the brush to Carol's house. Dewey and his ex-wife were still good friends. He used her phone to make arrangements while Jeff and Burt caught their breath.

At five they all watched the news and learned of Nick's capture at the pancake house. Although severely injured, he was expected to live.

For a moment Jeff felt sure he was going to cry. But he reached for a bottle of Jack Daniel's instead.

Around ten that night Carol drove Jeff and Dewey to John Wayne Airport, dropping Burt off at a friend's house on the way. Burt didn't want to go to Mexico. "I'm cool," he insisted. "I got some friends up in Santa Barbara. I'll lay low for a while."

He never made it to Santa Barbara, though. His friend went out for pizza later that night. Burt was all set to pig out when the SWAT team burst in.

By that time, Jeff and Dewey were in a Cessna over Baja, a rich Newport Beach chickenhawk at the controls. The guy turned Dewey's stomach, but he *did* have the plane and he owed Dewey a favor.

Jeff lit a joint. "Fuck," he said. "They're gonna burn him."

"Nick?"

"Yeah." Jeff took a hit. He wasn't going to need

much, he was exhausted. He passed the joint to Dewey. "You think Nick knows any good lawyers?"

Dewey looked at the joint. It had gone out. "I don't know, Jeff. I really don't know."

38

Randy didn't look much like an attorney, he looked like a shitkicker. Especially now, five days without a shave, Levi's and stetson caked with sweat and mountain dirt, he could have passed for a young rancher as he drove his battered Ford pickup past the San Francisco City Hall.

Scott rode shotgun, looking almost as bad. Or good. At times like this, Randy couldn't help noticing how much Scott resembled Nick; he was like a younger, blond version of Randy's old boyfriend, at least when he let himself go.

Although Randy seldom wore a suit out of court, Scott almost always did, in keeping with his role as the respectable half of the team. He was dashing on Montgomery Street, stylish at Pacific Heights cocktail parties, quietly conservative sipping tea with the mayor.

But on weekends, and holidays like this, Scott let himself get raunchy—wearing torn, faded Levi's, neglecting to shave—because he knew it turned Randy on.

The reason it did went back to Nick. Nick had done something to him, though Randy hadn't really understood what until long after Nick was gone from his life. Though Randy had been with many men before Nick, there'd been an intensity to the sex in their early days together he'd never known before.

Or since. It was true that at a certain point he'd become disillusioned with Nick, feeling that sex was all they really had in common, and that wasn't enough. And it was true that he'd fallen in love with Scott, and that feeling had evolved over the years into a fuller relationship than he could ever have had with Nick.

But Nick's sexual imagery was still burned into Randy's mind. How often—he could never tell Scott— he still saw Nick when they made love. Even this weekend hiking on the John Muir Trail was a repetition of a trip he'd made with Nick. The sex in the woods, the same.

Maybe that was why Nick was on his mind, more consciously than usual, as he turned on Castro Street, heading for home.

"Skin," Scott said, checking out the men as they crossed Eighteenth Street.

He was right. In the eighty-five-degree weather, a heat wave for San Francisco, the hordes on Castro were stripped down to their bulging gym shorts—in some cases beyond, a cock accidentally hanging out here and there. The sexual heat was nearly as intense as anything being generated by the sun. And Randy found himself getting more turned-on the closer they got to home.

Climbing the steps of their restored Victorian, Scott said, "I can hardly wait to take a shower. I feel *so* fuckin' raunchy."

"Yeah?" Randy kissed Scott's blond-stubbled face in the doorway. "Me, too."

A short time later Scott had his pants down in the kitchen. He braced himself against the counter, groaning with pleasure as Randy plowed him, wishing the goddamn TV wasn't on. It was distracting to say the least: gibberish commercials, then back to the news.

Randy thought so, too. Especially when he looked at the screen and saw Nick in an ambulance just as he came.

39

Carlos was seriously committed to living out a hard-core Zapata fantasy, Jeff realized right from the start. He and Dewey could hear shots for several miles before they reached the red brick house overlooking a skimpy beach south of Manzanillo.

María was driving the Jeep; she weighed in at about two-fifty. Gretchen, her lover, was riding shotgun. They lived in a house a half-hour back up the dirt road from Carlos' place. Jeff was pretty sure he'd seen Gretchen's picture on a post-office wall in the early seventies, when the FBI had been obsessed with radicals, but he didn't ask her about it.

Carlos was out behind the house, firing his .357 Magnum. At twenty-five, he was hard, glistening muscle jammed into a pair of faded fatigues, filthy leather bandoliers crossing his smooth brown chest. His target was a faded gringo poster of a smiling Cheryl Tiegs. Firearms clearly excited him; an erection stretched his fatigues.

Carlos holstered the .357 and greeted Dewey with a bear hug. "It's about time you came down anyway, man," he said after Dewey filled him in on what had happened. Carlos gave Jeff a firm handshake and they all went into the house.

The house had not always been Carlos'; in fact, it had only recently come into his possession. The decor was gutted mid-seventies L.A. organic: heavy wood-frame couches, oak tables, crypto-Navajo fabrics, a Pioneer stereo with a bunch of soft rock albums, including a worn copy of Fleetwood Mac's *Rumours*. It looked like the gringo owners had left suddenly—and Carlos had moved in just as suddenly, kicking back furniture, gatuitously busting things up, deliberately trying to make the house look like a commandeered battle station in an ongoing war. Jeff didn't ask Carlos, or Dewey either, about the details of the change of ownership, about where the "gringo couple" had gone or why. All he knew was that it had had something to do with dope.

The first day they took it easy, at least Jeff did. He drank beer and went through the gringo couple's record collection. He was astonished to find a copy of Jennifer's album, *Sweet Surrender*. It had a Thrifty's $1.98 bargain-bin sticker on it and that absurd picture of her, hair ratted high like a fierce 1970 Vegas whore, wet lips fixed in an imitation–Tina Turner sneer. He played side one, which began with a manic disco version of the Rolling Stones' "Wild Horses." Demented at best, and now the record was warped. Her voice lurched as if she was about to throw up. Jeff lifted the needle.

Dewey made calls to the States and to his other connections in Mexico. Cool at first, he became increasingly irritated as he tried to convince people that he was still on top of things, that anything he'd done back in the States, he could do just as well from here. But people weren't buying it.

"It's okay," he told Jeff. "We just have to let the dust settle. Anyway, I *do* have everything worked out for the visas and new IDs and all that. We're okay for now."

Dewey did his Soto Zen meditation out on the veranda, trying to cool himself out. But he flinched when the birds screeched, and for every thought that made him want to smile, there were at least a dozen others he found himself, contrary to practice, trying to push from his mind.

When a couple of rough-looking Mexican guys, who were tight with Carlos, showed up with the IDs and visas, they were less than pleased that Dewey couldn't pay them on the spot. A unpleasant discussion ensued, but in the end Dewey worked out "an arrangement."

Except for the rough-looking Mexican guys, the only people who came around were María and Gretchen. They brought in some food and stayed for dinner.

That night Carlos left in the pickup. Jeff and Dewey slept in a double bed with dirty sheets. Jeff got up in the middle of the night to take a leak from all the beer he'd drunk. He stepped on something crawling on the floor and shouted, waking Dewey up. When Jeff came back to bed, Dewey reached over and tried to hug him. Jeff recoiled. "It's too hot," he said.

The next day Carlos came back with a three-day-old *Los Angeles Times* and a canvas satchel Jeff was pretty sure held some sort of firearm.

Jeff read the paper on the veranda. There was a two-column story on the third page about Nick's capture. SPREE ENDS. Jeff and Dewey, the story said, had vanished. Authorities believed they were in Mexico. Dewey was described as a "notorious Orange County underworld figure." Jeff and Dewey laughed at that—"notorious Orange County underworld figure"—although they both knew that, despite the ridiculous sound of it, it was true.

Jeff quit laughing when he heard an automatic weapon being fired behind the house. He went and looked. Carlos was shredding what was left of Cheryl Tiegs with a severely chopped Heckler & Koch MP5 submachine gun.

Jeff looked at Dewey as if to say, What the fuck is going on?

Dewey seemed to read Jeff's mind. "We gotta get some money," he said.

40

Nick felt great—his brain was bobbing like a buoy in a sea of Demerol—but he looked like shit: scabs, an IV in his arm, stitches, bruises, gauze crammed up his nose, his left eye swollen shut, dried blood caking his lips. He didn't know how long he'd been in the hospital, or even which hospital it was, though he was reasonably certain it was somewhere in Orange County. He vaguely remembered the cops reading him his rights and trying to get him to sign a waiver so they could go ahead and question him without an attorney present. He was pretty sure he'd told them to get fucked, because they were still standing around out in the hall, looking anxious and pissed off.

In an odd way, Nick thought, he'd almost lucked out, getting wasted by those asshole Christians or whoever they were. If the cops had got their hands on him in a healthy state, he was certain he'd have ended up walking into a few doors or falling down a flight of stairs or having some other typical in-custody mishap that could have left him with his brains "accidentally" trickling out his ear on the strip-cell door.

Nick was listening to his urine trickle into the bedpan when he heard Randy's voice out in the hall, "Why don't you just tell him I'm here, okay?"

Even though it had been nearly five years, there was no mistaking that arrogant slur. Nick's heart started pounding like a white-knuckled fist in a padded cell.

Randy made his way in through the cops. When he saw how bad Nick looked, he tried to cover his shock with a jokey, sardonic attitude: "Jesus fucking Christ, all you need is a bunch of flies buzzing around your head and you'd be all set. I sure hope, for your sake, you don't feel as bad as you look."

"I feel bitchin'," Nick said with some difficulty. "Demerol." But his stomach felt like a sack of butterflies that was being slowly twisted and crushed by a pair of big sweaty hands. Jesus fuck! He'd never expected to even see Randy again, certainly never like this. For a second he was afraid he was going to cry. But he wasn't about to give the cops the pleasure of seeing that. "So what are you doing down here?" he said, trying to sound sarcastic. "Checking out Knott's Berry Farm?"

"That's right. Americanaland, too."

"I see. And you heard I was in here . . . getting my hemorrhoids clipped."

"Yeah. That's what they said at the pancake house. They also said you left without paying your bill."

"Lousy service. I was gonna write a comment to that effect on the back of the check."

"So how are your hemorrhoids?"

"Chokin' me, man. I can hardly breathe."

Randy smiled. "Well, at least you've still got your sense of humor."

"You bet. This is the funniest fuckin' thing that's ever happened to me. Maybe I'll write a humorous book and become the next Erma Bombeck. What do you think?"

"I think you need an attorney. A very good attorney."

Nick licked dried blood from his lips. "So how good are *you*?"

"Probably about as good as you're going to get."

"Good enough to get me out of this?"

"I don't know if anybody's *that* good."

"Maybe I better wait for F. Lee Bailey."

"That might be a long wait."

"Think so?"

"Yeah. Besides, F. Lee Bailey doesn't love you. I'm the one who loves you."

Nick smiled. "I always knew you'd come crawling back to me someday, saying just those words." It was supposed to be a joke but it sounded like he meant it.

Now Randy felt like he was going to cry. But he didn't. "You're going to be arraigned in L.A. day after tomorrow," he said. "You'd better start telling me what happened."

The L.A. arraignment got ugly. A number of Christians from the Orange County church interrupted the proceedings, shouting demands that Nick be remanded back to Santa Ana to stand trial for armed robbery and "Carl Hinds' murder." Deputies were clearing the courtroom when a pretty young girl spit in Nick's face. Nick was shackled and couldn't wipe off the spit. It trickled down his cheek until Randy took out his handkerchief and wiped Nick's face.

Sweaty, trembling, in a sullen rage, Nick pleaded not guilty to all twelve felony counts, including kidnapping and first-degree murder. Overhead, the fluorescent lights buzzed.

The deputy district attorney who got the case ducked into the men's room and jacked off in a stall to celebrate his lucky break. He was young, extremely ambitious, a hotshot who'd read *Helter Skelter* five times, and he promised to pull out the stops. "This is the best argument for capital punishment since the Manson family went on their rampage a decade ago," he told reporters, poking the air like his idol Vincent Bugliosi.

Nick was placed in the high-power section of L.A. county jail, a special isolation unit for prisoners the DA didn't want stabbed or fucked to death before they could stand trial. Nick had his own cell and the only time he saw any of the other prisoners was when the deputy took him down for his shower. They all took separate showers—much to the disappointment of the black rapist/murderer with the disfigured face. "Hey, can I take my shower now too?" he'd say as the deputy took Nick past his cell. He smiled with lips that looked like they'd been laid open with a can opener. Nick ignored him.

Nick and Randy began meeting daily in the conference room off the high-power unit. Nick sat at the steel table, chain-smoking cigarettes, telling Randy in exhaustive detail about everything that had happened.

Scott was busy up north, but he flew down as often as he could. "I'm going to need all the help I can get," Randy told Nick, realizing Scott's presence might open old wounds.

"Fuck all that," Nick said. "That's all ancient history. I never blamed Scott for us breaking up. We were on the skids anyway. We just weren't meant for each other. No big deal."

"I'm glad you feel that way," Randy said. But he figured Nick was bluffing.

He wasn't. Nick still liked Randy—in fact, he was starting to like him in a way he never could have before—but he'd realized early on that he wasn't *in love* with Randy anymore. Actually seeing Randy again had somehow put an end to the nostalgia he'd nurtured through the years since their breakup. It still sounded a little insipid, but maybe Randy was right: they'd had what they were supposed to have. Randy was clearly a lot better off with Scott. They had all their legal interests in common. They could fuck their brains out, then loll in bed for the next three hours discussing writs and motions and appellate-court rulings and crap like that. And Scott seemed like a nice-enough guy, contrary to what he'd expected. Intelligent, quick-witted, if a little naïve, refreshingly unaware of how good-looking he was. They were a good match. Nick wasn't jealous. He wasn't bitter anymore either. What had happened with Jeff, he realized as he talked about it endlessly, had shown that he wasn't as jaded and emotionally damaged as he'd thought. He'd really cared about Jeff—and still did. Even now, in jail, he felt more connected to Jeff than he had to anyone in as long a time as he could remember.

One afternoon Randy leaned back in his chair next to Scott and made his pronouncement: "You were traumatized."

"You're fuckin' A we were traumatized." Nick picked at the scab over his eye. "You're fooling around in the sack and suddenly Adam-Twelve and Erik Estrada bust in on you like they're ready to blow away the fuckin' Freeway Killer in the act or something—"

Scott leaned across the table, the sunlight catching his blond mustache. "What Randy means is that's going to be our defense. Sure, you were traumatized by their barging in on you, but more important, you were *severely* traumatized by the way they subsequently treated you. Your faith in the police was completely shattered."

Nick lit a Camel. "I never had any faith in the police in the first place. There was nothing to shatter."

"That's fine," Randy said. "But the point is, I think we can show that as a result of what happened with Burke and Rodríguez, the idea of surrendering was literally unthinkable. You and Jeff were pushed into a kind of irrational fear/panic state. You were following your instincts, and in the light of what was happening to you, resistance was an entirely understandable response. Technically, you weren't even resisting arrest. There were no grounds for arrest because you hadn't broken any laws. They were just harassing you and, in Burke's case, subjecting you both to the sickest kind of physical abuse imaginable. Kicking you in the nuts when you're cuffed. Attempting to rape Jeff by instrument. I mean, Christ! *They* were breaking the law! You had every reason to feel that the police had lost their capacity for fair and lawful behavior."

"I never believed they had any capacity for shit, man. The cops are always a bunch of fuckin' animals— especially if they know you're gay."

"True, L.A. cops aren't known for their warmth and humanity," Randy said, "but in this case I think it's fair to say they went much further than usual."

"I don't know." Nick stubbed out his cigarette. "Maybe it'd be simpler if I just said I ate a Twinkie."

Randy sighed. "Look, Nick, you've got to understand that the jury is probably going to be basically white, basically middle-class, and almost certainly straight. You can be sure the DA's going to challenge anybody over twenty-five who's still single. We'll be looking at people who are predisposed to think of the cops as basically decent. We're going to have to bring them around very carefully, so they'll see that if they'd been in your shoes, they would have been afraid to surrender, too. You were afraid to surrender *initially* at the apartment because the cops had just proved themselves incapable of respecting your most basic legal and civil rights—"

"And subsequent events," Scott said, "definitely reinforced your fear. The way they handled the baths raid—"

Nick winced. "That poor fuckin' guy. How is he, anyway?"

"He's alive," Randy said. "His name's Greg Stovey. I'm going to talk to him later in the week. He's staying with his parents out in Palos Verdes."

"Aw, Jesus, you're not gonna have to call him to testify, are you?"

"I may have to," Randy said. "He might be a very good witness. I know it's ugly, but it *did* happen and I want the jury to know about it. The homophobia of the LAPD is going to be a major aspect of this trial. They would never have treated you and Jeff like that if you'd been a straight couple, for Christ sake. And they would never have stormed the baths and started shooting if they hadn't tacitly placed a lower value on gay lives."

"So what's going on with Brundl?" Nick said. "They give him a medal yet?"

"Everything but," Randy said. "It's really disgusting. The review board ruled that the baths shooting was a regrettable accident occurring during the legitimate exercise of police force in the pursuit of known felons. In other words, tough shit."

"Jesus!" Nick snorted disgustedly.

"It's not surprising though," Scott said, "given Brundl's reputation. He's practically an icon. The other cops all love him. There was a book a few years ago, a novel. *The Stiff Gun.*"

"The *what*?" Nick laughed.

"I know," Scott said. "But that's what it was called. Some ex-cop wrote it. It's an incredibly sick book, virulently antigay, but *obsessed* with the subject, if you know what I mean. And the lead character's based on Brundl. He and his vice-squad buddy go around busting pansies with poodles, that sort of thing. It's incredibly odious, but it made Brundl a hero in the department."

"The sickest thing," Randy said, "is that a lot of the stuff in the book is based on fact. Brundl should be in prison right now. He's a murderer."

"The Riley case," Scott said.

"Right. A black guy, a church organist from Watts. Brundl and his partner busted him in a Hollywood porno theater for lewd conduct. Witnesses saw him being taken from the theater, handcuffed, docile. Crying. He was dead before they reached the station. Brundl and his partner said he resisted arrest. He'd been bludgeoned and beaten, died of internal injuries. His family sued, but nothing happened, of course."

"The dean," Scott said.

"Oh, yeah. That one's really played for laughs in the book. This college dean they caught pounding his pud in a park men's room. He was epileptic, and when they cuffed him, he went into a fit. In the book they just stand there and watch, cracking jokes as he convulses on the floor. 'Gee, Max, you think this guy's on PCP or what?' He finally bites off his tongue, and Brundl says, 'Hey, faggot. You just got blood all over my nice clean shoes.'"

"Whew." Nick looked a little ill. "Nice guys."

"Yeah," Randy said, "a couple of humanists. Sounds like good material for one of those liberal cop shows to me. In real life the dean recovered enough to blow his brains out. He was a conservative family man and all that. His wife killed herself a few days later. None of that's mentioned in the book, though. I guess it wasn't funny enough. Another interesting real-life detail: guess who Brundl's partner was."

"I don't know," Nick said. "Heinrich Himmler?"

"Burke."

"Jesus, you mean *the* Burke?"

Randy nodded. "They were vice-squad partners and they were still close pals at the time of Burke's death. That's why they put Brundl on the case. They knew he was in a rage because he thought a couple of fruits had killed his buddy, and they knew he'd stop at nothing to apprehend them."

"Shit." Nick shook his head. "You think you can get any of that admitted? I mean, it's all old stuff. Isn't there a rule against that?"

"We'll have to be careful," Randy said. "But I think if we set it up right, by the time the DA realizes what we're doing, it'll be too late to stop us. Not that he won't try."

"You'd better be *real* careful," Nick said, and his tone of voice indicated he didn't just mean in court.

"I know what I'm doing, Nick. Don't worry."

"I don't know." Nick looked in Randy's blue eyes. "I mean, granted, my recent experiences may have colored my view somewhat. But it's a known fact the LAPD doesn't fuck around. You start throwing stones at their big hero—"

"I'm an attorney, Nick. From here on in, everything's in the *legal* arena."

"Maybe so. But if I were you, I'd keep my address to myself."

* * *

Randy and Scott were staying at the home of a friend in Ocean Park. It was a restored Victorian house a block from the beach, its green-shingled turrets barely visible through the fog as they pulled up that night and parked. They sat in the car a minute as Scott finished telling Randy about the reaction—or lack of it—to Nick's situation up north.

"There's been nothing in the gay press," Scott said. "They won't touch it."

"Did you talk to Marvin?" Randy said, referring to an attorney with the ACLU.

Scott sighed. "Everybody feels the same way."

"It's really disgusting."

"I understand the argument," Scott said. "The gay-rights movement has entered a crucial new, respectable phase. It's more important than ever to show people that gays are not a bunch of psychopaths or criminals or child molesters. But to just dump Nick, out of political expediency—it's really infuriating."

Randy opened the car door. "But not surprising. All these assholes concerned about being 'politically correct'—they want everybody to think gays are a bunch of clean-cut businessmen and lesbian realtors who secretly dream of being Ozzie and Harriet. With a couple of poodles named David and Ricky."

They got out of the car, crossing the narrow, cramped street to the house, their voices carrying through the fog.

"What about your writer friend?" Scott said.

"Ed?"

"Yeah. Doesn't he live down here now?"

"Yeah, he moved back last year. But I think he does mostly entertainment stuff now." Randy unlocked the front door.

"Yeah, but he used to do investigative stuff, didn't he? Didn't he do that story about the police in Utah, when they killed that activist guy?"

Randy stepped into the dark hallway. He switched on a light. "Yeah, he did that."

Scott went into the living room, where the night-light was burning. The house was quiet. Paul, the owner, was still out. "Whatever happened with that?" Scott said.

Randy went up the dark hall toward the bathroom. "They had an investigation," he called. "But nothing happened. That's what always happens." There was a light on in the bathroom. He reached for the knob. "*Nothing.*"

Randy jumped as the bathroom door flew open. "Jesus!"

The teenage girl was startled, too. "Oops!"

"Where the hell did you come from?" Randy figured she was a young friend of Paul's; he was a straight rock musician.

"The guy said I could wait. Are you Randy?"

"Yeah. Who are you?"

Scott switched on the hall light.

"I'm Michelle, Michelle Rainey. My mom's the manager of the building where Jeff Gifford used to live."

Oh, my, Randy thought. "No kidding," he said. "Well, hello, Michelle."

"Look, my mom would kill me if she knew I was here. But I had to talk to you." She pushed her hair back. "I mean, the cops are lying. I don't understand it. I gave them a statement and everything. Maybe they lost it or something."

Scott looked at Randy. "Oh, wow."

Randy studied Michelle. Pretty, innocent, touchingly naïve. Credible. "Michelle," he said, "can I offer you something to drink? Some tea or a Coke or something?"

"No, that's okay," she said. "I already have a beer in the kitchen."

41

Sandy was giving Mark head behind the counter. It was almost three in the morning and everybody else in the Club Paradise Playa Grande village was in bed. There was something extraexciting about getting head in the lobby like this, Mark felt. There was always the chance another couple would get up and go for a moonlight stroll and walk in on them.

Sandy gave pretty good head. Mark liked looking down and watching her do it.

All in all, he had it pretty good. Where else could you be a hotel clerk and get to wear a skimpy sarong night and day that showed off your gorgeous bronze pecs and rock-hard stomach and get head or ass or both off a different chick almost every night? Mark knew he'd been hired primarily for his looks. He was everybody's fantasy of the perfect Club Paradise guy, the kind of hunky blond jock who grinned from the pages of the slick brochures.

A lot of the gals and guys who came to Playa Grande were pale and dumpy. Especially the guys. Sometimes the gals weren't too bad. Every once in a while they were more or less foxes, like Sandy. Except for the Wonder Bread thighs. "Easy, babe," Mark said, "watch your teeth."

Mark was glad the sarongs were loose-fitting. Sometimes he got a hard-on out by the pool, when he knew the gals—and let's face it, some of the guys—

were eating him alive with their eyes. He thought
about that, he thought about showing off, and he was
just about to blow when he looked up and saw the
three masked men.

One of them was obviously Mexican: he had those
bandoliers strapped across his bare chest like somebody in a sleazy spaghetti Western. He was holding
something that looked like an automatic weapon without a barrel. But barrel or not, the hole in the end
was pointed at Mark's head.

The other two men, who were covering the doors,
had similar weapons and their faces were also hidden under bandannas, but they certainly weren't
Mexican. They both had blond hair—on their heads
and bare chests.

When Sandy saw the men, she pulled away from
Mark and screamed—waking up most of the village.

Carlos told her to shut up. When she didn't, he
fired a few rounds into the ceiling, as Mark, out of
terror and excitement, shot off.

Dewey and Jeff saw lights snap on all over the
village, guys and gals coming out to see what the hell
was going on.

Carlos tossed Mark a bag. "Everything in the safe."

The guys and gals came up through the patio,
converging on the lobby. But they froze when they
saw Dewey and Jeff standing in the doorways with
their MP5s. At least most of them did.

One paunchy guy started to run. "Hold it, fuckhead,"
Dewey shouted. The guy stopped.

"Stop right there!" Jeff shouted at another man
who was trying to sneak away.

When the man kept going, Jeff squeezed the trigger
of his MP5, aiming for the sky above the man's head.
The man stopped in his tracks as a bullet mussed his
blow-dry hair. Piss ran down his sunburnt legs.

Jeff smirked. He felt charged up and powerful. His
cock jerked when he saw a good-looking young guy
with a nice round butt. He wondered what it would

be like to just grab the guy and fuck him on the spot
with everybody watching.

Mark shakily emptied the contents of the safe
drawers into the bag. There were rings and watches,
and most important, the wallets. Money was not
needed in Paradise; the guests payed for meals and
drinks with seashell tokens.

"Everything," Carlos said, indicating some cheap-
looking turquoise jewelry in the last drawer.

A few minutes later, it was over, the bandits van-
ishing into the jungle as quickly as they had come.
Then everybody was shouting indignantly, demand-
ing to know how something like this could happen to
decent people in a friendly country. Sandy's husband
was especially livid, stepping barefoot on a sticky
substance on the cool tile floor.

Jeff felt incredibly turned on as he and Dewey and
Carlos dashed through the black jungle back to the
road where they'd left the pickup. Leaves brushed
his bare chest, the strap of the MP5 tugged against
his sweaty pecs, every nerve was tingling, he was
both terrified and ecstatic. He hadn't felt like this
since he was a kid playing fantasy adventure games
at night in the suburban alleys of La Jolla. Jesus, he
thought, adrenaline was almost as great a high as
sex.

42

"**M**ichelle saw the whole thing," Randy told Nick the next day at the county jail, almost glowing with jubilation.

"What whole thing?"

"She saw you guys in the court. She saw Cowell shoot Burke from the rooftop across the alley."

"You gotta be kidding."

"She was watching from her bedroom window. And that's not all."

"You've got my attention."

"She *heard* everything, too."

"What do you mean?"

"Just that. She watched Burke and Rodrïguez enter Jeff's apartment, then she went into her mother's bedroom and listened through the window. *She heard every word.*"

"Jesus."

"And she just turned eighteen and moved away from home, and she's willing to testify that her mother lied her brains out, that she's a religious nut."

"Jesus, are you sure? I mean, is she reliable? What if the DA tries to make out like she's a little slut or something?"

"She's *not* a little slut. She's practically Marie Osmond." Randy was gleeful. "Nick, I'm telling you, this is going to be the biggest turnaround in the history of criminal law."

Scott was more guardedly optimistic. "It's a break in our case, Nick."

"All right!" Nick said. "Hey, who knows, maybe I'll be out in time to spend Christmas with the family—" It was supposed to be a joke.

"Yeah," Scott said. "Christmas, 1992." That was supposed to be a joke, too, but nobody laughed. It was an awkward moment.

Randy tried to save it. "Nick, one way or another, you're going to walk away from this. I've never been more sure of anything in my life." He squeezed Nick's hand.

Nick tried to look earnest and moved, as if he really believed what Randy was saying—but in his heart he knew he didn't stand a chance in hell.

Sure, Randy was smart and clever. Michelle's testimony might give the jury pause, depending on how much of it they could bring themselves to believe. Randy might succeed in reducing Rodríguez and Cowell to whimpering, remorseful basket cases (unlikely); he might even manage to transform cop-hero Brundl into a raving Godzilla (very unlikely); but in the end the equation would still come down to: who are you going to believe, ladies and gentlemen of the jury, the cops or the queer? The prosecution rests.

And then, Nick realized, he'd probably have to go through the whole thing again in Orange County. It would be worse down there—he pictured a jury of born-again moms and gun-club dads—and in the end it would all come down to the same thing: life in prison. San Quentin, maybe Folsom. Doing what? Trying not to get fucked to death by the black guys, Nick thought as the deputy walked him past the black rapist/murderer's cell.

At night Nick lay on his bed and felt more lonesome and shitty than he ever had in his life. Under similar conditions a lot of guys might have thought about suicide, but Nick didn't think about that. He thought about Jeff. It made him feel good to think about Jeff, it made him feel good in a way he didn't completely understand.

Sometimes, he couldn't even remember Jeff's face. It had all happened so fast. A three-day weekend, most of it without sleep, guts locked with terror, nerves charged with speed. But there was something about Jeff that kept coming back. If it wasn't his face, maybe it was his voice, but it wasn't really that either. Maybe it was just the feeling Nick had had when he'd been with Jeff, the feeling that he wasn't alone. Before Jeff, Nick had always felt alone, it had even quit bothering him for the most part. It was just the way it was. Even when he'd been with Randy in Mendocino, even when it had been at its best, he'd still felt like an actor in the wrong play.

Nick still liked Randy, he liked him a lot, and he knew Randy was doing more than he could ever have expected him to do. But Nick's real hope was Jeff— that was what was irrational. There was no reason to believe Jeff could do anything. He could come back and corroborate Nick's story, but Nick didn't believe for a second that would save either of them from anything. What else could Jeff do? Nick fantasized action-movie commando raids, helicopter rescues, Jeff and Dewey leading an armed assault on the county jail, automatic weapons blazing.

Reality didn't seem to work that way. Unfortunately.

Sometimes Nick *did* remember what Jeff looked like. He remembered Jeff's curly sun-bleached hair, his red nose that afternoon when they were scared shitless, trying to coolly hitch a ride out in Malibu. He remembered Jeff's body, the blond hair on his chest, the way it felt to kiss Jeff's chest, the salty taste of Jeff's sweat. He remembered Jeff's soft hairy butt, his hard cock, the way they'd made love that first night. Sometimes when Nick remembered Jeff that way, he reached in his rough denim trousers and pulled on his cock and jerked off. He was doing that one night, an image of Jeff fixed in his mind, and he was just about to come when harsh reverberating laughter ripped across his body like a jagged machete.

Nick looked up and saw a black deputy and a white chicken-chested deputy, laughing through the bars as as they watched him come. He wanted to kill them.

43

Harvey Berringer wanted to die. Instead, he grabbed Bess by the elbow and whispered, "Darling, don't be an ass."

Bess shook free and tossed back her sixth glass of wine. "Ass?" she said. "Who's being an ass? I'm serious! You *should* make a movie out of it." She glanced across the table at Michael Reed. "You could play yourselves, both of you! And the, ah, houseboy or whatever he was, he could play himself too!" She laughed, much too heartily. "Colostomy bag and all! I think it would be absolutely hilarious!"

If looks could have killed, Michael's glare would have blown Harvey's chic young alcoholic wife across Das Tamale and out the door. Heads turned in Hollywood's newest *in* restaurant. A hush fell over Michael's table. The portly business manager stared at his sauerkraut enchilada; the studio vice president excused herself to use the ladies' room; Cary, Michael's stunning "new boy," whistled under his breath.

"Bess, for God sake, please," Harvey whispered, glancing around, breaking into a nervous sweat.

"But I'm *serious*," she said with renewed demoniacal glee. "Let's see, what should we call it? *Malibu Fags on Parade*? No, that's already been done—"

Michael set his fork down with a clank. "That does it," he said. "Get her out of here, Harvey."

"Bess, come on." Harvey got up and tried to pull Bess to her feet. "Let's go, darling—"

"I'm not going anywhere," she said, grinning like a demented schoolgirl. "I'm going to finish my chili Bavarian—and think of more titles. Let's see. How about *Fistfucker Beach*?"

"That's enough," Michael said through gritted teeth. He glared at Harvey. "This woman should be in a sanitarium."

Harvey pulled Bess to her feet. "Come on, Bess. You've humiliated me for the last time."

"*I've* humiliated *you*?" She stumbled into the table, Quaaludes spilling out of her Gucci handbag like loose Certs.

She steadied herself against the table and glared at Michael. "You think you can pay everybody off, don't you? Well, you can't pay me off. I'm going to call the tabloids and give them the whole story. All about you and your *boy* with his teeth in your behind, and my own *darling* hubby with his fist up that young man's—"

"Shut up!" Harvey screamed.

Humiliated beyond redemption, Harvey yanked Bess across the dining room, shouting angry obscenities to drown her out.

Harvey grinned fiercely a few minutes later and waved to a movie-star couple as Bess threw up between two Rolls Royces in the parking lot.

Michael Reed was in the bathroom of his Burbank Studios office, watching Cary masturbate—God, the kid looked just like James Dean!—when Harvey called later that afternoon to apologize.

"Not to worry, Harvey. The ravings of a pathetic if beautiful drunk. I doubt that any of our Das Tamale-for-lunch bunch had the slightest idea of what she was talking about."

Cary ejaculated through a shard of sunlight, like an image in a secret pornographic outtake from *Rebel Without a Cause*. Michael shuddered. Watching was the future, he'd decided.

"Actually, Harvey, I was just about to call you. I've

been thinking. All hysteria aside, it's *not* a bad idea.
The film, I mean."

In his frigid Century City tower office, Harvey broke
into a sweat. "You've got to be kidding."

"But, Harvey, it's perfect," Michael yelled. "We
can make a fortune and protect ourselves at the same
time. I mean, really, what else is there?"

Harvey stared out across the West Los Angeles sky-
line and he felt sick.

But later that afternoon he called Randy and told
him Michael Reed wanted to buy the rights to Nick's
life. "He sees it as a book first, of course. An as-
told-to sort of thing, although a ghost job isn't out of
the question. They'll do the screenplay simultaneously.
Michael sees it as a cross between *Badlands* and *Dog
Day Afternoon*." Harvey mentioned two hot young
stars Michael was thinking of for the leads. "They'll
have to tone down certain elements, of course, probably no actual touching. But all that can be worked
out later."

Randy relayed the message to Nick the next morning. "By the way, Michael Reed wants to buy the
rights to your life. They see it as a book first, then a
movie." Randy mentioned the young stars Michael
had in mind.

Nick laughed. "That fucking dick."

"They're talking six figures, Nick."

"And you want a cut, is that it?" Nick instantly
regretted the remark. He knew Randy was preparing
to hock everything he had to cover the trial costs.
"Hey, I'm sorry."

"It's your life, Nick."

Nick looked out the barred window. "Then tell
him to get fucked. I wouldn't let that manic queen
touch anything about me. He'd probably turn the
whole thing into a fucking musical and make one of
us a girl. Tell him he can eat shit."

Randy said he'd relay the message.

*   *   *

Nick was still thinking about Michael's offer later that day as the chicken-chested deputy took him down for his shower. The two stars were all wrong; neither one of them looked anything like Jeff or him. Besides, they were simps; neither one of them could act. Hollywood, *shit.*

"Hey, can I take my shower now too?" the black rapist/murderer said as Nick passed his cell.

For once Nick acknowledged him. "Hey, fuckhole," he said, "what happened to your lip?"

The black rapist/murderer's mutilated lip formed something—but it wasn't a smile. "Come here and kiss me and I'll tell you all about it," he said.

"You fuckin' wish."

Nick peeled off his denims and got into the shower. He turned on the water, trying to ignore the chicken-chested deputy, who, as always, leaned in the doorway and watched him.

Nick sang "I Fought the Law," his voice echoing through the tile shower room.

"This is where Charlie used to take his shower," the deputy said, cutting into Nick's singing.

"Charlie?"

"Manson."

Nick soaped up his crotch. "So was that the high point of your life, watching Charles Manson take a shower?"

"At least he wasn't no fuckin' faggot."

Nick lathered up his ass. "You're sick."

"Charlie was a *real* criminal. Had his own harem and everything. Fuckin' those little hippie chicks right and left. Had a pretty big dick on him, too, for a little guy."

"No kidding? You get down on all fours and measure it?"

A scowl split the deputy's forehead. "You're really asking for it, aren't you, Krieger?"

"Sure. There's nothin' like a blow-job from a dumb cop. Take out your dentures and go to work."

"You suck dick, faggot!"

"Pithy, man. You're a real Noël fucking Coward."
Nick rinsed off his ass.

"That's it, queer. Clean that pussy real good."

"I'm gonna clean your mother's pussy real good."

The chicken-chested deputy rocked on his heels,
trembling with rage. For a second Nick thought the
dippy little guy was going to punch him out. Instead,
he broke into the broadest shit-eating grin Nick had
ever seen. Then he backed out the door.

Nick rinsed off, straining to see down the corridor.
He heard a cell door open, wondered what the hell
was going on. He also had a sick feeling he knew.

A moment later, the black rapist/murderer strolled
into the shower, whistling, naked. He turned on the
faucet next to Nick, his cock becoming erect.

The chicken-chested deputy leaned in the doorway,
grinning.

At the same time, Randy was dropping Scott off at
LAX. "I'll see you Wednesday," Scott said. Then he
kissed Randy, drawing a glare from a woman in a
copper-colored hairdo.

Randy watched Scott go through the automatic
doors and had a crazy premonition. The plane was
going to crash; he should go after Scott and stop
him. No, that was crap. The plane wasn't going to
crash, for Christ sake.

Maybe he just didn't want to face what was next
on his agenda. He'd postponed it as long as possible,
but he had to talk to Greg Stovey about the night at
the baths.

"It was a complete shock. Needless to say." Greg
laughed ironically and took a swallow of beer.

His manner was pleasant, disconcertingly cheerful,
considering what he'd been through. He certainly
looked good. His lifeguard tan was fading, but he
still had the fresh-faced good looks endemic to that
line of work. He wore only a pair of warm-up pants.

His swimmer's chest was subtly defined, achingly smooth.

"I had no idea there was anything going on. The steam room's soundproof. I couldn't believe it when I stepped out and saw all the cops."

Randy felt his skin crawl. He stared off at the ocean view from the backyard of Greg's parents' house in Palos Verdes.

Gret continued in a harrowingly calm tone of voice. "I still don't understand how it happened. The cop who did it ... he wasn't really that far away. You would have thought he'd have been aiming higher, if he was trying to hit the suspects."

Randy's throat was tight with rage. "You really should pursue this. If I can be of any assistance—"

"My parents have already talked to several lawyers. But I don't know ..." Greg's voice trailed off. He seemed momentarily lost in thought. "I hear it really ruined the baths. People quit going there after it happened. They're all going to that new place, the Glory-hole. It's supposed to be real hot."

Randy nervously finished his beer. "Greg, I hate to ask you this, but would you mind testifying about this in court?"

"No, I don't mind. *Really.*" Then, disjointedly, "I still have some of it. It's not like I'll never be able to have sex again. I can still come. But I don't think I'm going to go to the Glory-hole. I don't think I should do that, do you?"

Randy realized Greg was far less emotionally recovered than it had initially seemed.

"Well, look—" Randy got up. "I appreciate your talking to me about this."

"Don't you want to hear about the sickest part?" Greg said. He was smiling, but it wasn't a healthy smile.

"Maybe I can come and see you again later—"

"He took it," Greg said. "The cop who shot it off picked it up and put it in a plastic bag and took it. We asked about it later, at the hospital. They said

they didn't have it." Greg started shaking. He squeezed
the arms of the aluminum lawn chair till his knuckles turned white. "You want to know what I think? I
think he kept it."

Then, in a way Randy found unbearable, Greg began to groan: a ragged, guttural groan, the sound of
a beautiful animal being tortured by jealous, sadistic
creeps.

Greg's parents came running from the house. They
tried to calm him, with no success. They tried to get
him on his feet, and Randy tried to help, but they
told him to leave.

Randy was still quaking as he got on the freeway.
He took the Harbor turnoff and headed downtown.
He wanted to talk to the goddamn DA.

The black rapist/murderer disengaged from Nick.
Nick was dazed, his face against the tile, the water
running cold down his back. He hadn't resisted, there
was no point. The black guy was bigger and stronger.
But he was raging inside.

"Okay, now you can blow me," the black guy said.

Nick hesitated. Then he got down on his knees.

The chicken-chested deputy still watched from the
doorway, but he'd quit grinning some time ago. He
looked awed now, excited and guilty.

"Like this?" Nick said to the black guy. And bit
down hard!

The black guy howled and jerked back, blood sprin-
kling the tile walls.

Nick saw the deputy coming at him. He pushed the
black guy into the deputy *hard.*

"I want Brundl off the streets *now,*" Randy said to
the astonished district attorney in the eleventh-floor
hallway of Criminal Courts. As several deputy DAs
shook their heads and laughed incredulously, Randy
told the DA about Greg Stovey's accusation.

"That's the most disgusting thing I've ever heard
of," the DA finally said. "And the most ludicrous. It

was an unfortunate incident, but Max Brundl is one of the most respected men on the force."

"He's an animal and you know it. Everybody knows it."

The hallway was crowded with jurors and witnesses, with cops and families of defendants, and everybody was looking.

"Stovey's upset," the DA said. "Understandably."

"Why don't you get a warrant and search Brundl's house? He's probably still got it. It's probably in a pickle jar on his goddamn mantel."

"This is too farfetched. I'm sorry." The DA started to move on.

"You just don't want to make waves," Randy shouted. "You're scared of the cops, too, aren't you?"

That pissed the DA off. "Look," he said, "maybe you can get away with this kind of behavior up north. But this is Los Angeles and I don't have to take it. You'd better watch your step."

The DA hurried off down the hallway. Randy stood there a moment, blood pounding in his head, aware that everybody was looking at him. A couple of deputies exchanged knowing smirks. One of them laughed sharply. Randy heard the other say something about a "fruit attorney."

Randy's guts were still grinding when he got back to Ocean Park; he was enraged and frustrated, and he felt completely alone. And that was the fucked part. He shouldn't feel alone, he shouldn't be the only one on Nick's side.

If people knew the truth, he wouldn't be. That was why he decided to call Ed.

In spite of everything, Randy couldn't help smiling a little as he thought about Ed. Ed was such an asshole. Brilliant but an asshole. Good-looking, God knew, with a full reddish-brown beard and a hunky quarterback body, but an irredeemably manic-extrovert loudmouthed asshole. He'd been too much for Randy, their affair in the mid-seventies had lasted about a week. But Randy still respected Ed as a writer. In his more sober moments, Ed had written a number of courageous investigative pieces for gay publications and, significantly, for the mainstream press as well. Lately, he'd turned to movie-star pieces, gushing over Barbra, writing breathlessly of Mel. But if this story didn't stir his old iconoclastic spirit, Randy believed, nothing would.

He'd go crazy when he heard about Burke and Rodríguez and the frame-up, when he heard about Max Brundl and *that* piece of sick business, when he talked to Michelle; he'd go crazy and write a masterpiece. And to hell with the timid gay press and their "positive image" bullshit; Ed would sell the piece to *Rolling Stone* or *California*, and it would be the turning point.

There'd be a massive outpouring of sympathy for Nick, a Nick Krieger Defense Fund. Even the cautious gay powerbrokers would be forced to belatedly champion Nick's cause. It would lead to an independent investigation of the LAPD's actions in the case. There'd be such a storm of outrage over what had happened to Greg Stovey that the DA would be compelled to seek an indictment against Max Brundl. By the time Nick's case came to trial, he'd be a hero, a modern-day outlaw who, like the men who'd rioted at Stonewall, had had the guts to fight back.

Psyched up to a state of near euphoria, Randy got Ed's number from information and dialed it.

"He's in Palm Springs," said the drawling character on the phone, punk music blasting in the background.

"You have his number there by any chance?"

"Gee, no. You might try the Betty Ford Center. Oh, hey, just kidding."

Randy left a message, though he doubted that Ed would get it. He'd just hung up when the phone rang. "Hello."

"Randy Schaeffer, please."

"You're talking to him."

"You're Nick Krieger's attorney?"

"Yeah. Who's this?"

"This is Deputy Woodman, L.A. Sheriff's Department. Just thought you'd like to know your client was involved in an altercation at county jail this afternoon. He's being held at L.A. General Psychiatric pending the sanity hearing."

"What? What the fuck are you talking about?"

"Looks like he attacked a deputy and another prisoner. They're both in intensive care, the deputy with a broken back. Your client's a real animal, Mr. Schaeffer."

"Jesus. What about Nick? How's Nick?"

The deputy snorted disgustedly and hung up.

44

N ick tried to escape during the sanity hearing. Although shackled and pumped full of Thorazine, he broke away from the deputy and made a mad dash for the courtroom door.

He got as far as the elevators, where he banged his head against the Down button before several dozen cops of various departments converged on him.

They threw him to the floor amid much shouting and kicking. When Randy tried to intercede, a husky black lady deputy caught him in a choke-hold.

By that time it was all over, anyway. The psychiatrists had all testified. According to the state doctors, Nick was a "paranoid psychotic," a "violent sexual psychopath," with "pronounced schizophrenic tendencies."

The defense doctors had admitted Nick was "highly distraught," "agitated," and in need of "rest and therapy." But when one of them tried to explain to the judge, "Your Honor, if you had been anally and then orally assaulted, you, too, might have been tempted to defend yourself as best you could," he was ruled out of order.

In the end Judge Whitley was alone in his courtroom, everybody else was out in the hall where all the commotion was, when he signed the order committing Nick to an indefinite period of treatment at the

California State Mental Hospital at Atascadero. He felt certain he was doing the right thing. It might not be fashionable to say it these days, but in private he still believed that just being queer was in and of itself a form of mental disease.

45

The he take from the Playa Grande job was only seven thousand, considerably less than Dewey had hoped for. They could get a couple thousand more for all the IDs, but by the time they gave Carlos his cut, paid off his buddies for their fake IDs, and slipped Carlos another two grand for "the authorities in Manzanillo," Jeff and Dewey didn't have much left. They were covered for maybe three months, Dewey said, but they'd have to start planning for the future now. Jeff didn't ask what that was going to entail. He had a pretty good idea when Dewey began pumping Carlos for information on a number of the resort developments scattered along the coast between Puerto Vallarta and Manzanillo.

Carlos taught Jeff to shoot. Jeff practiced behind the house, with a .357, a .38, and a .45 automatic. He got the hang of the MP5, but with the .357 especially, he got so good he could blow Eydie Gormé's face off a Mexican magazine cover at a hundred feet.

Dewey began sleeping with Carlos at night, which left Jeff alone in the double bed. It was fine with him. He liked Dewey and still found him attractive, but for some reason Jeff didn't feel like having sex. Not with Dewey or anybody.

He'd gone through periods like this before. In his teens when he'd first realized he had gay feelings and suppressed them. Again, after it had ended with Jennifer. Of course, he'd had herpes then, even though it had probably been psychosomatic. Now he felt the same way. After Nick.

Jeff thought about Nick a lot.

Sometimes he thought about him when he went to bed, right before he fell asleep, when his unconscious mind was taking over and his thoughts were almost dreams.

One night he saw himself in a room in a house by the ocean, a cool, dark room, in contrast to the bright hot beach outside. Through the window he saw Nick coming up from the beach, his hairy chest wet, a pair of wet baggy Hawaiian swim trunks showing off the shape of his cock. Nick came into the room, skin flushed from the sun, in need of a shave. Smiling at Jeff, he peeled off his swim trunks and stretched out on the bed. Jeff stepped over and Nick drew him down to the bed, but they didn't have sex. They just held each other lightly and laughed and talked, listening to the voices of people having fun out on the beach.

Jeff wondered about these dreams or fantasies or visions or whatever they were. He couldn't decide if they were premonitions, or just a way of playing out futile desires.

Sometimes Jeff woke up in the middle of the night, slick with sweat. He'd sit up in bed and bite his fingernails, worrying about Nick, imagining what he must be going through. He'd usually have to get up and take a few hits off a bottle of tequila before he convinced himself there was really nothing he could do to help Nick now.

Jeff was down on the beach one day soaking up the sun when Dewey came down with a week-old *L.A. Times*. "Bad news."

Jeff sat up. "What?"

"They sent Nick to Atascadero."

Jeff took the paper from Dewey and read the story. " 'Considered mentally unfit to stand trial,' " Jeff read, " 'after an altercation with detention personnel and another prisoner.' What the fuck?"

"That's where they sent Phil," Dewey said.

"Phil?"

"A guy I went to high school with. Gay. Real effeminate. I never knew him that well, I avoided him. I was a real closet case in high school. But I heard about it."

"About what?"

"These different treatments they gave him. Stun shots."

"Stun shots?"

"Yeah, they'd shoot him up with some drug that simulated a heart attack. Supposed to make him see the light, I guess. Then they tried aversion therapy. Wired him up and zapped him while he was looking at slides of naked guys." Dewey paused. "When that didn't work, they cut off his nuts."

Jeff was stunned. "They cut off his nuts? You mean, literally?"

"That's what I said."

"Jesus, why? What did he do?"

"I don't know. I think he jacked off in public or something. You know, a whole bunch of times. Like they busted him twenty times or something and he just kept doing it, so they finally sent him to Atascadero."

"Christ."

"Of course, that was almost ten years ago," Dewey said. "I don't think they do stuff like that anymore. They're more advanced now."

Jeff tried to think about something else but he couldn't. He picked up the newspaper and reread the story on Nick.

46

Randy was worried, too. He drove out to the UCLA Research Library and looked through the back issues of a national gay newspaper, searching for an article he remembered from a few years before. He found it, took the bound volume to a desk by the window, and reread the interview with William Corman, a fifty-year-old family man from Palo Alto, California.

Q. What were the circumstances of your arrest?

A. Well, I was a Scoutmaster in Palo Alto and I was having an affair with one of the boys in the troop. He was fourteen. It was by mutual consent, but his parents found out about it. They pressed charges.

Q. The court sent you to Atascadero?

A. That's right. In January of 1977.

Q. What happened there?

A. Not too much at first. Group therapy with the other patients. That's where they send all the so-called sexual criminals. Some of them *were* pretty bad. *Real* child molesters. I never thought of myself as a child molester. With Don and I, it was mutual. If anything, he pursued me. I mean, I was too scared to do anything at first. But Don was very persistent. Teenage boys are extremely sexual—

Q. So there was group therapy—

A. Yes, but it was a farce. Everyone was on drugs. You know, Thorazine and so forth. The nurses, the psych techs, none of those people cared about the patients. It was more like a prison than a hospital. The only person I felt any real connection with was Dr. Staner.

Q. The doctor who eventually performed the surgery?

A. That's right. I felt comfortable with him immediately. He didn't act superior or condescending. He was more like a friend, an equal, like another Scout father I might have known on the outside.

Q. How did he describe the surgery to you?

A. He said it was a new kind of treatment for homosexuality. He stressed that it was nothing like a lobotomy, even though it did involve inserting probes into the brain. He showed me the probes. They resembled very fine needles. He said the idea was to get into the brain and in essence switch the nerve tracks at a particular point, so he could reroute the sexual impulses and make me straight. I'd never heard of anything like that before, but he was very convincing. He described it as a minor operation and promised I'd be exactly the same as before, that I'd have all my faculties and intellect and all that, only I'd be straight.

Q. And you gave your consent?

A. Yes. I was thinking of my family. And I wanted to get out of the hospital. And I believed him. I thought it would work. He's a very highly respected pioneer in this field, I found out later, but even then he seemed like a very nice man and I was eager to become straight. I was not very liberated, I have to tell you. Being gay was something I'd tried to repress all my life, and when it periodically erupted, it was almost always disastrous.

Q. What was the outcome of the surgery?

A. I became completely impotent and lost all interest in sex, either gay or straight. Dr. Staner assured me that was a temporary condition. I was released last year, on probation, and returned to live with my family in Palo Alto. The situation has remained the same. Nothing of a sexual nature, gay or straight, interests or stimulates me. It's hard to describe. Part of me *wants* to be interested, but it's as though something has been blocked—or cut. This has led to periods of severe depression, alternating with a great deal of rage. I was taking medication for a while, but I've stopped now.

Q. Why did you decide to sue and go public with this?

A. I had already 'gone public' as a result of the arrest. I discussed it with my family—and I must say they've been incredibly supportive through all this—and we decided we had to take some action. I feel I was misled and taken advantage of. I've learned since that the surgical process—it's called microcoagulation—is still considered highly experimental. I feel I unwittingly served as Dr. Staner's guinea pig. And I have reason to believe the same surgery was performed on other patients, without their full knowledge of the likely outcome, or in some cases, even that the purpose of the surgery was to alter their sexual orientation.

Randy skipped the rest of the interview and read the postscript: "William Corman committed suicide in July of this year, shortly before his lawsuit was scheduled to be heard."

The next day, Randy filed a motion with Judge Whitley requesting Nick's transfer to Chino, on the grounds that the Chino facility was more appropriate for short-term psychiatric treatment.

"In light of the evidence," the elderly judge said, "I

see no reason to believe Mr. Krieger's treatment will *be* short-term. These sexual psychosis cases can drag on forever. Atascadero's the best place for him. Motion denied."

Randy was furious, but he didn't show it in court. The judge had the power to approve any treatment the Atascadero doctors requested, which was why the last thing Randy would have done was mention his real concern for Nick's safety, relative to Benjamin Staner. It'd be just like Whitley to say, "Never heard of *that* before. But if it'll straighten him once and for all, it might be a good idea."

Randy played it cool. He was already developing another strategy.

So, in his own way, was Max Brundl.

The district attorney, as it turned out, had actually mentioned Randy's accusations concerning Brundl to the chief, and in a highly perfunctory manner, Internal Affairs had questioned Brundl about the matter. The ten-minute session at Parker Center had broken up amid loud guffaws and references to the whole thing as "a load of crap."

But word got around. Some cops joked about it: the idea that Max Brundl had kept Greg Stovey's cock as a souvenir was generally regarded as too absurd to believe, obviously the fevered imaginings of some desperate fruit attorney. But some cops—especially those who knew or had worked with Brundl, and most especially those who had actually seen the fucking thing in the peanut-butter jar in Brundl's workroom before he flushed it down the toilet—had funny glints in their eyes as they joked about the absurdity of it, the kind of look Vietnam veterans might have if they were drunk and only half-trying to deny a wartime-atrocity story.

Brandl himself treated it lightly enough. "I used it as bait on my last fishing trip," he said, feet on desk at Hollywood Division, cigar in mouth.

"Catch anything, Brundie?" one of the other detectives said.

"Yeah." Brundl smirked. "VD."

The other cops howled. Brundl might take first place, one of them said, if there was a cop night at the Comedy Store.

But Brundl wasn't cracking jokes when he cornered Eddie Sepúlveda in the men's room of the Fortune Bowling Alley in South Gate. Eddie was a piece of worm-infested Chihuahua shit disguised as a human being. But he owed Brundl a favor, and the cop had come to collect.

"Yeah, yeah, okay, okay," Eddie said, trembling at the urinal next to Brundl, too scared to pee.

This was too heavy, he figured Brundl must be insane or something. But for a thousand dollars he was ready to do anything the cop said.

47

Some of the buildings were pink, others were lemon yellow. They all looked like part of a neatly landscaped California high school, except that the windows in the pink buildings had lemon-yellow bars and the bars in the windows of the lemon-yellow buildings were pink.

The walls of Nick's room were white. There was a bed, a toilet in the corner, a caged light overhead beside a closed-circuit TV camera with a wide-angle lens. There was a steel table bolted to the floor, a door with a grilled window in it, and a window in the wall with lemon-yellow bars.

Beyond the lemon-yellow bars there was a lawn with a few scrawny trees and a chain-link-and-razor-wire fence. Beyond the fence there was a row of boarded-up blue stucco tract houses and an empty white stucco church. Crows nested in its weathered steeple. Hawks swooped through the sky all day.

When the orange sun was going down, the view was almost picturesque, Nick thought, like a picture in an arty photograph book or one of those paintings that looked like a photograph.

One evening Nick was looking out the window when he saw a dirty white '68 Camaro pull up to the abandoned church. Two men got out and went inside.

They were still there in the morning. Nick watched them come out. One man was shirtless, well-built, with a blond beard. He stretched.

The other man took a leak in the weeds. He wore faded jeans, a white T-shirt, and he was blond, too. He seemed to be looking over at the hospital complex.

For a moment Nick imagined the men were Jeff and Dewey, come to rescue him. Though he knew it was a fantasy, his heart started pounding.

He watched the men walk back to the Camaro. Just before they separated to climb into the car, the shirtless man gave his buddy a pat on the ass. Whether it was a gay or straight gesture of affection, Nick couldn't determine.

Who cared? he thought. What difference did it make?

Benjamin Staner cared. He studied Nick intensively. He studied him in person, in friendly discussions. He studied the results of a battery of psychological and physiological tests. He studied Nick's rapid-eye movement and masturbation habits on videotapes recorded at night in Nick's continuously illuminated room.

The friendliness of the discussions was facilitated by Nick's medication, a constantly adjusted combination of Haldol, Evavil, Thorazine, and Ritalin, designed to keep Nick in a calm but expansive mood. Staner wanted as much data as possible.

Nick Krieger, Staner concluded early on, was a man with a male brain. In every respect, Nick was a masculine man: appearance, speech, body language, genital endowment, ejaculatory prowess, all 100 percent male. And he had a history of extreme hypermasculine combative behavior, an intensely aggressive/assertive personality—in short, in the most desirable attributes of the ideal male of the species, all the drives necessary for achievement, social productivity, and procreation, but all inverted, twisted into a horrendous pattern of self-destructive and sociopathic behavior, stemming from a compulsive sexual psychopathology that had, it seemed, been contracted as a result of a fluke encounter with a carrier of the disease.

"I was sitting in the back row of this movie theater in Detroit. I guess I was about thirteen. It was some biker movie with Nancy Sinatra. So this guy sits down next to me. He's about twenty, you know, kind of a jock-type. He was pretty good-looking. And he says, 'Hey, these biker movies are really bitchin', huh?' Only before I can answer him, I realize his leg is kind of pressing against mine."

"What happened then?"

"What do you think? I couldn't fuckin' believe it. I got a huge fuckin' hard-on. And the guy finally reaches over and unzips my pants. The second he touches my cock, I explode."

Staner smiled. "So that was your first gay experience?"

"Yeah, I guess you could say that. After that, I couldn't get enough of it. It was like all my fantasies had come true."

Staner laughed heartily. "So this guy was a jock. He was pretty butch, huh?"

"Yeah." Nick laughed. "I guess you could say that. At least till we got to his apartment."

It was easy to trust Staner. At forty-five, he was quite good-looking. Although he'd been a rather insipidly pretty teenager, with rosy cheeks and red sensuous lips that had evoked cruel remarks from his peers in the butch Eisenhower era, he'd become a strikingly distinguished-looking gray-haired man. Especially in his drugged state, Nick found Staner's gentle paternal air highly flattering and reassuring.

The doctor took Nick's side. He nodded and smiled compassionately when Nick talked about his ordeal with the cops. His expression didn't change when Nick described the altercation in county jail.

"I don't blame you," Staner said. "I'd have done the same thing."

Nick appreciated the thought, though it was difficult to imagine Staner being forced to his knees in a shower room.

Before long Nick was spilling his guts. He talked

about the marines, the 7-11 robberies, the insanity of his speed-taking days. He talked about his mother's death, his guilt feelings over Father Timothy's suicide.

It felt good to get this stuff out. Nick had never taken many people into his confidence. He'd always figured they didn't want to hear about all your painful, negative experiences. But no matter what Nick told him, Staner just nodded and smiled compassionately.

This Staner guy was all right, Nick concluded. The fact that he was straight didn't even seem to matter. He seemed unshockable, though Nick detected that his own sexual experience was limited. Sometimes his stilted attempts at locker-room banter amused Nick.

"So you like to get a b.j. more than anything, huh?"

Nick cracked up. "A b.j.?"

"Isn't that what you call a blow-job?"

"In Oklahoma maybe. In 1955."

Staner cleared his throat, embarrassed. "But you like that? More than anything?"

Nick tried not to laugh; he knew the doctor didn't mean it as a come-on. "No, I wouldn't say that. I mean, a blow-job's okay, especially if you're in a hurry. But there's no contest between that and fucking. Fucking's about my favorite thing in life, as a matter of fact. After Haagen-Dazs ice cream."

Staner laughed wholesomely. "Well, I guess we have something in common after all."

Nick smiled too, his mouth dry from the drugs, his lips sticking to his teeth. "Yeah. Maybe so."

"You ever think about girls, Nick?" He tried to make the question sound impulsive.

"Girls?"

"Yeah, you know. Girls?" Staner laughed, indicating he knew he might as well have said Martians. "I mean, having sex with them."

"Not really." Nick cracked his knuckles. "Should I?"

"Not necessarily. It's just that sometimes people aren't all one-way."

Nick sniffed. "I like being gay."

"Do you really?"

For the first time in all their hours together, Nick caught something strange in the air. Staner was looking at him with the same expression of compassion as always. But for some reason Nick felt like a bug.

Another doctor poked his head in the door, breaking the mood. "Doctor, we have an emergency."

Staner excused himself, patting Nick on the shoulder, and stepped into the hall. It wasn't the kind of emergency he'd expected, though. It wasn't medical; it was legal. There was some "homosexual attorney" out at the front desk.

"We have a legal right to see him," Randy told the wavy-haired physician for what seemed like the fifteenth time.

"It's not up to me," the doctor said. "You can't just walk in here without making arrangements and expect us to click our heels. This is a state hospital."

Randy tried not to blow up. "This is completely outrageous," he said as calmly as possible. "I demand that you let us see Nick Krieger right now."

Bill, the psychiatrist Randy had brought along to examine Nick, was equally adamant. "Look, you must be aware of the law. You can't refuse to let us see him."

The wavy-haired physician shrugged. "I'm sorry you drove all the way up here for nothing."

"I want to talk to the doctor in charge of this case," Randy said in a voice that turned heads.

The nurses behind the counter scowled. A patient giggled sharply. A couple of brown-uniformed guards were already hustling up the corridor toward the reception area.

"Dr. Staner's in charge of that case," the wavy-haired physician said blandly, "but he's out of town right now."

Randy blew up. "Now you listen to me. If you let that demented quack touch a hair on his head, I swear to you, when I'm finished with you guys, the Nuremberg trials are going to look like traffic court in Boise."

The wavy-haired physician sighed. He didn't have to call for help, the guards were already there, palms resting on their revolvers. "Just get them off the grounds," he said.

Nick shuffled up the corridor, a black psych tech leading him back to his room. He tried not to think about the odd moment of tension with Staner; he'd probably imagined it anyway.

He thought about dinner. Let's see, tonight it was beef with gravy. Then he'd take a bath and his evening medication, and watch *Dynasty* on the dayroom TV until it quit making sense.

"Looks like more rain," said the black psych tech with a lispy voice.

Nick didn't bother to look through the pink barred windows they were passing. If he had, he would have seen Randy and Bill being shown to their car by the guards.

48

"Actually, it's the best thing that could've happened," Randy said as he swerved around a tank truck on the way back to L.A. "I'll go to court Monday and get an injunction and an immediate transfer to Chino."

The tank-truck driver blasted his horn.

"Randy, for Christ sake, watch it, will you?" Bill said. "Look, you want a Librium? You want me to drive?"

"I'm okay."

"Randy, they can't do anything without a hearing. You can't just arbitrarily start cutting somebody up—"

"I don't even care about that," Randy shouted. "It's not even a factor. Nick'll be out of there by Tuesday at the latest!" Randy pushed the car past eighty.

They got back to L.A. around ten. Randy dropped Bill off, then went back to Ocean Park, where he called Scott in San Francisco and filled him in. They were talking when Randy noticed a scrawled message by the phone. From Ed, the writer. "I'll call you back," Randy told Scott, explaining why, immediately dialing Ed's number.

"Hey, Randy!" Punk music blarred in the background.

"Ed, I've been leaving messages for the last two weeks. I've got to talk to you. It's about Nick."

"Randy, I'm just on my way to a big party, you wanna come? We can talk on the way."

Randy hesitated. Ed already sounded pretty ripped. "Yeah, okay," he finally said.

Randy called Scott back long enough to tell him he was going out with Ed.

A short time later, Randy was hurtling down PCH in Ed's Firebird convertible, the tape deck blasting the Dead Kennedys, headlights reflecting in Ed's mirrored shades as he took gulps from a bottle of Metaxa. "I can't get enough of this shit," he shouted, indicating the music. "But I'll put on *Summer and Sweat* before we get to Malibu—"

Randy felt his guts flip-flop. "Don't tell me we're going to Michael Reed's—"

"Look, I know what you're thinking—but it's money!"

"What?"

"The picture!" Ed shouted. "I know it'll be a piece of shit, but that's what people want now! I don't want to spend the rest of my life barely surviving as a journalist, Randy."

"You're writing a picture for Michael Reed?"

"Keep your fingers crossed. I should know next week. That's why tonight's so important."

"What kind of picture?"

"I told you, a piece of shit. It's a science-fiction musical fantasy. *Brigadoon* in outer space." Ed giggled. "Don't ask me. It's *his* idea."

Randy indicated the tape deck. "You mind turning that down?"

Ed lowered the volume imperceptibly. "Randy, it's money! Three hundred thousand dollars! Christ, I can get a new car! Do you know how humiliating it is, driving on the lot in this piece of shit? People take one look and peg me as a loser."

"Ed, I want to talk to you about Nick—"

"You're goint to *love* this party, Randy. I promise you, it'll be the tackiest, most tasteless party you've ever been to. I don't take any of this seriously—"

Randy shut off the music. "Ed, if you don't want to talk about this, take me back."

Ed made a sharp turn at Carbon Canyon, paying no attention to the car behind them as it made the same turn. He pulled off the road a few hundred yards from the highway and shut off the engine. "So what is it?"

"I want you to write a story about Nick. There are a lot of facts that haven't come to light. People have been buying the police version of what happened."

Ed leaned back, stared up at the clear night sky, and sighed. "Oh, Randy. Randy, Randy, Randy—"

"There are facts, Ed. About the police. About Max Brundl—"

"Who?"

"The cop who shot the guy at eight-six-o-three."

A car rumbled down the canyon road, momentarily catching Ed and Randy in its headlights. Neither of them realized it was the same car that had followed them when they'd turned. It reached the highway and turned toward Malibu. It was quiet again.

"Look, Randy." Ed was still staring at the sky. "I know you're defending Nick. I know you were involved with him at one time—"

"There are other facts, Ed. Michelle, the landlady's daughter, was a witness. Nick didn't shoot that guy, the SWAT shooter did it!"

Ed sighed again. Randy waited for his response. "Nick *is* pretty hot." Ed took another hit off his bottle of Metaxa and offered it to Randy, who waved it away. "At least in his pictures anyway. I can see why you liked him. I'll bet you guys used to have a lotta fun—"

"He's a nice guy." Randy suddenly realized Ed was fondling himself. He tried to pretend it wasn't happening, but it was.

"I'll bet he's got quite a cock on him."

"Oh, Christ."

"But, then, you've got quite a cock on you—as I

recall. Of course"—Ed unzipped his pants—"I'm not doing so bad myself."

Ed stroked his cock with his left hand and, with his right, tried to feel Randy's crotch. Randy pushed his hand away. "I don't fuckin' believe this. Take me back."

Ed shrugged and giggled. He started the engine, turned on the tape deck, and screeched out, not bothering to stuff his cock back in his pants.

As they reached PCH, Ed said, "Look, Randy, I'm sorry. It's no big deal, right? I'm just in a frisky mood tonight. I'm real jacked up, I took a couple Preludin earlier. Come on, come to the party with me, we can talk afterward."

"No, fuck that."

"Come on, I said I was sorry." Ed took a right— toward Malibu.

Randy blew up. "Take me back to Santa Monica. I don't want to go to any fucking party at Michael Reed's."

"Jesus, you've turned into a real old lady, Randy."

"Yeah, and you've turned into a mindless queen. You make me sick."

Ed screeched to a halt. "So you wanna go back, go back! I'm already late."

Enraged, Randy climbed out of the car. "You're pathetic, you know that."

Ed screeched away.

Randy stood there a minute, staring at the traffic, finding it difficult to believe he'd actually been involved in such a cheaply melodramatic scene, nobody'd ever kicked him out of a car before. On some level, it was almost funny.

He crossed the highway and stuck out his thumb.

Almost immediately, a light green '64 Impala slid up beside him, the door opening.

"Hi," Randy said to the four Latino men as one held the seat so he could climb in back.

"Hi," one of them replied, as Eddie Sepúlveda stepped on the gas, cranking up Ritchie Valens' "Donna" on the radio.

Max Brundl made sure he had an alibi that night. He stayed glued to a barstool at a popular cop hangout in Pasadena, cracking jokes, tossing back doubles, until two in the morning.

His wife, Trudi, was asleep in front of the TV when Max got home. He woke her up and took her into the bedroom.

He did something then he'd only done one other time.

"No, honey, please. Not that," Trudi said.

But Max was drunk and mad and not about to take no for an answer.

Pictures flashed through Brundl's mind as he sodomized his wife. Gloating boys in a barn, long ago. The face of the man he'd shot at the bathhouse, the look of shock when he saw that his cock was gone.

"Max, please stop. It hurts."

"Quiet."

He saw Randy in the men's room at Criminal Courts, standing at the urinal. Brundl had been combing his hair at the mirror. Randy's firm round butt, covered with corduroy. Brundl held that picture as he came.

50

Jeff called Randy's Ocean Park number in the morning. It had taken him a while to get it. Randy's San Francisco office had wanted to take a message, but Jeff couldn't leave one, not with Dewey listening over his shoulder. Dewey was worried about the phone. Finally, Jeff had called while Dewey was out, identified himself to Randy's secretary, and got the number. He tried it around ten. No answer. He called a dozen more times throughout the day. It just rang.

That night in bed Dewey tried to reassure him. "I'm sure this is the same guy Nick lived with for a while up north," he said of Randy. "Nick told me they were real hung up on each other at one point. I'm sure he won't let anything happen to Nick."

"Yeah, I guess," Jeff said, but he still felt funny and he knew Dewey did, too.

Dewey held him as he stared out the window at the rain.

They'd begun sleeping together the week before, after Dewey lost his self-control one afternoon while they were sunbathing naked on the beach. He'd leaned over and kissed Jeff, and Jeff had not exactly tried to fight him off. He'd had to admit it, he'd been horny for a long time and he'd always been attracted to Dewey. The sex was good, more friendly than romantic, but what Jeff liked most were moments like this, when Dewey gently held him at night.

Dewey had been getting increasingly anxious, though. He'd made a number of calls to the States, trying to get a big dope deal off the ground. But people had hung up on him when they heard the strange clicks on the line. In Orange County, his former attorney had been indicted on charges stemming from his business deals with Dewey; his ex-wife was certain she was under surveillance; and Burt was supposedly about to make a deal with the feds. This last item was especially disturbing because Burt knew about the Mexican hideout.

Carlos was a problem, too. He had been doping heavily. He'd come back one day with a cache of ludes, coke, and speed. "I have a bad feeling Carlos didn't pay off the federales," Dewey had confided to Jeff. "I think the money went for the dope instead."

Not long after Dewey had quit sleeping with him Carlos had come home with a dog, a mangy, smelly, emaciated mongrel. Dewey had refused to let it in the house at first. But Carlos bathed it, groomed it, and cooked horsemeat for it, and now it was sleeping with him at night.

Jeff called Randy's number again the next day, still getting no answer. He was trying it that afternoon when he heard Carlos playing with his dog on the veranda. Jeff peered through the window, watching Carlos kiss the dog and scratch its stomach, talking to it in Spanish, letting it lick him on the face. Carlos seemed at that moment innocent and childlike. Although Jeff knew it was the corniest bit in the world—a boy and his dog—he was moved.

It rained hard that night. The next morning Jeff saw the dog pawing and growling at something back by the edge of the jungle. He went out to see what it was. There were thousands of flies and the smell was pretty awful. It was the gringo couple who had owned the house. They were in a shallow grave.

51

The Staners went to church that morning, a perfect Protestant family in the stained-glass light. That afternoon Ben took Betty and the twins to a Mexican restaurant in San Luis Obispo, then to a movie at a nearby mall.

Summer and Sweat had been a blockbuster all summer and most of the fall, but now the Michael Reed production was near the end of its run. The print the Staners watched was scratchy, the original Dolby sound now monaural and low-fi, but the theater was packed, mostly with talkative teens. The girls in the front rows were especially bad. Die-hard *Summer and Sweat* fanatics, they squealed when the hunky young star took off his shirt (which was often), sang along with every song, and worse, spoke key lines of dialogue a second ahead of the actors, creating a grating out-of-sync effect.

No one told them to shut up.

Certainly Betty hadn't. She stared straight ahead, smiling prissily, as if absolutely nothing were wrong. That was Betty, all right. The perfect little homemaker who never complained. A bit dowdy, it was true, with her harlequin glasses attached to a chain; but Ben still knew he'd lucked out, finding a good wife, a good mother for his children, in an age of strident man-eating Amazons with masculine brains.

The twins were restless, Ron and Pete, age eleven.

They squirmed in their seats. A normal response. To an effeminate film.

Musicals, Benjamin Staner thought, watching the bare-chested male dancers cavort on the screen: family entertainment infested with queers.

And not just queers, but repulsive, swishy, effeminate queers. The hopeless variety. Not like Nick.

Staner smiled as he thought of Nick. He really liked Nick; he liked him as a person, as a pal, the way one normal guy liked another. He pictured Nick straight, with a family, as a typical dad. Romping with his kids in the rumpus room. Laughing with a bunch of his straight jock buddies in a bar, like guys in a beer commercial. It was easy to picture Nick like that. He pictured Nick coming home from work in a three-piece suit, rushing in to hug and kiss his pregnant wife. He pictured Nick on a family picnic, he saw him strolling with his pretty devoted wife on a beach at sunset where similar couples strolled. He imagined Nick at peace, content at last, smiling the kind of smile that said more than words of gratitude could ever say. Benjamin Staner felt his eyes grow damp.

Thank you, God, he thought, for getting rid of that fruit attorney.

52

"**T**hey found his body down on the beach,"
Scott told Jeff on the phone that after-
noon. "He'd been stabbed fifteen times.
Multilated."

Scott sat in the dark Ocean Park living room, his
eyes red from crying, an empty fifth of Jim Beam on
the table in front of him. Ed the writer was talking to
Paul at the front door. He was red-eyed, too, and
wanted to see Scott. Paul was telling him to fuck off.

"Do they know who did it?" Jeff said, Dewey listening over his shoulder. Carlos was raving dementedly
in the kitchen, falling into things, loaded on PCP.

"They said he was down there cruising," Scott
answered. "They said he probably just cruised the
wrong guy. But that's bullshit. We didn't step out on
each other. I know that beyond any doubt."

"Then who?" Jeff said.

Scott told him about Brundl, about Greg Stovey's
allegation, and Randy's confrontation with the DA.

"Jesus, you think Brundl did it?" Jeff said.

"I don't know," Scott said. "Maybe some of his cop
friends helped. Or maybe he hired somebody else to
do it. But it was him."

"Christ." Jeff was stunned. "What about Nick?" he
finally said.

"That looks bad."

Carlos screamed in the kitchen—a shrill, terrified
scream—as angel dust demons attacked him. Jeff

covered his ear as Soctt told him about Benjamin Staner. "Oh, fuck," Jeff said more than once as he listened.

After he hung up, Jeff told Dewey what Scott had said.

"Micro-*what*?" Dewey looked incredulous.

"It's brain surgery. Some kind of brain surgery."

"Oh, Jesus."

Jeff and Dewey exchanged looks, both thinking the same thing. Through the window they watched Carlos lurch across the veranda, naked and foaming at the mouth, a machete in his hand. He was going to kill his dog. The dog saw him coming and took off. So did Jeff and Dewey.

Twelve hours later they were climbing from a Cessna at a small airfield in a surburb of L.A. They didn't have much luggage, just a couple of knapsacks and a heavy canvas satchel that looked like it could have held some sort of firearm.

53

Scott tore a centerfold from a *Drummer* magazine, "America's Mag for the Macho Male," and drew a map of Atascadero State Hospital on the back as Jeff and Dewey watched. Victor was in the kitchen, whistling, fixing dinner.

Victor had been glad to help when Jeff called. He wasn't pissed off about what had happened. He'd been very concerned. "Besides," he told Jeff, "it was all for the best, my brother finding out I was gay and everything. Now I don't have to fake it anymore. Plus getting evicted on account of the neighbors complaining about naked guys was a blessing in disguise. I found *this* place for twenty-five-bucks-a-month cheaper."

It was a cottage in Mount Washington on a large overgrown lot. Hedges hid the windows and the nearest neighbors were old and deaf.

"Here's the entrance," Scott indicated the map. "Here's the reception area. Here's where the AA meeting is." He drew another row of buildings. "Nick should be in this building here. This is where they put you if they're going to do a closed-circuit observation routine. Once you're on the grounds, you'll need to get a set of keys."

"Do they check you very closely," Jeff said, "if you're just going to the AA meeting?"

"I don't think they check you at all." Scott still

looked bad. His eyes had put on about ten years. "Dress square. Wear a sport coat or something."

Jeff and Dewey looked at each other. Dewey indicated the canvas satchel. "I don't think that's going to be too useful here. This looks like a pistol situation to me."

Scott suddenly buried his face in his hands and groaned. Jeff was sure Scott was about to start sobbing.

Instead, he looked up at Dewey. "Okay," he said coldly, "I've helped you, now you can help me."

"What did you have in mind?"

"I need a gun." Scott ground his teeth.

Dewey sighed. "You don't need a gun. You're a young hotshot lawyer with a big future. You don't want to fuck it up now."

Scott glanced at the canvas satchel. "Look, I know you guys have guns. Let me borrow one of them. I only need it for about a day. I'll bring it back tomorrow." Scott's face was twisted with hate.

Jeff couldn't take it. He went into the kitchen, where Victor was boiling spaghetti and singing an old Donna Summer song under his breath. When he saw Jeff, he went into a campy go-go dancer routine that never failed to crack Jeff up.

Jeff smiled. He really loved Victor. It made him feel sad to realize it was never going to be like it had been: he and Victor would never talk for hours on the phone again, about nothing, just bullshit and gossip and trash, they'd never laugh till their guts ached again.

"Hey, Victor—"

Victor quit dancing. "What, babe?"

"You got a sport coat I can borrow?"

54

Nick was coming back from his evening bath when the lispy black psych tech mentioned the surgery. "I don't know what it is, they stick some wire in your brain. It's no big deal. It's not like a lobotomy. You still have your memory and all that."

Despite a high dose of Haldol, Nick found this information disturbing. "What are you talking about?"

"I just didn't want you to worry when you found out. One guy last year went totally berserk. It's an opportunity, really, for a whole new life. How many people have that kind of choice?"

Nick suddenly felt more clearheaded than he had in a long time.

Around three that morning, Nick managed to loosen the screws in the lighting fixture in the ceiling of his room. He took out the fixture and, with great difficulty, crawled through the hole. He worked his way through the crawl space, reaching a ventilation grille at the end of the building. He saw the stars through the grille. He heard the crickets and smelled the jasmine in the chill night air.

He was still trying to kick out the grille two hours later when, with considerable difficulty, the guards managed to pull him from the crawl space.

Nick was taken to a new room and strapped to the bed. Staner came to see him around nine that morning, along with four other physicians who were planning to observe the surgery. Nick strained and shouted, "You goddamn fuck! I trusted you! You fuckin' piece of shit—"

A nurse gave Nick a shot that turned him to jelly.

The doctors conferred.

Nick's tongue lopped out of his mouth.

A doctor with a weak chin said, "I'd like to take a look at his genitals."

Staner made a gesture that said, Be my guest.

The doctor with the weak chin lifted Nick's gown. "Hmm," he said.

55

It was raining hard by the time Jeff and Dewey reached San Luis Obispo. The visibility was so bad they nearly missed the Atascadero turnoff.

The '56 Chevy Nomad leaked, the rubber around its windows rotted out. The tuck and roll upholstery stank, and the red temperature light was flashing.

"What do we do if this thing dies on us?" Jeff scrunched around in Victor's plaid sport coat, two sizes too small for him.

"It's not going to," Dewey said at the wheel, looking even dorkier than Jeff in Victor's ten-year-old rust-colored leisure suit. He swerved up the tree-lined road that led into the hospital parking lot.

Jeff felt the cold barrel of the .38 against his groin. Dewey had a .45 stuck in his belt. He'd got the guns from the same guy who'd sold them the Nomad, an old biker in the City of Commerce. The guy had practically creamed when he'd seen the MP5 submachine gun, but Dewey had been unwilling to trade it. Now he wished he had. What if the car wouldn't start when they were ready to go?

They parked in the lot and dashed through the rain to the brightly lit glass-fronted reception building. People turned to look at them as they pushed through the doors.

The reception area was crowded. There were nurses, a couple of guards, but mostly there were the guys, about twenty regular fellas in polyester sport coats, smoking cigarettes and laughing robustly, trying hard to bring a sense of healthy joy to the grim institution. One of them came over, a genial gray-haired fella with a broad Harry Von Zell grin. "Hi, I'm Bob." He stuck out his hand. "I take it you fellas are here for the AA meeting."

"Yes." Dewey shook Bob's hand. "I'm Jack."

"I'm Pete," Jeff said, also shaking Bob's hand.

"Well, it's always good to see new faces," Bob said with boisterous good cheer. "How long do you fellas have?"

"What do you mean?" Dewey said.

"Sobriety. When did you have your last drink?"

"A long time ago," Dewey said. "A couple years ago. I don't drink."

Bob looked slightly puzzled, but he grinned again. "Well, I'll tell you, Jack, that's the name of the game!" He looked at Jeff. "How about you, pal?"

"I don't know. I think I had a beer day before yesterday."

"But ya don't know, huh?" Bob laughed heartily. "Well, that's par for the course. Stick around till the fog lifts, Pete. And believe me, we know how it is, we've all been through what you're going through right now."

Bob waved to the other guys. "Come on," he said to Jeff and Dewey, "I'll introduce you around."

Jeff and Dewey went along, shaking hands and making small talk with the other fellas. Eventually, the group began moving up a corridor toward a grilled security entrance. Jeff's heart was pounding.

"Were you into drugs, too?" a younger guy asked Jeff.

"Yeah, anything I could get my hands on." He glanced nervously at Dewey.

Thunder boomed as they reached the grilled doors. A guard buzzed them through the first door. After it slammed shut, he buzzed them through the second.

Just like the baths, Jeff thought. He jumped when Bob slapped him on the shoulder.

"The first few days are always the roughest, Pete. You still have the craving, don't you?"

"Yeah, I do," Jeff said. "I'd give my left nut for a pint of Jack Daniel's right now."

Bob looked mildly disturbed, but laughed robustly as the group reached an exterior door. "Well, you're in the right place, Pete! Just keep coming back!"

The rain was coming down hard, inundating the pink and lemon-yellow buildings in the distance. Several men opened umbrellas.

The single guard accompanying the group was hanging back, unwilling to brave the rain. Good. Jeff and Dewey exchanged looks as the first men took off.

"Watch your step, Jack," Bob said to Dewey. "That concrete gets mighty slippery."

Jeff and Dewey fumbled with their jackets to make sure they'd be the last.

They braced themselves and took off, following the last of the other men up a sidewalk that went around the corner of a lemon-yellow building. They saw a pink building up ahead, the last of the men ducking through the door. Abruptly, Jeff and Dewey cut off the sidewalk, ducking behind some bushes near the lemon-yellow building.

"Is that everybody?" they heard a man say.

"Guess so." A door closed, the lock clicking over.

Twenty minutes later Bob looked around the meeting room. A patient was speaking, a man with a gray ponytail and unsettling blue eyes. "My wife and I killed seven girls and dumped their bodies in the desert," he said. "But I didn't have to pick up that first drink."

Bob wondered what had happened to Jack and Pete. They'd chickened out, he decided. That happened with newcomers. Perhaps just as well. This was not the most inspiring speaker Bob had ever heard.

* * *

Jeff and Dewey crouched in the bushes across from the pink building Scott had indicated on the map. They were soaked, Jeff's teeth chattering. "This is fucked," Jeff said.

"Easy."

"Shit. We should've brought raincoats."

Dewey snorted. "We should've just written this punk off as a lost cause. I must be out of my fuckin' mind."

At that moment Jeff liked Dewey more than he ever had. Although Dewey could be a real prick at times, when it came to helping a friend he had guts and a kind of purity that was almost embarrassing. The only reason he was doing this, Jeff knew, was because he loved Nick, too.

Finally, the door in the pink building opened. Jeff and Dewey got ready as two figures stepped out, buttoning their raincoats. One was using a key to lock the door when Jeff and Dewey grabbed both of them from behind.

Dewey slammed the weak-chinned doctor against the pink wall, holding the .45 to the back of his neck. Jeff shoved Benjamin Staner against the door, placing the .38 under his chin.

"All right," Jeff said to the distinguished-looking physician. "You're going to take us to Nick Krieger."

"Don't know him." Staner's heart was racing, but his voice was calm.

Dewey pushed the weak-chinned doctor's face into the wall. "Look, you fucking dicks, we know you know who he is. You're going to take us to his room and unlock the door."

If he weren't the one involved, Staner couldn't help thinking, this might be quite fascinating. "We're just consultants," he said smoothly. "We don't know every patient in the hospital."

But the weak-chinned doctor was crumbling. "Maybe we should do what they want, Dr. Staner."

"Staner?" Jeff ripped open Staner's raincoat and saw his nameplate. "This is the guy! This is the fucking guy!" Jeff drilled Staner with a look of pure hate. "Open the fuckin' door."

Suddenly the weak-chinned doctor started screaming, but not for long. Dewey smashed his head with the butt of the .45. He slumped to the steps, rain spattering the blood in his hair.

Jeff pushed Staner against the door. "Get out your fuckin' keys!"

"He's not *in* there," Staner said brittlely, his calm gone.

"Where is he?"

"Over there." Staner looked off at a yellow building in the distance.

Jeff looked in Staner's green eyes. "If you're shitting us—"

"I'm not shitting you," Staner said snidely.

Jeff looked at Dewey. "Let's go," Dewey said.

It was a long way off. They slogged across the lawn, the rain passing over them in sheets. Reaching the building, they could see through its glass doors. The interior was white, brightly lit, like a regular hospital.

Entering, they startled an old nurse with a leathery face. Dewey aimed his gun at her. She dropped her charts.

"Which room?" Jeff said to Staner.

"Up there." He indicated a side corridor.

Dewey covered the nurse. "Come on, honey."

They went up the side corridor, past a nurse's station. It was empty. They saw another nurse going from one room to another, but she didn't see them.

"In there," Staner said as they reached the last room. The door was open. It was an ordinary white hospital room. A curtain hid the bed.

Jeff pushed Staner into the room, Dewey bringing in the nurse. Covering Staner, Jeff pulled back the curtain.

Nick was sleeping. There was an IV in his arm. His mouth was open, his eyelids red and swollen. His head was shaved.

There were no bandages, just little stitched knots smeared with translucent orange antiseptic about an inch above either ear.

Dewey cringed. "Oh, goddamm it."

Jeff began trembling, his .38 pressed behind Staner's ear.

Staner looked at Jeff out of the corner of his eye. He knew who the young man was and could not resist a smirk. "You're too late, Jeff," Benjamin Staner said.

When the first shot went off, the old nurse shrieked and Nick opened his eyes. The shot was deafening, the nurse's shriek excruciating—like cat claws shredding a baby's skin. She quit shrieking after the second shot.

Jeff pumped all six rounds point-blank into Staner's head. The doctor's skull disintegrated, his brains flying everywhere, sticking to the wall, to the old nurse's uniform, like bloody Kleenex. When Staner finally dropped to the floor, he was just a body, there wasn't any head.

Dewey was still cringing, covering his ears, when he saw Nick trying to sit up. Jeff was shaking like an epileptic going into a fit. Dewey grabbed Jeff and slapped him hard across the face. "Jeff! Come on, Jeff!"

Jeff looked at Staner's body and threw up the Whopper he'd wolfed down in Santa Maria a few hours before.

Dewey removed the IV and tried to help Nick up. Nick tried to talk but the syllables came out jumbled.

"Help me, Jeff!" Dewey yelled. "For Christ sake—"

Jeff went to Nick and helped him to his feet. Nick reeked of antiseptic, his mouth was cruddy, his breath foul. Jeff caught his eye for a moment, and Nick tried to speak again, but couldn't. But he was still there, Jeff saw. In his eyes, even though they were red and unfocused, he was there.

Dewey checked the corridor. Then he scooped up Staner's keys and grabbed the old nurse by the arm. She was a rigid mummy now. "Okay, honey bunch," Dewey said to her, "you're going to show us the way out." She made a funny little sound in the back of her throat.

Patients peered from their rooms as Jeff helped Nick into the corridor, Dewey covering the old nurse. Another nurse was on the phone in the nurse's station. She ducked below view when she saw Dewey holding a gun to her co-worker's head.

The nurse used Staner's keys to unlock a door at the end of the corridor. It led to a stairwell. They were going down the stairs when the alarms went off.

At the bottom of the stairs, she unlocked another door; it led to the parking lot. They stepped out into the pouring rain and locked the door leaving the old nurse there. Dewey helped Jeff with Nick, who was soon drenched, the wind blowing back his hospital gown. Search beams were combing the grounds behind them as they reached the Nomad and helped Nick in the back. Dewey took the wheel. The engine started on the first try. They tore out as a search beam slashed across the lot.

Dewey saw flashing red-and-blue lights, cops closing off the tree-lined exit road. He drove off the road, careening through a muddy picnic area, plowing through a chain-linked fence. He roared past the boarded-up pastel tract homes, past the abandoned church, until he reached a winding two-lane road that led to another two-lane road that eventually went south. They'd studied the map in advance, certain the highway patrol would be out in force on 101.

In the backseat Nick was soaked and shaking. Jeff removed Nick's hospital gown and wrapped a heavy wool blanket around him. For the next five hours he held Nick, cradled him, trying to keep him warm. He rubbed Nick's arm through the blanket and kissed his cold shaved head.

They were going up a hill near Lake Cachuma when the engine died. Dewey got it started again, but he knew the car was doomed. "Don't worry," he said, though he was sweating. "I know a guy who's a doctor. He lives near Goleta. He's cool."

56

The Nomad coasted to a dead halt in front of Chet's house, a glass and wood architectural showplace set in a grove of trees on a cliff overlooking the Pacific, north of Santa Barbara. Chet lived there with his wife, Joyce, a professor at UCSB. Chet was an orthopedic surgeon at a local Catholic hospital. Dewey knew him from the mid-seventies, when Chet had worked his way through medical school selling drugs. Since then, he'd settled down quite a bit, and seeing Dewey, a known fugitive, at his door at three A.M., was an unwelcome stab from the past. But when he saw Nick, he let them in.

"He needs to be hospitalized immediately," Chet said. Nick lay trembling on the bed in the guest room, his teeth chattering violently. Rain beat against the plate-glass window.

"That's not possible," Dewey said.

Chet was stocky, prematurely gray, and balding. His manner normally was low-key. Joyce watched from the bedroom across the hall, eager to draw Chet aside and ask him what was going on.

"He's undergone neurosurgery," Chet said

"They stuck some hot wires in his brain at Atascadero," Dewey said, "to try to burn out his being gay. We just busted him out."

"Dear Lord." Chet felt Nick's forehead and took his pulse. Nick looked like a sick dog that had been left out in a storm to die. "Let me call the hospital—"

"Chet, we can't go to a hospital."

"I don't see any alternative."

"Chet," Dewey said without relish, "Memorial Day, 1975."

Chet closed his eyes and sighed, almost with relief, as though he'd been expecting Dewey to mention this eventually, as though it were the real reason he'd let them in at all.

Joyce scowled in the doorway. "Honey," she said, "what the hell is going on?"

"You'd better get dressed," Chet said to her. "I'm going to need some things from the office."

Jeff sat in a straight-back chair by the door, his heart still pounding. His shirt was splotched with blood. He looked at Chet. Chet's forehead was shiny with sweat. Jeff wondered what had happened on Memorial Day 1975.

From his bed in the guest room Nick watched Joyce as she watered the potted plants out on the deck. There was something about her he really liked, a quality he hadn't encountered in many women. In her mid-thirties, she had an air of mellow sensuality Nick usually associated with European actresses, women who could be sultry without becoming camp. She certainly wasn't like the vacuous blond centerfolds you saw strutting around L.A.

Of course the guys in L.A. were just as bad. Vacuous plastic hunks. People in L.A. were disgusting anyway. They went around with their sex organs in wheelbarrows, huge balloon cunts and pricks attached to brains the size of a pea. And their hearts were a speck.

Especially the guys. Guys. It seemed like a long time ago.

Nick thought about different men he'd been with, random images flashing through his mind. But he felt as if he were looking at dirty pictures over another guy's shoulder. Maybe the other guy was turned on by the pictures, but Nick wasn't. He stared at them and saw himself in them, but it meant nothing. It was like being paralyzed from the neck down and staring at his legs.

He thought about Jeff. He looked at *those* pictures. He tried to remember how it felt when those things happened. The harder he tried, the more it began to feel as if his brain was going to split in two.

He looked up as Chet and Jeff came in.

"Well, you're awake," Chet said. "How do you feel?"

"I've got a headache."

Though he still felt a little ragged himself, Jeff sat down on the edge of the bed and took Nick's hand. It tore his heart out when Nick cringed and pulled away.

If Chet noticed, he ignored it. "You're going to have headaches for a while, Nick. You might as well learn to live with them."

"Sure, fine, Doc. But in the meantime, why don't you give me a fuckin' Percodan before I go nuts, okay?"

"Percodan?" Chet said with mock indignation. "What do you want? To get well or high?"

"Right now, both."

Jeff went back to the living room, upset over Nick's rebuff. Maybe he was just being overly sensitive.

Dewey was on the phone, mad. "Right," he said with astonishing bitterness. "I knew I could count on you, you rancid fuck!" He slammed down the receiver and looked at Jeff. He didn't have to say it, but he did anyway. "We got problems, man."

Jeff knew they did. They'd lost their return flight to Mexico. With every cop in the state looking for them, the pilot got scared and took off.

They had another problem, too. They were broke.

Chet stepped from the bedroom, closing the door behind him.

"So what do you think?" Dewey said.

Chet measured his words carefully. "Frankly, moral considerations aside, Staner was an excellent surgeon. I don't forsee any complications in that respect."

"What about his headaches?" Jeff said.

"Oh, well, a lot of that's psychosomatic. It's natural, when a patient knows he's undergone neurosurgery, to believe his head *should* ache afterward."

"What about his intelligence ability?" Dewey said. "Is he going to be impaired?"

Chet smiled faintly. "You tell me," he said, "you knew him prior to surgery. But I'd assume Nick never possessed what one might describe as a brilliant intellectual mind. Correct me if I'm wrong," Chet said jokingly, "but the chances of his ever being interviewed on PBS were rather remote." He laughed softly at his own remark. "I'd say he seems generally cognizant of his immediate surroundings. I haven't detected any significant deterioration so far. Have you?"

"No," Dewey said. He didn't like Chet's attitude. Neither did Jeff.

Jeff sat down on the sofa, staring at the medical journal on the coffee table. It was folded open to an article, "Homosexuality: Psychosurgical Cures. A Preliminary Report." By Benjamin Staner.

"Objectively speaking," Chet said, indicating the article, "it's really rather fascinating—"

Jeff stared at the type on the page, and for perhaps the thousandth time since it had happened, he heard the gun go off and saw Staner's brains splatter the old nurse's white uniform; he heard her shriek and felt a surge of nausea.

"The site of the micro-coagulation," Chet said, "is extremely minute. Rather like a tiny pinprick on either side of the hypothalamus. Simply a matter of severing infinitesimal connections."

Jeff looked out the window at the pine trees rustling in the breeze, at the bright-blue ocean. He tried to force himself back into the present. "So is he gonna be asexual or what?"

"Frankly, Jeff, I don't know," Chet said. "I suspect the best we can hope for is that the surgery has in fact been successful."

Jeff glared at Chet. "What the fuck does that mean?"

"All I'm telling you is that there's a very good chance that if Nick's sex drive returns at all, it's going to express itself along heterosexual lines. The 'gay connections,' so to speak, have been severed."

"Severed?" Jeff walked over to the window. "How do you know? I mean, what the fuck." Jeff was trembling with rage.

"Look, Jeff, I think it goes without saying I don't condone this sort of thing. It's a moral atrocity. Whatever one may feel about certain excessive aspects of the so-called gay life-style, there's a great deal of evidence that homosexuality is in fact biologically natural. I find the idea of forcibly reordering someone's sexual orientation totally abhorrent. It smacks of fascism, there's no getting around it. But the fact is, it may be possible."

Jeff stared at the ocean. "Thanks for your opinion, Doctor."

"Well, you know, Jeff," Chet said with a vaguely snide tone of voice that reminded Jeff of Staner, "there are worse things than being straight."

57

The Atascadero story was big news for several days. Benjamin Staner was described as a gifted medical pioneer and beloved family man. That he'd taken a special interest in the case of a hardened sociopath like Nick Krieger was cited as further evidence of his humanity. The brain-surgery rumors were vehemently denied.

The manhunt for the fugitives was intense. Police in San Francisco swept a notorious cruising park where a man matching Dewey's description had been seen. Cops in San Diego burst in on three men having sex in a motel room after the clerk made a positive ID from the fugitives' photos. When these and other leads proved false, the story began to fade, except for periodic statements from frustrated law-enforcement officials, stating that a capture of the fugitives was "imminent."

The fugitives stayed in the house, watching TV.

Nick's physical recovery was rapid. Except for the headaches, he seemed to be fine. Of course, there was one other problem that might be considered physical, but nobody had the courage to ask him about it.

He showed no signs of mental impairment, no loss of memory. Maybe Chet was right: it was a relatively minor neurosurgical process leaving all of Nick's capacities intact except one. Burned cells now blocked the microscopic channels of desire.

In some ways Jeff loved Nick more during those

weeks at Chet's than he ever had. He felt a kind of tenderness toward Nick, a protectiveness, that was made even more acute by the fact that he couldn't show it, at least not in the way he wanted to. It wasn't the absence of sex that was painful. He couldn't even touch Nick. More than anything he just wanted to hold him, but he sensed that he shouldn't try to, that Nick was too raw, too confused. He knew that he had to leave Nick alone.

One afternoon, Jeff watched Nick sitting out on the deck by himself. The sun was bright, but it was cold and Nick was bundled up. A knit cap Joyce had given him covered the scars on his prickly head. He looked old, Jeff thought, like an old man sitting in the sun. And Jeff wondered if, in some other context, they might have grown old together. Or if, in any way, they still could. More than anything he wondered if Nick still cared about him. Or if, really, he ever had. A three-day weekend of insanity, that was all they'd really shared, wasn't it? Was everything else just in his mind?

Nick got shitty with Jeff at times. He could turn hostile for no apparent reason. The worst time was when Nick, Jeff, and Dewey were eating lunch out on the deck and Joyce came out in skimpy running clothes. She smiled—though her smiles were becoming increasingly brittle—and went down to the beach, where she did stretching exercises.

Nick watched her as he munched his sandwich. Dewey sensed from Nick's attitude what was coming, but saw no way to stop it.

"Not bad," Nick said, meaning Joyce.

"Huh?" Jeff said, not catching on.

"That is what I call a hot bod." Nick was strident, posturing, a terrible pain just below the surface.

"You like it, huh?" Jeff said.

"Yeah. Yeah, I think I do." He had a swaggering attitude, as if he was aping, or trying out, a macho straight persona.

"Good," Jeff said. "That's fine. Great."

"Yeah, I think she's hot for me too."

"Do you?" Jeff looked at his plate.

"Yeah, yeah, I do. In fact, it might be fun to find out what a *real* woman's like for a change. As opposed to a bad imitation, like certain people I could mention, but I—"

Jeff threw his sandwich in Nick's face, exploding in bitter rage. "You *ass*hole—"

Nick grabbed for Jeff across the table. Jeff took off running. Nick took off after him, chasing him down to the beach.

He caught Jeff and threw him to the ground, but Dewey pulled him off before he could do any real damage.

"He's confused," Dewey told Jeff later. "He didn't mean anything. Really."

"Yeah, I know," Jeff said. "I didn't mean anything either. Nobody meant anything at all."

That night Chet and Joyce had a fight. Jeff and Dewey heard it through the walls.

"It's not my fault you ruined your life," she screamed. He had evidently told her about Memorial Day, 1975. Doors slammed as she ran from the house in tears, Chet going after her, spitting out clenched obscenities.

Dewey sighed, looking at Jeff in the single bed set at a right angle to his. "You know, I think it may be time to move on."

Jeff agreed. But where?

Mexico was out. Carlos, they'd learned, had been gunned down by the federales a few days after they'd left. Dewey was sure their role in the Club Paradise robbery was now known. "I'm afraid they're gonna consider us bad for tourism," he said.

Victor was out, he was under surveillance. Scott was still in L.A., but the last they'd heard, he was still obsessed with the idea of killing Brundl.

"If we had a lot of money," Jeff said, "that would pretty much solve all our problems, wouldn't it?"

Dewey yawned. "Let me put it this way. Yeah."

"What about, say, half a million?"

Dewey punched out his cigarette and rolled over. "Jeff, I've been racking my brains to come up with something."

"So have I."

"What you guys should've done was take that hit. You'd have been heroes to gay America by now."

"You're probably right. But it's too late now."

Dewey had checked. The contract had gone to an ex-Green Beret transsexual with Agent Orange leukemia and nothing to lose.

"Anyway," Jeff said, "I wasn't thinking of a hit."

Dewey pulled up the blanket and began to doze off. But he sat up and reached for his cigarettes when Jeff told him what he had in mind.

58

"Oh, Harvey, its beautiful!" Robbie studied himself in the three-panel mirror, adjusting the supple olive-green leather pouch hooked rakishly to his belt. "It's just what I've always wanted. A Gucci colostomy bag!"

He threw his arms around Harvey and gave him a big moist kiss.

"I'm glad you like it," Harvey said as the phone rang. The funny thing was, he really meant it. Sure, he'd picked up Robbie's medical bills initially just to keep the kid's mouth shut, but something else had happened somewhere along the line. It might be too soon to call it love, but whatever it was, it gave Harvey a warm glow he hadn't known since his cocker spaniel ate poisoned hamburger when he was ten.

He took the call. "Yes?"

"Harvey? This is Jeff Gifford."

Harvey nearly dropped the phone. "Jeff, good Lord. Where are you, you poor boy?"

Jeff didn't waste words. "Harvey, Nick and I want to make a deal for the rights to our story. Can you negotiate it?"

This was too much. Could he negotiate it? With Michael salivating? "That's a stiff order, Jeff. Considering."

"Look, we know you tried to buy Nick's story for Michael," Jeff said.

"That was a while ago, Jeff. A lot's happened. I'm not sure Michael's still interested."

"Don't jerk me around, Harvey. We want five hundred thousand. For exclusive rights."

"You have delusions of grandeur, Jeff."

"Harvey, I know what it's worth. Books, a movie, paperback rights. I know about all that crap. I was going to be an agent, remember?"

"Shop around, Jeff. I think you'll find your story plunged in value with that Atascadero episode. Blowing a distinguished doctor's head off—hard to play that for sympathy, if you know what I mean."

"You'll find a way. Five hundred thousand. Firm."

"Let me talk to Michael."

"I'll call back this evening. Tell your service to put me through."

"Will do, kiddo. Talk to you then."

Harvey called Michael at the Burbank Studios.

"Oh, my God," Michael said. "This is too rich, Harvey. Too rich and too perfect."

When Jeff called Harvey that evening, Harvey told him, "Two hundred thousand."

They settled on three.

"In cash. Small bills. Tomorrow night. Ten o'clock." Jeff told him where.

"Jesus Christ, Jeff. Tomorrow's Sunday. It's gonna be a madhouse out there."

"That's the idea."

Harvey hesitated. "Okay, Jeff," he said finally. "We'll be there. You sign the papers, we'll give you the money. We'll both be happy."

When Jeff hung up, Dewey said, "What do you think?"

"I don't think anything," Jeff said. "They want it. They're willing to pay for it. That's the way Hollywood works."

"You'd have made a good agent, Jeff," Dewey said. But he seemed preoccupied.

Jeff looked at Nick, stretched out on the sofa. Nick still wasn't too keen about the idea of Michael Reed mutilating his life but had finally agreed with Jeff and Dewey that if Michael didn't do it, somebody else would. Anyway, the money was the main thing now.

Nick looked good with his beard, which had grown in more quickly than Dewey and Jeff's. But they all figured nobody would recognize them; it would be relatively safe. At least that was what Dewey said. It was his favorite place for this sort of transaction. Nothing could happen in a crowd.

"So how do you feel?" Jeff said to Nick.

"Excited." Nick yawned. "I've never been to Americanaland before."

"There's a first time for everything," Jeff said.

59

Sunday morning Nick read the *L.A. Times* in bed. Toward the back of the Calendar section he noticed an Americanaland ad. The Payne Family—those icons of wholesome American values—was opening there tonight. When Dewey came in, Nick showed him the ad. "Maybe we ought to go early and catch the show."

Dewey snorted. "Yeah, right." He looked at the family portrait: three rows, encompassing four bouffanted, blow-dried generations, beaming at the camera with insipid smiles and dead eyes. The centerpiece was Bud, the blond toupeed dad of the family, an arm around each of the beloved Breck Girl twins.

"It's sad, in a way," Dewey said. "A bunch of robots. Except that guy at the end." He indicated an unctuously pretty young man. "I'll bet anything he grows up to be a fruit. Which would sure frost Bud, seeing how much he hates fags. I heard him on some religious show once, talking about how Jesus could remove the desire to . . . you know—"

Dewey stopped in embarrassment when he realized what he was saying. Nick had turned back to the paper, avoiding Dewey's eyes.

Flustered and angry, Dewey excused himself. "I've got to get some breakfast."

As soon as Dewey left, Nick put down the paper and stared at the wall. He felt a wave of depression and futility. As he had many times in recent days, he looked at the .38 resting on the dresser. He imagined getting up, walking to the dresser, putting the gun in his mouth, and pulling the trigger. He imagined Joyce sobbing as she scrubbed his blood from the walls.

He didn't know what he felt anymore. He still liked Dewey, that hadn't changed. Dewey was his friend. And he appreciated the risks Jeff had taken on his behalf—at least he did intellectually. But on a visceral level there were times when Jeff drove him right up the wall, and he didn't know why. There were times when Jeff made him sick, and he wished Jeff was dead. But there were also times when he missed Jeff so much he thought he'd go crazy, when he felt as if Jeff *was* dead, even though he was only in the next room.

Fuck it, Nick decided. It was definitely not a day for rumination. He got up to take a leak.

Nick jumped when he opened the bathroom door. Jeff was already there, drying off from a shower. Nick looked at the body he remembered fantasizing about when he'd been in county jail. He looked in Jeff's blue eyes.

"Sorry. I didn't know you were in here."

Jeff looked at Nick, at his body, at his face, his brown eyes. He wanted to touch Nick's black beard, he wanted to kiss him so bad. He wanted to put his arms around Nick, but Nick backed out the door before he could.

Around noon Dewey came back with a car, a blue '71 Malibu with a peeling vinyl roof that he'd stolen from the airport parking lot at Goleta. "It's been there awhile," he told Nick and Jeff. "Hopefully, they won't come back at least until tomorrow."

Late that afternoon, Dewey and Nick and Jeff got in the Malibu and drove away. Chet and Joyce were glad their part in the ordeal was over. Dewey had promised not to come back.

They reached the San Fernando Valley around seven, the traffic backed up because of a wreck. Dewey was driving, Nick in the middle. Jeff took gulps off a quart of Coors, trying to sooth his nerves without getting drunk.

They reached West Los Angeles. Nick looked better than he had in quite a while. He'd taken a nap before they'd left, and a Percodan, and he was in a cordial, almost genial mood. Even with Jeff. Then Dewey made a reference to Randy and Nick's mood turned dark.

Nick had never really reacted to Randy's murder. When Dewey had told him about it, he'd withdrawn into a kind of numb depression that was not really grief, nor anger. It had been as if he didn't dare give in to the rage he really felt; there'd been no way to express it. The same thing had happened when they'd heard about Brundl. Far from being investigated in connection with Randy's murder, Brundl had actually been named commander of the special task force set up to apprehend them. Jeff and Dewey had gone through the roof. Nick had gone to the guest room, taken two Percodan, and turned on the TV. Nick's only vague expression of anger came when Dewey told him about Scott's request for a gun so he could go after Brundl. "You should've given him one," Nick had said blandly, curled up in a blanket on the bed.

Dewey glanced at Nick now as they swept through the empty flat vistas near the Harbor Freeway and felt a terrible sadness. For Nick to lose what he'd lost seemed unbelievably cruel, since in a way it was all he'd had. The rest of his life was just shit jobs with no future, drudgery and exhaustion. He'd lived for sex, Dewey knew; it had been the only thing that kept him going.

They crossed the Orange County line. Nick played with the radio for a while. He found an old Jim Morrison song, then lost it. Finally he shut off the radio and leaned back, resting his head on Jeff's shoulder—a small gesture of trust and affection.

"Tired?" Jeff said, his voice unsteady.

"No," Nick said softly.

Then he took Jeff's hand. For a long time he seemed to study it, gently rubbing the veins and knuckles and fingers.

Finally, he kissed Jeff's hand and buried his face in Jeff's lap and sobbed.

The way Nick sobbed, his whole body shaking, made Jeff start to cry too. He rubbed Nick's shoulders, his back. Nick's cap came off, the scars on his prickly head showing in the freeway lights.

Dewey looked straight ahead. His eyes were wet too.

Sobbing, Nick kissed Jeff's crotch, his tears spotting the faded denim. Then he sat up and kissed Jeff hard on the mouth. "I love you," he said. "I love you so fucking much."

Nick kissed Jeff's neck and began unbuttoning Jeff's shirt. Tears rolled down Jeff's cheeks, glistening in his blond beard.

Nick kissed Jeff's chest, his stomach. Jeff moaned as Nick's hand closed over his crotch. Nick unbuttoned Jeff's Levi's and took out his hard cock. Nick bumped Dewey as he leaned over, nearly causing a wreck.

His face shiny with tears, Nick sucked Jeff's cock, breathing in Jeff's salty taste and odor. Jeff moaned, his knee brushing Nick's crotch. Nick was hard.

Jeff pulled Nick up and kissed him deeply, unbuttoning Nick's Levi's. Nick shuddered as Jeff reached inside. He groaned as Jeff bent down and sucked him.

Wiping tears from his eyes, Dewey stared at the freeway and the full yellow moon up ahead.

Jeff came first, involuntarily, excited by the pleasure he was giving Nick. Then Nick came too, in hard convulsive bursts. He cried out as a burning pain stabbed his groin, even as an excruciating joy flooded his brain. He closed his eyes and saw white.

In the peaceful space that followed, Nick and Jeff

held each other, gently fooling around, kissing, joking with Dewey, as mile after mile of streetlit Orange County suburbs slid by. But they pulled themselves together, stuck their cocks back in their pants, and checked their guns, when they saw the red concrete volcano looming up ahead against the black night sky.

~~~~~~~~~~~~~ **60**

The vast parking lot was nearly full. Attendants directed Dewey along lanes that led farther and farther away from the park entrance. "This is fucked," he said, and made a turn up the last aisle and doubled back.

Near the western train-station entrance, Dewey caught a family backing out in a station wagon, a little kid puking candy out the rear window. Dewey grabbed the space and cut the engine. "Okay." He looked at his watch. "It's fifteen to ten."

They had a clear view of the entrance turnstiles. The silver-bullet train shot by overhead on its elevated tracks. Everything seemed normal. An average Sunday night crowd: hordes of Dacron tourists, families, teenage couples, everyone as mundane and boring as could be. Two security guards in Cavalry uniforms stood near the information booth. They were old and looked bored. Just beyond the turnstiles, the beloved Americanaland Rat skipped around with its hands on its bulbous white-costume hips, greeting the delighted new arrivals.

Nick checked his Levi's jacket to make sure it covered his .38. Jeff zipped up his red windbreaker. "Let's go," Nick said.

He and Jeff got out. Dewey was going to stay in the car. When he saw them come out, he'd pull up.

Nick leaned down to Dewey. He wanted to kiss

278

Dewey badly, but a family was walking by. "If we're not back by ten-thirty, call the cops."

It was a dumb joke, but Dewey smiled away. It was just the kind of dumb joke Nick would make at his best.

Dewey watched Nick and Jeff buy their tickets. He watched them go through the turnstile, the white Rat greeting them with a jaunty cartoon-style salute. Jeff returned the salute. Dewey watched them disappear into the crowd.

Nick and Jeff walked up the Anytown Promenade, past the dementedly quaint gingerbread buildings. A ragtime piano tinkled. The smell of fresh popcorn and taffy filled the air. Jeff felt oddly reassured. He'd been here a lot as a kid. Even though it looked different now—much brighter and harsher, more obviously fake—it still brought back memories of an innocent childhood age, before sex, when den mothers baked apple pies and dads knew best. Jeff could still recall those long, hot summer nights when the family had gathered in front of the Magnavox to watch the Americana Sho<u>w</u>. For years he'd been lost in that fantasy world, his sense of wonder, of right and wrong, derived more from the Americana cartoons than from anything he ever heard in Sunday school.

His sense of poignance too. He still got misty-eyed when he thought about Butterfly, whose wings were burned off just as he emerged from his painful cocoon. Jeff's first moment of real terror surely came from the Halloween attack of the Trolls. His first sense of guilt had no doubt been instilled by the prissy, scolding blue Hornet. Though he knew it was silly, his skin still crawled when he thought of the cute little boy who disobeyed his parents and got stung. His head had swollen up until it filled the whole room, until it was red and shiny and ready to pop, while the blue Hornet buzzed at the windows, shaking his finger, warning, This is what happens to bad little boys.

Jeff saw the Hornet now, up ahead by the talking Sitting Bull attraction, strutting and prancing for a group of little kids. He nudged Nick. "You'd better be good or you're going to get stung."

Nick finished the Hornet's famous rhyme, changing it the way a number of rebellious kids always had: "Shut up, you fuckin' Hornet, or I'll rip out your tongue."

Nick and Jeff laughed, passing the Hornet, as they moved on toward the square.

Dewey sat in the car, watching the crowd at the entrance, a ZZ Top song on the radio. He looked at the jaunty white Rat and smiled.

There was something kind of nauseating about the Rat. Something cloying and insipid. The red button eyes, the softheaded grin. Something disturbingly sexless. A eunuch Rat.

Dewey felt his guts lock. The eunuch Rat was speaking into a walkie-talkie.

Nick and Jeff were approaching the square when Jeff said, "I have to take a leak." He started for the men's room behind the Wounded Knee snackbar.

"Jeff, Christ—"

"Look, I drank a lot of beer. You want me to go in my pants? I'll be right back."

Jeff entered just as a group of dressed-up dads, probably there for the Payne show, came out.

Dewey got out of the Malibu and unlocked the trunk. He took out the canvas satchel and loosened the strap so he could wear it over his shoulder. He knew it might make him look fruity, like a dated unisex fag with a shoulder bag, but he'd just have to take that chance. He bought a ticket and entered the park.

*   *   *

Nick leaned against the lamppost, waiting for Jeff, trying to seem casual and relaxed.

A lovey-dovey couple drifted by. The girl's lips curled slightly when she noticed the paranoid glint in Nick's eyes, the sweat shining on his forehead. She whispered something to her boyfriend. He shot Nick a dirty look.

Nick felt someone else looking at him, and glanced over his shoulder. But there was no one. Just some little kids, laughing as the Hornet scolded them.

The men's room was immaculate. No glory-holes here. Jeff could still hear the ragtime piano as he took a leak. He thought he was alone until he heard someone tearing off toilet paper in one of the stalls.

He buttoned his jeans and washed his hands, checking himself out in the mirror. He looked good with his blond beard. He was drying his hands when he noticed the black furry feet under the stall door. The Skunk was taking a dump. Jeff smiled. The Skunk flushed the toilet.

A second after Jeff left, the Skunk stepped from the stall, his black plastic head in his hands. Officer Rodríguez didn't look so good. He'd been drinking more than ever lately, and it showed in his dull eyes. He put his bulbous head back on. In his costume pocket a walkie-talkie crackled.

"Jesus Christ, what took you so long?" Nick said to Jeff as they continued on toward the square. "People have been checking me out with a microscope."

"Nick, please don't get paranoid now." They cut past the Gay Nineties trolley. "It's okay. I know it."

"Yeah, you said the same thing at the baths."

"Yeah, but this is not the baths." Jeff looked up ahead at the Valhalla Citadel. "There they are."

Up on the Citadel balcony, bathed in pink and blue floodlights, Michael Reed and Harvey Berringer were waiting, right where they were supposed to be.

*   *   *

Dewey walked rapidly up the Anytown Promenade. He felt queazy and started to sweat. People seemed to be deliberately blocking his path. A fat woman in tight puce pants rammed into him. Her werewolf husband glared. He stumbled through a brigade of gurgling wheelchair spastic kids. A pregnant woman with a baby in a stroller lurched in front of him. A family of Mexicans seemed to leer. He pushed on toward the square, unzipping the satchel, slipping his hand over the pistol grip of the MP5.

Nick and Jeff approached the Valhalla gate. Jeff waved to Michael. Michael waved back.

Nick felt increasingly paranoid. He looked up at Michael and Harvey, their faces flat in the pink light, their expressions impossible to read. He scanned the rooftops of the surrounding buildings, especially those along the promenade. People screamed on the volcano snake ride. A wave of applause wafted through the air from the Futurama stage, where the Payne Family show was under way. Couples lingered at the Valhalla pond holding hands and nuzzling. Everything seemed perfectly all right, but Nick felt as if he was going to shit from fear at any second. "Let's get out of here—"

"Nick—"

"I mean it. Fuck the money."

"*Shit.*" Jeff was completely exasperated. "Three hundred thousand dollars! Are you saying fuck three hundred thousand dollars? Are you nuts?"

Nick's eyes darted over the crowd. "I don't like it. I don't like all these people, I don't like this place. Let's go."

Jeff couldn't see it. Everybody looked so bland and innocuous. Just everyday average Americans, anybody's neighbors, for Christ sake. "Come on," he said, and started toward the Valhalla gate.

Suddenly the sky above Valhalla exploded with fireworks. Red, white, and blue pinwheels cascaded

over the Citadel towers. Clusters of firecracker pops
and cracks reverberated through the night air. It was
a stupendous display—yet disordered, everything
going off at once, as if they were trying to make as
much noise as possible. As if they were trying to
mask the sound of something else.

Even Jeff knew it was wrong. He looked at Nick
and understood the fear in Nick's eyes. "Oh, man.
Oh, fuck."

From their vantage point on the balcony, Michael
and Harvey saw Dewey crossing the square before
Nick and Jeff did.

"Oh, dear," Michael said. "Here comes the other
one." He wasn't speaking to Harvey.

"Nick!"
Nick and Jeff whirled around, jolted to see Dewey.
His face was pale and shiny, his glasses fogged.
"It's a trap!"

Michael watched the three fugitives in the square
below. He sighed when they turned heel, heading
back toward the promenade. "I'm sorry. I had a
feeling it wasn't going to work."

"Don't worry," said the Orange County SWAT
commander, "We'll pick them up on the way out."

Michael's eyes flitted over the crouching commander, the dark-green uniform covering a Jeff Chandler
physique that was simply to die for, the rakish cap
pulled down over his brow like something straight
out of a Tom of Finland illustration. Michael fingered his Nikon. God, if he could only get a picture.

The SWAT commander flipped a signal to the men
who were covering the balcony stairwell. Taking care
not to be seen from below, they clattered down the
stairs. The commander slung his automatic rifle over
his shoulder and pressed his walkie-talkie to his thin-
lipped mouth. "Suspects are returning to the main
entrance—"

*   *   *

They were still on the promenade when Dewey spotted two of the Trolls up ahead by the entrance. One had removed his gargoyle head and held a walkie-talkie to his ear. Dewey recognized his craggy cop face.

"Oh, fuck." Dewey motioned Nick and Jeff back into an alcove by the Elf Bar. "It's Lieutenant Spivey! He's an *L.A.* cop. That means it's a joint fucking effort. It's probably that task force, and the Orange County sheriffs, and the local cops, and God only knows who else."

Nick shook his head. "This sucks so bad I don't even fucking believe it."

"We can't go out the front," Dewey said. "They're probably going to try and nail us in the parking lot."

"What about the bullet train?" Jeff said. "That goes over to the hotel."

"No, that sucks." Dewey looked beyond the red volcano to the geodesic spheres of the Futurama complex. "Over there. There's got to be a service entrance in Futurama. Come on."

They ducked back up the promenade and cut across the crowded square. The hordes of people still seemed innocuous, but Nick especially felt that almost any of them could be cops. That woman with the Dolly Parton hairdo and the big shoulder bag: was she a police bitch? What about her husband, a fat bear in a tight Dacron shirt? If he didn't look like a cop, nobody did. Even that woman in the Indian sari could be a Latino cop in drag; they did stuff like that. Nick's heart was pounding in his ears.

They cut past the red volcano, the snake ride clacking through the plastic jungle at the base of the structure, people in the cars screaming with glee.

Michael Reed was beside himself as he and Harvey hurried from the rear exit of Valhalla. What would have been a rather ho-hum, abrupt few seconds of violence in the Citadel stairwell was now—Michael felt in the pit of his stomach—about to become something much, much more horrific. And he wanted a view. "Harvey, come *on*." Michael started toward the Bavarian skylift station.

"Michael, I'm afraid of heights. I mean it."

"Don't be silly, Harvey, it's not that high. Hurry, before something happens." Michael frantically adjusted his Nikon.

Nick, Jeff and Dewey crossed the Futurama Plaza, pushing through the crowd lined up for the Demolition Starship ride. Nick kept his hand on his .38, barely hidden under his denim jacket. He bumped into a rabbity dad and nearly pulled the trigger. The man recoiled when he saw the look in Nick's eyes.

Dewey looked back and saw the SWAT team fanning out through the crowd in the plaza. People stared at the armed men, dumbstruck, as if they were watching a movie being shot, as if the idea that someone might fire real bullets in Americanaland was too farfetched to even consider.

Dewey was hoping that was the case. They wouldn't fucking dare, he told himself. Not here.

Dewey led the way up a concrete walkway that ran behind the main Futurama dome. It looked as if it might lead to a service entrance, but it didn't. It led to a propped-open steel door.

They ran thought the door, up a flight of concrete stairs, and found themselves backstage.

A Payne twins duet reverberated through the cavernous backstage area as Nick, Jeff, and Dewey cut past an enormous flat, the hot lights shining through the canvas, the Payne Family swaying in silhouette as the girls reached the inspirational climax of their song.

A stagehand shouted at them, and Jeff looked back— just as two steel doors flew open. The SWAT commander and four of his men burst through the doors, weapons ready, and they didn't yell, "Freeze!"

They saw the suspects running past the flat, and they just opened fire. It was a blistering, deafening fusillade. Bullets ripped throught the canvas as Nick, Jeff, and Dewey lunged out across the stage. Silhouettes jerked like puppets on yanked strings.

Dewey collided with one of the twins as she caught a bullet in the back. The last thing she saw was Dewey's face—his glasses fogged, his eyes insane with fear—as she collapsed in his arms and slid to the floor.

Bud Payne took a bullet in the eye. His mouth seemed to lock in a permanent smile as his blond toupee blew off in a spray of blood.

The second twin ran to her father, a bullet striking her arm as she slid to the 'floor. Her unctuously pretty young brother threw himself on top of her. As he did, a folded page torn from a gay guidebook slipped from his pocket, the Orange County listings quickly soaked in his father's blood.

Nick, Jeff, and Dewey ducked through the screaming Paynes and jumped into the orchestra pit.

There were screams from the audience too, but mostly there were wails of disbelief. People were more stunned than anything those first few moments after the shooting stopped.

The SWAT men were stunned, too, and lost sight of the suspects, who pushed through the crowd and reached the lobby.

The SWAT commander was devastated. He tried to tell himself it hadn't really happened. He wanted to go back a few seconds and undo it. He stood there and stared at the dead Payne twin, a pool of blood spreading from beneath her white chiffon dress. He felt as if he'd just bayoneted the Christ child in the manger. The girl's husband was wailing like a wounded animal, her brave brother streaked with tears as he rocked her wounded twin sister. Grandma Payne, a wrinkled woman with a silver bouffant, looked like she was having a stroke. Bud, still smiling, eyes sparkling, rested on a pillow of his own brains. Oh, Christ God, it was too much! And this angel, this precious blond angel! The SWAT commander took off his rakish cap and knelt over the girl he had killed, and sobbed.

His men didn't need his orders. They were already pushing through the crowd in pursuit of the suspects. And the mood of the crowd was changing, the wails of disbelief replaced by shouts of rage. But not rage at the SWAT men, though they might have been the logical target.

A fresh face in the third row finally spoke the words that galvanized the crowd. Vicky, the late Carl Hinds' secretary, was traumatized those first few moments like everyone else. Her boyfriend, Dale, his face scarred permanently pink from Nick's act of self-defense at the pancake house, tried to shield Vicky's eyes from the carnage onstage. He tried to stop her from saying anything, but it burst from her with a lacerating shrillness that cut through the sobs and shouts. *"It's those queers!"* she screamed. *"It's those queers who killed Carl! It's those dirty queers!"*

"There they go," shouted a man who saw the suspects cutting through the lobby.

"Get 'em!" screamed a girl in a wheelchair.

The enraged crowd stampeded through the lobby, cutting off the SWAT men.

Michael Reed watched everything from the skylift bucket as it rocked gently toward the crater of the red volcano. He saw Nick, Jeff and Dewey dashing across the Futurama Plaza; he saw the mob of enraged, screaming Christians coming after them. Michael trembled with adrenaline as he feverishly aimed his Nikon and clicked away. "Oh, God, Harvey. This is more than I could ever have wished for." He was thinking of the eventual film. "It's the Odessa steps sequence in Orange County! It's *Day of the Locust* all over again! It's *Dawn of the Dead* with real people!

You must look, Harvey, you must! It's going to be a slaughter."

Harvey couldn't look. He white-knuckled the rim of the steel bucket and stared at the floor.

Michael was right.

The mob cut off the walkway to the square, trapping the suspects in Futurama. Jeff remembered the bullet train. "Up there!" He pointed to the elevated platform.

They reached the escalator just as the first Payne fans caught up with them. A screaming blond girl dug into Nick's shoulder with her fingernails. Her boyfriend grabbed Nick around the neck. Nick threw the man back in the crowd, tore off the girl, and tried to help Jeff fend off an enraged stocky dad. A brawny jock slugged Nick in the face while a shrieking Boy Scout kicked him. Nick pulled out his .38, but dropped it as the Scout bit his hand.

Vicky charged Dewey. He leaned back against the escalator rail and kicked her away. Then he pulled the MP5 from the satchel, rocked back, and opened fire.

People couldn't believe it when they heard the pops and saw the muzzle flash and the stocky dad fall back. They couldn't believe it when the brawny jock's face exploded like a bursting red flower, when the blond girl caved in and the top of her boyfriend's head blew off.

Dewey spun around as a man with a scarred face lunged at him. He squeezed off a three-round burst, blowing Dale back into the mob. People shoved and screamed, trying to get away.

Jeff saw the SWAT men pushing through the crowd. Nick saw the bullet train coming around the volcano, slowing as it approached the platform above. He saw something else, and heard it, too, whomping. A police chopper veered in over the Citadel. He grabbed Dewey's arm. "Come on. The train."

"Go on!" Dewey yelled. "Grab the conductor!" He held his stance on the moving escalator steps.

Nick hesitated, then followed Jeff on up to the platform as Dewey fired another burst over the heads of the mob below. Dewey looked up as the chopper came in over the plaza, its search beam rippling over the mob.

People disembarking from the bullet train had no idea what was going on, but they screamed when they saw Jeff's gun. He and Nick moved quickly to the front of the train as the passengers scrambled for the down escalator.

Jeff grabbed the young conductor and stuck the gun in his ribs. "Just stay real cool."

Through the Plexiglas bubble window, Jeff saw the chopper hovering over the plaza. "Where's Dewey?"

"I'll get him," Nick said.

Dewey was near the top of the escalator when Nick called to him. "Dewey, come on!"

Dewey turned from the mob and took the final few steps. He was right at the top when the chopper search beam nailed him. Nick shielded his eyes from the blinding light. A shot cracked. Dewey fell facefirst on the platform.

Nick ducked down to him and pulled him back out of range. There was a neat little hole in Dewey's back, a large ragged gash in his chest. But Nick saw life in Dewey's eyes and was about to lift him when the chopper, lower now, nailed both of them with its beam.

Nick lunged for the MP5, jammed his finger over the trigger, rocked back, and fired point-blank into the blinding light. He held the trigger down and let the weapon chug.

He hit the light. It cracked and blew out. He blew something else out, too, although he didn't realize it immediately.

Nick slug the MP5 over his shoulder and helped Dewey up. "Oh, Jesus." There was so much blood. He carried Dewey to the conductor's car.

"Oh, shit, no," Jeff said when he saw what had happened to Dewey. Then he looked through the window and saw something else.

Nick and Dewey saw it too. So did the conductor. So did the mob in the plaza below. Everybody in the park saw it. It was hard to miss.

Wobbling like a bird suffering a stroke, the chopper crashed into the red volcano.

At first it was just a crunching, scraping, wrenching crash as the rotor blades ground into the red concrete and snapped off, as Plexiglas tore, steel crumpled, and debris flew through the air. For a few moments it looked as if the twisted chopper body was going to come to a silent rest in the crater. It did, for a second. Then it blew up.

"Fuckin' shit," Nick said as the explosion lit up the entire park like an enormous flashbulb.

Orange flames engulfed the volcano. Its plastic lava ignited and oozed for real down the rough concrete facade. Black clouds of toxic smoke billowed from the crater, blotting out the yellow moon.

"Jesus." Jeff's eyes sparkled with the glow.

Dewey grinned weakly.

Even the conductor was spellbound. "Oh, Lord."

It was, in a way, quite beautiful. It would have been stupendous in a Michael Reed production, an awesome special-effects finale, stunning in 70-millimeter and Dolby sound. Certainly, Michael would have thought so had he been watching it in rushes in a private screening room.

But from the skylift bucket, rocking relentlessly toward the crater, aesthetic distance was difficult. Michael and Harvey got an idea of what was going to happen to them when they saw another bucket, being pulled in the opposite direction, emerge from the billowing clouds of black smoke. The people in it were screaming. Understandably. They were on fire, burning plastic dripping from their skin. Harvey started screaming too.

Michael dropped his Nikon and shouted to people below. "Help! Somebody stop this thing! Stop it!"

People heard him, but they just pointed and stared with horrified fascination.

Michael keened as his synthetic-blend shirt began to melt into his skin. Harvey's shirt was cotton, though that didn't help him much. Flames singed the hair on his arms and chest and head. Michael's blond rockabilly cut ignited in a flash, like an old nitrate film. A screaming head of fire, he disappeared in the smoke—a final fade-out as the bucket rocked over the crater.

Jeff watched the burning bucket emerge from the clouds of smoke. He didn't know Michael and Harvey were in it, but somebody clearly was. "Jesus."

"Let's go!" Nick shouted at the conductor.

Whimpering now, the conductor pushed the stick forward, moving the bullet train out of the station.

Nick looked back as the train picked up speed. The platform appeared deserted now. But a second after Nick turned back to Dewey, a fuzzy blue insect lunged across the platform and jumped into the last car.

The bullet train shot through a grove of trees, the burning volcano flickering through the leaves, flames reflecting in the bubble window. The screams of the mob faded. Finally, it was almost quiet, almost calm, as the bullet train whoshed across the park.

Nick held Dewey in his arms. Dewey's white T-shirt was drenched with blood. So were the blue plastic seats and floor. Dewey's breath gurgled. "You guys better drop me."

"No way," Nick said. But he knew it was hopeless.

There was a dull boom as another explosion shook the volcano. Nick saw the glow in Dewey's eyes.

Dewey smiled faintly. "They're not going to forget us, are they, Nick?"

"They're not going to forget us," Nick said, "because this is just the start. This ain't it."

"Look." Dewey squeezed Nick's hand. "There's going

to be cops at the hotel station. You'd better bring this thing up over the highway and then jump."

"We'll all get off. Me and Jeff'll help you." Nick tried to make himself believe it, but his eyes were filled with tears.

Dewey smiled. "I don't think so, Nick."

They shot across the parking lot, a cold wind blowing through the open window. Sirens warbled in the distance.

Dewey tried to sit up. He looked at Jeff, who was still covering the terrified conductor. "Hey, Jeff—"

"Yeah." Jeff looked at Dewey, but had to look away. He felt more insane than he ever had in his life.

"You used to surf." Dewey coughed up a spray of blood.

"Yeah. When I was in high school."

"Where'd you go?"

Jeff stared at the flat, streetlit horizon. "Trestles. Rincon. Bolsa Chica. We went to Bolsa Chica a lot."

Dewey grinned. He pictured the sun-drenched waves, squirting through the turns on a hot summer day. Then, sweetly exhausted, baking the saltwater into his body on the white sands of Bolsa Chica; finally, losing himself, at peace, watching the red-orange sun go down. "Yeah. Bolsa Chica used to be bitchin'." Dewey coughed more blood, then smiled again. "You know . . . you guys really fucked up my surfing."

Nick brushed back Dewey's sweaty blond hair and kissed his forehead. Tears ran down Nick's cheeks.

"I loved you a lot, Nick."

"I know. I loved you too." Nick sobbed.

"I loved you more than anybody. You were always the one, you know that?"

"I know." Nick looked in Dewey's blue eyes and saw the life going out of them. Before it was all gone, Nick leaned down and kissed Dewey very gently on the mouth.

Nick's lips had barely touched Dewey's when a

deafening blast shook the car. Dewey's head jerked back, a hole in his skull squirting blood.

Nick howled. The conductor started screaming.

Jeff swung around and saw the Hornet clinging to the roof of the train, his .38 smoking. Jeff fired at him through the open window. He hit the Hornet in the head. Not the right part of the head.

The Hornet fired at Jeff, hitting the conductor in the back. Jeff fired again, but the Hornet was gone.

The conductor slumped over the controls, blood spreading from the hole in his back.

Nick was still howling as he dropped Dewey's limp body to the floor and picked up the MP5. "Fuck!" He climbed through the open window with a rage that was toally insane. Nobody had to tell him who the Hornet was. He knew.

His ears ringing, Jeff looked ahead and saw the hotel station coming up fast. "Nick!" he shouted. For a second he thought he was going to black out. "We've got to get off. Nick . . ."

Nick looked down the length of the bullet train's curving roof, the wind pounding his face. The Hornet wasn't there; he'd already climbed into one of the other cars.

Jeff poked his head out the window. "Nick—"

Nick ignored him and started crawling along the curve of the roof.

He reached the first car. It was empty.

Jeff crawled out after Nick as the train shot over the highway, clacking furiously into the hotel station.

The hotel station was full of cops, but they couldn't see Nick and Jeff on the far side of the roof, and they didn't open fire. It was obvious the two men in the front car were dead.

Jeff worked his way along the curve of the roof after Nick as the train shot back over the park.

Nick reached the next car. It was empty, too. The train shot over the floodlit pink and purple dreck of Fairytale City. A new chopper veered in around the burning volcano, momentarily disappearing behind the billowing clouds of smoke.

Nick reached the next car, where a family of blacks screamed. Startled, Nick almost opened fire. But the Hornet was not among them.

The bullet train shot back toward Futurama, heading into the loop around the base of the volcano. Nick crawled on to the next car.

Jeff looked up and saw the chopper, glowing in the volcano's flames. He felt the heat as the train entered the loop.

Nick swung around to the window of the next car, his fingers on the trigger of the MP5. The car was empty.

There was only one more car.

The train clacked around the base of the burning volcano, where the plastic jungle was engulfed in flame. Jeff shielded his face. The heat throbbed through his Levi's, his red nylon windbreaker began to smolder and stink.

Suddenly, the train lurched, its brakes squealing. It was grinding to a halt, its braking system activated from some distant point of emergency control. Jeff nearly fell off.

Nick clung to the frame before the last car as the train ground to a stop over the glistening turquoise dolphin pool. The heat from the volcano was still intense, scorching the left side of Nick's face. He didn't feel it. He swung into the last car, the MP5 chugging.

An Indian tourist couple cowered behind the plastic seats. Nick stopped firing before he hit them.

The emergency door in the back of the car was open. Nick saw a blue splotch running down the elevated railframe. He scrambled to the emergency door and opened fire.

He got off a single round, and that was it. The clip was empty. The blue splotch kept running.

Jeff reached the last car. "Nick—"

"Give my your fuckin' gun!" Nick grabbed Jeff's
.45 and steadied his arm against the edge of the
emergency door. Carefully, very carefully, he aimed
the .45 at the running blue splotch and squeezed the
trigger.

Nick hit the Hornet in the small of the back. The
Hornet lurched, pirouetted, and tried to keep from
falling off the railframe. But he missed his step.

The Hornet came down crotchfirst over the rail
that powered the train. Electricity churned through
its smoothly padded crotch and charred its blue felt
skin. It emitted a high-pitched fizzing sound as its
guts popped and cooked, and its silly-ass grin spewed
smoke.

Sparks crackled up and down the rail, tripping
circuit breakers. The park went black. The bullet-
train cars went dark, the turquoise lights in the dolphin pool blinked out, the Anytown Promenade shut
down. Everything was dark, except the volcano, which
continued to flash and glow.

The sugary stench of burning flesh wafted through
the breeze. Sirens wailed. The chopper search beam
zeroed in on the Hornet's rigid smoldering remains.
The Hornet's neck jerked. Its melting plastic head
fell off and plopped in the water below. Max Brundl's
face was red and blistered, his eyes squinched shut,
his mouth locked in a silly-ass grin just like the
Hornet's.

Nick coughed as plastic fumes seared his lungs.
Jeff looked down at the dark pool, the plastic dol-
phins frozen on their tracks. Jeff nudged Nick. Nick
nodded. They jumped, breaking the reflection of the
burning volcano on the surface of the pool.

It was ten minutes before the lights came back on.
By the time the SWAT team secured the bullet train,
Nick and Jeff had climbed from the dolphin pool and
scrambled through the miniature Monument Valley.

By the time the cops reached the miniature Monu-

ment Valley, Nick and Jeff had slipped through a
service gate behind Valhalla, and made it out to the
freeway, where they pulled a shirtless young me-
chanic from his metallic-blue '68 Camaro and took
off in the car, heading south toward San Diego.

Around midnight, the highway patrol chased a
metallic-blue '68 Camaro doing ninety down the San
Diego Freeway near Oceanside. They finally pulled it
over. It was a man and his wife-in-labor. She gave
birth to a perfect baby boy on the shoulder of the
fast lane of the 405. The cops were helping as best
they could, and didn't see the other metallic-blue '68
Camaro shoot by.

Epilogue

Three months later, police in Winslow, Arizona, found the '68 Camaro abandoned behind a motel. Caked with dust, it had clearly been there for some time. Searching it, they found two Dexedrine Spansules in the crack of the driver's seat, an empty fifth of Jack Daniel's, a flattened .45 cartridge box, a family-size jar of Vaseline with several blond pubic hairs in it, two crushed amyl nitrite ampules, and a fetid box of Kentucky Fried Chicken. The trail was cold.

For a long time Victor was worried, then he was mad. The least Jeff could do was call, or send a postcard with some sort of coded message. But the months passed and there was nothing. Victor made excuses. Perhaps Nick and Jeff were holed up in the States and considered communication too risky. Or perhaps they were still on the move, their immediate survival of greater concern than keeping in touch with old friends. There was a good reason, Victor was sure of that. He was certain he'd hear from Jeff eventually.

In the meantime, he continued hanging out at Revolver, where he drank too much and bragged about his part in the story. Under normal conditions, Nick and Jeff's outlaw mystique might have rubbed off, transforming him into an irresistibly butch trick, but normal conditions had ceased. A black cloud was rolling across the gay world. Fearful, Victor turned from casual sex to casual eating and quickly put on thirty pounds.

Sometimes, back at his house in Mount Washington, Victor drank vodka into the night, playing old records from the great days of the past when Jeff had been his best friend. How casually he'd treated it all at the time, Victor reflected, never suspecting how abruptly it would end. Sometimes he'd play old Donna Summer records and dance drunkenly around the room, doing the campy go-go dancer routine that had always cracked Jeff up. He'd stop, sweaty and embarrassed, when he caught a glimpse of himself in the mirror. There he would be, fat and fucked-up, a burnt-out disco dolly living in the past. Not even thirty and his best years behind him.

How he wished that the phone would ring, that it would be Jeff calling to arrange a rescue. He'd hop the next jet to wherever, diet, detox, join a gym (in Rio? Saint-Tropez?), get a tan. Live happily ever after in the paradise he was certain Nick and Jeff had found.

Most nights Victor passed out in the chair in front of the stereo, the speakers popping static in the dark.

Randy's murder had a profound effect on Ed the writer. He quit his screenwriting job with Michael Reed and, in the weeks between Randy's death and the Americanaland catastrophe, dedicated himself to discovering the truth of Randy's killing.

His progress was swift. Acting on an early tip, he began to frequent the Fortune Bowling Alley in South Gate, where he soon learned that Eddie Sepúlveda had been less than discreet. Drunk, he had bragged that he'd killed a fruit attorney for Brundl, and now had the famous cop by the balls. Ed soon made contact with the wife of one of Eddie's low-rider accomplices. Her husband, she said, had been an innocent witness; he'd had no idea a murder was planned. Yes, she'd heard Eddie discussing the crime.

In fact, the men had come back to the house the night it happened, all of them covered in blood—all except her husband, of course. And now he had disappeared. Ed taped her statement, and later that night went to see Scott in Ocean Park.

Scott was drunk and had a gun. He also had Brundl's home address. He was getting up his courage when Ed came to the door. He was about to tell Ed to fuck off, when Ed said he knew who'd killed Randy and had evidence that would put Brundl away.

Ed had barely begun to explain when a bulletin interrupted the movie on TV. Scott's attempt to kill Brundl that night would have been futile. The detective was not home; he was miles away in Orange County. Ed and Scott looked at the TV and saw the red volcano flash and glow.

Scott laughed till he cried when he saw Brundl's charred costumed body stuck to the bullet-train track.

But Ed and Scott were enraged in the days that followed, as Brundl was posthumously cited for bravery, as Dewey took the rap for shooting the Paynes, as state authorities continued to deny the rumors about Nick's surgery, as Brundl began to emerge as a folk hero, the subject of quickie biographies, his face on magazine covers and T-shirts, his acts of valor soon to be portrayed in a major motion picture. Both men were disgusted, though hardly surprised, when Nick and Jeff, and Dewey were vilified as depraved psychopathic criminals, and even the president spoke of the all-out effort to apprehend the fugitives, "so that decent people everywhere can cease to live in fear."

Ed went through the formality of giving the district attorney a copy of his evidence pertaining to Randy's murder. But he didn't expect anything to come of it, and nothing did.

And so Ed began work on a book that would tell the true story. It was not without risk, a fact brought home when Eddie Sepúlveda was found in a South Gate dumpster with a bullet in his brain. Brundl's many friends, Ed was warned more than once, would stop at nothing to protect the detective's memory. Ed took a house-sitting job where he thought he'd be safe, and began talking to people.

He spoke to Michelle at length, getting an accurate version of the initial altercation in Jeff's apartment, and Burke's subsequent death. He spoke to Greg Stovey, who was now sueing the city for thirty million dollars, and located several other witnesses to the baths shooting. He spoke to Michael's former boy Tim, who gave him enough irrelevant dirt to fill a thick Beverly Hills novel as well as an accurate version of the Malibu episode.

Clandestinely, he met with several informants from Atascadero, including the lispy black psych tech, who gave him everything he needed to blow the lid off the practice of "therapeutic surgery."

He also spoke to Harvey Berringer, who had miraculously survived the Americanaland fire. But with a skin that now resembled Hawaiian-style potato chips, Harvey's courtroom and chic lunching days were over. The patrons of Ma Maison would have found it difficult not to gag at the sight of his pink-and-yellow poke-hole head. Now it was Harvey's turn to be taken care of, and Robbie was his loyal nursemaid. Though Ed had anticipated resistance from Harvey, the opposite proved to be the case. Harvey was warm and expansive in the living room of the modest Hermosa Beach apartment he shared with Robbie since leaving his wife.

One night after an interview, Ed watched the couple set out on a nightime stroll along the beach, Robbie's simple clear-plastic colostomy bag pearlescent in the moonlight, a lipless smile on Harvey's face as they locked hands and lightly nuzzled, the way lovers do.

Only Chuck MacDonald, the hunky high-school P.E. teacher, slammed the door in Ed's face and hung up when he called. Only Myron Gillet (aka Hatch) demanded money for his story. Ed declined. A week later a tabloid appeared with the wishful-thinking headline: I WAS FUGITIVES' SEX SLAVE. CLAIMS ADJUSTER TELLS ORDEAL.

Of course Ed spoke with Victor, who was the expert on Jeff and also knew a great deal about the Labor Day weekend events. But the person who knew the most about everything—other than Nick and Jeff themselves—was Scott.

They spent a number of weekends together, in L.A. and San Francisco, going over the details of the story. Although their relationship remained platonic, Ed knew that his feelings for Scott were growing. But Scott was not really over Randy. Though Ed sensed that Scott was beginning to care for him, too, the time just wasn't right yet. Ed wasn't used to waiting. But he sensed that what was developing with Scott would be worth it.

The afternoon Ed finished the book he knew would vindicate Nick and Jeff—and perhaps even allow Dewey's mother to face the neighbors again—he clicked off his typewriter and went for a drive.

Down to the Ocean Park beach. Where Nick and Jeff had met. Where Randy's body had been found. It was sunset. Runners were out.

Ed walked out to the lifeguard station, the focal point of the nighttime cruising. It was chilly, a fog rolling on. He zipped up his brown leather jacket.

Leaning against the ramp, he lit a cigarette and wondered again where the hell Nick and Jeff were. Why hadn't they contacted him? Hadn't they heard what he was doing?

A good-looking young man was walking his German shepherd along the shore. Ed noticed him, thought he was attractive, but didn't expect anything to happen, not before dark.

But the man came over. "Hi."

"Hello."

He was even better-looking up close, with a short black beard and a pleasant smile. He indicated the lifeguard station. "Down here kind of early, aren't you?"

Ed smiled. "Or too late."

"Yeah." The man smiled. "I guess it's not what it used to be. Mostly jerking off these days. At least that's what I hear. It was never really my scene."

"Mine neither," Ed said. He could still see the orgies on hot summer nights.

"By the way." The man put out his hand. "I'm Jeff."

"*Nick*," Ed said, shaking hands.

"Say, I just live over there. See that apartment building? Want to come over and smoke some dope, Nick?"

Ed sighed. Then he smiled and nodded. They trudged back across the sand.

The German shepherd took a quick leak against the lifeguard station, then took off after them as the fog rolled in.